DEATH BY PORK LOIN

"Well, the lab reports are in," Detective Bease said. "Cause of Death was a lethal irritant in the victim's throat. The speed with which the test results were returned speaks to the victim's high level of intolerance to whatever it was."

Sherry pondered the repercussions of this revelation. Detective Bease and Detective Diamond whispered a conversation between themselves before redirecting their attention back to the women.

"An allergic reaction to an ingredient?" Sherry shrugged.

"Not exactly. The substance was something not found in the traditional food pyramid. Another fact was just brought to my attention. The last dish the deceased victim consumed was"—Detective Bease glanced at his scribbled notes—"Chutney Glazed and Farro Stuffed Pork Tenderloin."

Sherry gasped. She shook out her hands, which had suddenly grown ice cold. "Mine?"

"You said we should hold off mentioning that," Detective Diamond hissed at his partner.

Overhearing the comment, Sherry slowly drew in her breath. Her sister shook her head subtly. Marla put her index finger up to her lips.

"Mr. Andime and the other two judges all gave statements to the police at the scene corroborating the fact Ms. Frazzelle's food was the last thing Chef Tony Birns, now deceased, was seen consuming."

Both men kept their eyes on Sherry until she felt as if she was being fried in a hot skillet like a catfish fillet . . .

Expiration Date

Devon Delaney

KENSINGTON PUBLISHING CORP.

www.kensingtonbooks.com

KENSINGTON BOOKS are published by

Kensington Publishing Corp.
119 West 40th Street
New York, NY 10018

All Kensington titles, imprints, and distributed lines are available at special quantity discounts for bulk purchases for sales promotions, premiums, fund-raising, educational, or institutional use. Special book excerpts or customized printings can also be created to fit specific needs. For details, write or phone the office of the Kensington sales manager: Kensington Publishing Corp., 119 West 40th Street, New York, NY 10018, attn: Sales Department; phone 1-800-221-2647.

KENSINGTON BOOKS and the K logo are Reg. U.S. Pat. & TM Off.

ISBN-13: 978-1-4967-1443-5
ISBN-10: 1-4967-1443-1

First printing: May 2018

10 9 8 7 6 5 4 3 2 1

Printed in the United States of America

First electronic edition: May 2018

ISBN-13: 978-1-4967-1444-2
ISBN-10: 1-4967-1444-X

Chapter 1

Sherry watched with curiosity as the woman wearing a press credential used two fingers and her teeth to open her OrgaNicks Cook-Off brochure. In her other hand, the woman juggled a recording device and overstuffed carryall. When the brochure slipped out of the woman's grasp, she sighed and watched it float to the well-worn linoleum floor. Before Sherry could offer assistance, the woman proceeded down the hallway, leaving the paper behind.

Having just left the ladies' room, Sherry inspected the hem of her apron to ensure she hadn't tucked it in to her pants. Satisfied she was presentable, Sherry reached down and recovered the abandoned brochure. She trotted up behind the woman and tapped her on the back. "Did you drop this?" Sherry asked as the woman turned around.

"Yes, thanks," the woman replied. "How do these kids ever get to class on time? The high school has tripled in size since I was a student here. Guess that's why the cook-off is being held here, plenty of room."

Sherry rolled her shoulders and shuffled her feet. She glanced at the giant clock on the wall. Her eyebrows shot up when she calculated six lost minutes.

"Wow, it's still here." The woman pointed at a trophy case along the wall. "Didn't know my high school accomplishments would stay relevant so many years later." She waved Sherry forward to join her, before putting her nose up to the glass. "That plaque's in honor of all the Hillsboro High School Yearbook Editors. Can you believe they didn't spell my name right? It's Patti with an I not a Y. Pretty ironic for an award given to kids whose job it was to find typographical errors. Why was it they always got my husband Rafe's name correct?"

Sherry transferred her weight from one leg to the other, then back again. She took a second look at the clock.

"I'm sorry, I see by your nametag you're a cook-off contestant. I'd better let you go. By the way, I'm Patti Mellit. I'm reporting on the cook-off for the paper. I'll be talking to you inside as you cook."

"I'm Sherry Frazzelle. Nice to meet you. Got to get cooking!"

"Don't mind me. I'm just strolling down memory lane. My husband and I were co-editors of our yearbook a million years ago. Time to get back to reality."

"Congratulations. The only award I ever got at school was for baking the most creative cupcake in Home Economics," Sherry called out as she turned toward the kitchen.

"Wait. Can I follow you?"

Without turning to answer, Sherry motioned Patti forward with a sweep of her arms. With Patti in tow, she jogged down the hallway. As she passed the school auditorium, Sherry paused, peeked in, and saw a large audience watching three chefs seated at a table on the brilliantly lit stage. Her heartbeat quickened. She ran her hands down the front of her apron and resumed her trot. When she reached the kitchen entrance, the beefy security guard standing vigil uncrossed his arms and broadened his stance.

Patti stepped around Sherry until she was face-to-face with the man. "Hey, Mike, good to see you again. I'm following my new friend, Sherry, inside to the kitchen."

Behind Patti, Sherry displayed her official cook-off contestant ID badge clipped to her apron. The guard nodded his approval.

"You're fine, Ms. Frazzelle, but I'm sorry, Ms. Mellit, I don't see your name on my list. You can't go in there."

"Don't be silly." Patti tossed her brown curls to the side to provide a clearer view of her press pass. "Right here, it says 'V.I.P.' Very important person. Where's Nick Andime? He'll vouch for me."

"The kitchen's off limits to anyone but the six cook-off contestants and event staff." The compact, yet imposing, man folded his arms and turned his body to better block the entrance. "Ms. Mellit, if you could just remain here while I find Mr. Andime, we can resolve this situation. I'm just following the instructions I was given."

Patti lowered her head, slithered past the guard,

and passed through the double doors. Sherry threw a glance at the man, whose jaw dropped open, mouthed an apology, and followed Patti. Sherry made her way back to the table that housed her recipe ingredients. The reporter stopped a few feet away. Sherry picked up her knife, checked her recipe sheet, and opened a bag of baby spinach leaves with the sharp blade. She spread the vibrant green leaves across her cutting board and began chopping.

"Hello, Patti. Better late than never."

Sherry peered up between knife cuts and recognized Nick Andime, the CEO of the OrgaNicks Corporation. His light blue suit screamed, "recycled groomsman attire." Sherry noted his shiny hair was closer to black than brown, but neither color could claim dominance. She settled on its similarity in hue to the burnt ends of a smoked brisket. All the strands of Nick's hair were held rigidly in place, reminiscent of a Lego figurine's snap-on hairstyle.

"I shouldn't have taken the Interstate," Patti explained. "Ridiculous backup on it. An overturned produce truck. What a mess! Vegetables all over the pavement! Anyway, let me get to work. I've got an article to write. And call off that Mike guy, will you? He's a little overzealous about his job. He tried to keep me out of the action."

Sherry quashed an involuntary snicker that bubbled up like vinegar when introduced to baking soda.

"He's harmless." Nick turned his head and peered at the doorway. "Don't forget the contestants' display table around the corner. It's where you can try a bite of the cooking when the contestants have completed their recipes. Don't let anyone see you, though. The audience won't get a chance to view those plates until after the judging is concluded, and I don't want anyone to think you've influenced the contest's outcome. I'm just doing you a special favor. It's our little secret."

"I owe you one then, thanks. That's going to make my job a whole lot easier if I can taste the contestants' food."

Sherry cleared her throat when Nick Andime underscored the word "secret." She stuffed her spinach in the measuring cup to the one-cup line and removed two leaves that sprang up in defiance. If Patti was going to watch while she prepared her recipe, Sherry wanted details to be perfect. As she held the cup up to check the measurement, she caught Patti's eye. Sherry's hand wobbled until she steadied it with a double-fisted grip.

Patti pressed the red button on her recorder and began dictating. "The tension is as thick as an overfloured roux here in the cook-off kitchen. With less than twenty-five minutes to go, it appears a food-nado has swept through the contestants' workstations. But I know better than to second-guess a competitive cook. From seeming chaos, delectable edibles will undoubtedly emerge. Right in front of me is a contestant furiously preparing pork tenderloin. This home cook is checking the accuracy of her ingredients down to a leaf of spinach. There's no pinch of this and a dash of that from these contestants. If their recipe says one cup of something, you can be sure that's the amount that lends to the perfect flavor and consistency."

Sherry smiled and returned her attention to her table. A ripple of panic hijacked her grin when she lost track of where she was in her recipe. She picked up the typed sheet of instructions but couldn't find her place. She ran her finger three-quarters of the way down the paper before things looked familiar. "Please let her move on to interview someone else," she whispered. Sherry puffed out her cheeks. "Come on, girl, just concentrate."

Patti clicked off her recorder but, much to Sherry's chagrin, stayed put. "So, Nick, how's my favorite brother-in-law? Do you mind if I include a biographical profile on you and your recent entry into the organic food market in my article?"

Nick groaned. "The focus should be on the contest itself, Patti. Nothing else is necessary."

"But it's so interesting how well your new venture is doing. I can see your gravy train pulling into the station any day now. And it's destiny your cook-off is held at the very same high school where you were voted 'Biggest Dreamer.' Here you are, living your dream!"

Patti leaned in closer to Nick. "You have a little something in your soul patch. Is that parsley?"

Sherry snorted, this time unable to restrain her laughter.

"It's a goatee, not a soul patch, and keep me out of the article." Nick turned his back to Patti.

"No problem, but your story would sell papers, if you ask me."

When Patti and Nick walked away, a sense of calm blanketed Sherry with the swiftness of a chug of brandy. Back on track, Sherry scanned the kitchen and felt a twinge of admiration that over two dozen people were functioning with relative proficiency in a room designed for half that amount. All the cook-off finalists performed their culinary magic side by side, in equally size-restricted prep areas. Men and women in OrgaNicks-logoed aprons moved seamlessly between cutting boards, refrigerators, and ovens. People were weaving around each other, like the latticework crust created by bakers to top the best fruit pies. Cooks were carrying everything from mixing bowls to sizzling skillets. Event staffers were dodging contestants while monitoring activities and offering assistance.

A wisp of Sherry's hair blew across her face, tousled by the breeze generated by a very familiar contestant.

"Hey, Sherry! Hot pan coming through." A woman in a T-shirt, jeans, cowboy boots, and an apron approached. "Don't back up, Kenny, or you'll get a hot cheese facial." She rushed from her workstation, deftly transporting dangerous cargo.

"Your sister's a gem. I've never seen a cook move as fast as her," Kenny Dewitt remarked from the neighboring table as Marla Barras scurried by him. He moved closer to Marla's unoccupied table. "You two don't seem at all alike. She's a bit scattered. You know, all over the place. Look at her table compared to yours. How can she find anything in that disaster zone?"

"We all have our certain style. Whatever way gets the job done is the right way. Marla can shimmy and shake with the best of them." Sherry cringed as she examined her sister's workspace. "Be careful. Marla's not going to like you crowding her space."

Before Kenny could step back, Marla appeared. "Can I help you? Why are you handling my ingredients?"

The can of organic chicken broth Kenny was holding slipped out of his hand, which Sherry noted was missing its pinkie finger, and crashed to the floor. Kenny reached down with his other hand and retrieved the dented can.

"Don't worry. It's mine." He pointed to Marla's chicken broth can that was obscured by bags of produce. "I know enough not to touch anyone else's stuff. Just checking out the competition. No harm, no foul." Kenny raised both hands in mock surrender. He left in a hurry with his ponytail swishing behind him.

The speakers mounted on the wall above Sherry's head crackled to life. "Approaching the seventy-minute mark, contestants. Twenty minutes and counting remaining in the OrgaNicks Cook-Off. Keep in mind, your dish will be judged equally for adherence to the contest theme, which is 'quick and easy entrees,' along with appearance, taste, of course, and creative use of at least one OrgaNicks product."

"Can you believe that Kenny guy?" Marla asked as she passed behind Sherry's prep table. "Hey, where did you go a few minutes ago? I didn't think we were allowed to leave the kitchen."

"My bladder is more active than yeast in warm water. I had to beg until the officials let me run to the bathroom." Sherry patted her stomach as if she were shaping pizza dough. "I met Patti Mellit, the reporter, in the hallway. She's covering the cook-off for the newspaper. There she is, right over there." Sherry pointed down the row of contestants. "She'll be by for an interview, no doubt, so be prepared to multitask. Anyway, must go. See ya."

Sherry strutted to the refrigerator, opened the stainless-steel door, and pulled out her specified ingredient bag. Confident she had a few minutes to spare, Sherry took her time returning to her workstation, hoping to check the progress of her fellow competitors. In front of her a woman wiped her brow with a dishtowel. The soiled towel left a leaf of some green produce just below her hairline. Another contestant held a timer at eye level while she babysat a simmering saucepan. The only other man in the competition, besides Kenny, was drinking a tall glass of something. As he lowered his glass from his mouth, his hand quivered, splashing the liquid in all directions. Sherry's gaze caught his. He greeted her with a lukewarm smile, which Sherry returned. He managed his drink safely down to his table, wiped his eyeglasses with a napkin, and returned to his cooking as Sherry carried her ingredient bag back to her table.

Chapter 2

As the final minutes of the cook-off ticked by, Sherry's center of attention was back on her knife and cutting board. Just as the final blow of the shiny blade minced the last of the parsley, someone careened into her table. The table vibrated, and the knife loosened from her hand. She tightened her grip to keep it from jettisoning toward her feet. Greens and metal measuring spoons tumbled to the floor. Sherry set down her knife, taking care to aim the blade away from her, and began picking up the debris.

Peering up from her squatting position, she caught a glimpse of Nick Andime as he brushed parsley bits off his seersucker pants. Sherry rose and involuntarily grumbled. She caught his eye, but he made no apology. After he passed her table, she watched him walk to the middle of the kitchen, where he took the microphone from the cook-off hostess. He clicked it on.

"Okay, cook-off contestants, finish up your dishes. It's almost time to get your food to the judges' table."

"Excuse me. I was told I was the timekeeper." Brynne Stark, the event hostess, approached Nick, hand outstretched. Her comment resonated across the airwaves.

Nick lowered the mic. The sudden jerk of the microphone created a screech that battered all eardrums in the vicinity. From her front-row seat to the exchange, Sherry backed up a step to lessen the impact.

"Well, if you recall, this is technically my contest, so who best to ring in the final thrilling moments but me?" Nick's sarcasm appeared to sting its recipient. "You might want to check the mirror. Your mascara is dripping."

Brynne dabbed her eyelid with the back of her finger. "I was hit with the mic during an interview. I'm not even sure how it happened. Let's just say the California contestant, Kenny Dewitt, was very enthusiastic about being interviewed. The eye that was hit started watering and only stopped a minute ago. Hazards of the job, I guess. By the way, you have parsley in your hair."

"We can still hear you," Kenny called out. "And sorry about the eye thing."

Sherry pointed to the power button on the microphone. Nick clicked the device off.

"Here you are, Ms. Stark." Nick handed the mic to Brynne. He shuffled away, clipping Sherry's table again as he passed by. This time she intercepted her parsley before it hit the floor.

Mac Stiles, the event photographer and Brynne's assistant, remained mute during her brief exchange with Nick. He had inched closer to Brynne, though, in what seemed to Sherry a show of solidarity. He even handed Brynne his cell phone, which Sherry guessed must have had the mirror app activated because Brynne scrutinized it as she wiped away the black makeup melting from her eyelashes. Following the kind act, Brynne mouthed a "thanks," and Mac gave her a smile and a wink.

Sherry blew a wayward strand of hair from her face. She wiped her hands on a towel and licked her dry lips. She began rehearsing a greeting for Brynne, who was moving closer. "I am so excited to be in the cook-off today." Nope, an underseasoned comment, not interesting enough. "OrgaNicks is a great sponsor of today's cook-off." Overcooked adulation. "I hope the judges like my stuffed tenderloin." The truth served up to perfection. She was ready for her interview. Sherry's chin lowered a bit when Brynne and Mac made an about-face and veered away from her.

A woman three tables down flinched when the hostess and photographer parked in front of her. Despite the fact that there were two active cooks between Sherry and the woman, the proximity was close enough to give her the opportunity to catch most of what was said.

"Amber Sherman. How is our contestant from Maine doing?"

"I'm doing the best I can," Amber replied with the strength of fat-free cheese.

Sherry strained to catch each word, knowing she might be next.

"Please speak up." Brynne guided the microphone closer to Amber's lips. "This interview is streaming live throughout the auditorium next door. We want the paying public to hear you loud and clear."

"It's harder than people would think, keeping it all on track and on time," yelled Amber.

The mic squealed with distortion.

"Oops, sorry." Amber placed her hand over her mouth. "Maybe now isn't a good time to talk. I really need to keep a close eye on my shrimp. Bad things can happen if no one's watching the pot."

"But if you watch it, it never boils, right? Isn't that how the saying goes?" laughed Mac. "So you're damned if you do, damned if you don't."

As the interview deteriorated, Sherry's oven timer went off. She squared her knife up to the edge of her cutting board, tidied her ingredient piles, and headed toward the ovens in the back of the kitchen.

"Are you finished cooking, Ms. Frazzelle?"

The sole of Sherry's shoe caught on a raised floorboard, and she stumbled. She righted herself and tried to pinpoint where the question originated. She noticed Mac crouched down, gathering his camera bags. At the same time, Brynne and her microphone found Sherry.

"Nope. Just a quick trip to check on things." Sherry fumbled with the hair in her eyes while she caught her breath. "My timer went off, but that was just to remind me to double-check the oven. My tenderloin may or may not be ready."

The photographer rose and moved to within an arm's length of Sherry. She assessed his ripped jeans, decaying sneakers, and grimy T-shirt. The outfit seemed better suited for changing his car's oil than for performing his current profession.

"Your shirt's inside out." Sherry gestured to Mac. Despite her efforts at discretion, Brynne's mic broadcasted the comment back to the attentive audience in the next room, and there was an eruption of laughter heard through the doorway.

"I'd like to say I got dressed in the dark, but what really happened was Nick Andime, Mr. OrgaNicks CEO himself, made me turn it inside out," replied Mac, while he smothered the mic with his hand. "He was pissed because I had a competing company's logo on it. I thought it was kind of a funny shirt to wear, but he freaked out. Guess 'organic' is a code word for uptight. He's kind of a cranky guy." Mac removed his hand from the microphone.

"Well, I better get back to work." Sherry turned her body with such conviction the strings of her apron loosened.

"Let's follow her, Brynne." Mac shadowed Sherry's steps toward the oven. "I'd bet anything, her plates are almost done, and I can get a good picture."

"Be careful, this oven's really hot." Sherry lowered the oven door just enough to release the meat's fragrance and the sound of the gentle sizzling of its olive oil baste. She sniffed in and grinned. Her cheeks warmed. "Not quite done, but extremely close." Sherry smiled at Mac. "After years of experience, the nose knows."

Mac clicked a photo of Sherry resetting her timer. Brynne and Mac followed her back to her workstation, where Sherry grabbed a large wooden spoon and a mixing bowl. She spooned farro from a saucepan to the bowl and began the process of seasoning the grain. A portion was stuffed in her tenderloin and the remainder would provide a bed for the meat when it was plated.

"We are here with Sherry Frazzelle, our Augustin, Connecticut, contestant," Brynne announced. "Sherry, do you have an ingredient in your recipe you're confident will 'wow' the judges?"

"And should we check your pockets for any super-secret ingredient you may have smuggled in?" Mac added.

"Don't even joke about that!" Sherry frowned and threw her hands up to her head. The wooden spoon in her elevated hand splattered mango chutney on Mac's camera. "I know the rules, and you have to cook with exactly the ingredients listed in the recipe you submitted to the contest. And to answer your question, Brynne, I do have a 'wow' ingredient. It's chutney. I love it so much I named my dog after it. My pup is sweet and spicy, just like the condiment."

"What a cute story! Thank you so much and best of luck to you," said Brynne.

Sherry flashed a fierce smile at Mac's camera.

Brynne clicked her tongue. "I'll do the interviewing, Mac. You stick to taking pictures."

Sherry nodded in agreement with Brynne. The pair left Sherry as she dabbed her work-weary hands on her apron.

After her perfectly roasted pork finished resting on her cutting board, she transferred slices to her plates. Sherry knew she had only one task left to complete. Having disposed of most of the parsley Nick Andime knocked to the floor, Sherry gathered up a sanitary half-dollar-size amount of the herb.

She visualized where on her plate to place the bright green pop of color. Sherry decided to let the garnish fall from her hand and land at will on her food. She pushed her two completed plates of food to the front of her worktable. The palms of her hands came together in triumph. She filled her lungs with the sweet air of accomplishment and exhaled only after savoring the moment.

"Time's up! Cooking is now over," announced Brynne. Along with Mac and Nick, she gathered in front of the cooks. "Thank you, finalists. Please stay by your plates until the judges are ready to taste test."

"Guess we just have to sit tight and be patient. Do you have any spare paper towels? I just ran out." Sherry pointed to Kenny's roll of towels.

Despite the fact the towels were easily within his reach, Kenny made no effort to retrieve them. "Help yourself."

Sherry stretched across his table, losing her balance in the process, and grabbed the roll of paper towels just before landing on her elbows with a thud. A slight twinge in her overworked back convinced her to correct her crooked stance. The muscles in her body were beginning to tighten, and she inhaled and exhaled in practiced intervals, in hopes of softening them.

"Are you okay?" Marla called to her sister.

"A little tired. It's been a long morning."

Sherry tore off some paper-towel sheets and blotted at the various foods splashed, squirted, and spilled on her apron. Her actions were futile, though, and only served to smear the stains together into a messy mosaic.

"Forget it, Sher." Marla wagged her finger at her sister. "Those stains are going to take hours of soaking to get clean."

"Why are you even bothering to clean up? See all the contest runners? They're here to do the dirty work." Kenny swatted some leftover tomato stems off his table onto the floor.

"I like order, not chaos. Plus, I need something to do with my hands now that we're done. You know, idle hands, devil's workshop and all?" Sherry stepped behind Kenny and placed the paper-towel roll back on his table.

"Suit yourself." Kenny shrugged. "I know I didn't come all the way from California to cook my best dish and then be expected to perform maid service afterward. Remember, we're doing the sponsor a favor giving them free recipes. I don't want to feel totally abused here. Speaking of the devil, here comes Slick Nick!"

"Please stay by your designated workstation." Nick Andime shot a sideways glance at Sherry. "The judges are winding down their presentations in the auditorium, and we need you to be ready at a moment's notice to bring your finished plates to them for scoring." Nick smoothed his well-oiled helmet of hair with all ten fingers before walking away.

Sherry, feeling unfairly singled out, tossed Kenny a glance laced with indignation.

"Hope he doesn't get any of his follicular bacon grease on his baby blue leisure suit." Kenny ran the back of his hand across his forehead. "That oil slick would be a bitch to clean up. It's an environmental disaster all on its own."

Sherry used all her strength to avoid staring at Kenny's four-fingered hand but failed. "Do you mind if I ask what happened to your finger?"

"A story for another time." Kenny plunged his hands in his pockets.

"Are you heading back to California today, Kenny?"

"On the red-eye, with a big check, hopefully!"

"Are you okay, Sherry? Your forehead is a road-map of tension creases." Marla stooped over across Kenny's table.

Sherry leaned in from the opposite side. "I'm worried about my pork. I wanted to taste it one more time because I'm not sure I used enough salt. Now I'm really second-guessing myself!" Sherry picked up one last parsley bit and tossed it in the garbage. She brushed her palm across her cutting board to feel for any otherwise undetectable bits to discard.

"I'm sure you salted your dish perfectly, as usual." Marla located a chair and pulled it up to her tiny cooking area. After sitting, she began tapping her leg with a soiled spatula. Each time the spatula made contact with her pants, food particles sprayed off.

Sherry was unable to contain her revulsion. "Marla, what a mess you're making."

"Relax. I'm not bothering anyone."

"How do you think you did?" Sherry brushed away a crumb from her shirtsleeve.

"I think my recipe came out pretty well. I just

hope the judges are partial to cheese, because I used a ton! My grits will be harder than the cow pies in my pastures, though, if they don't get to judging pretty soon."

Sherry noted the calmness in her younger sister's reply. Being so relaxed while under pressure was a trait Sherry wished she had the gene for.

"How 'bout you?" Marla asked.

Sherry flipped her hands palm side up. "I can't tell. I was pretty nervous when we started. My mind went completely blank, and I couldn't even remember my recipe. No matter how many times I do this, I can't shake the opening bell nerves. The nonstop interviews with the hostess and the media are necessary, I know, but so distracting."

Nick Andime burst through the kitchen doors. "Contestants, thanks for your patience. The judges' demonstration is running a bit long, but it's winding down now." Nick tucked his wayward necklace back into his dress-shirt collar and then dashed from the kitchen before anyone had a chance to question him.

"Well, the game is in overtime, and this team's grits may be going down for the count." Marla slapped her leg with her spatula, sending debris flying.

Kenny shook his head. "What are you talking about?"

"Gluey grits. They could send me to the penalty box." Marla gestured toward the empty chair behind Sherry. "Sit down, Sher. You might as well get comfortable and enjoy the show."

Before Sherry could turn around, Kenny pulled the seat up under his backside.

"Ah, I'm so happy to take a load off." Kenny let out an elongated sigh.

Sherry groaned.

Kenny put his finger up to his lips. "Shhh! I want to listen to this!"

Sherry's mouth dropped open. She lowered her gaze to the floor and concentrated on what was coming through the kitchen's speakers.

"And this final slide in the presentation is a gorgeous shot of the dish that launched my food truck when I was fresh out of culinary school in Philadelphia. Naïvely, I put all my resources into my truck I lovingly named 'Casa Rolls.' My menu specialized in personal-sized casseroles, and I spent a fortune retrofitting my truck to resemble a Rolls Royce. Genius, right? Unfortunately, Harry, of Harry's Ham-bulance, greased the palms of a city official and stole my selling location out from underneath me. He's in jail now, unrelated charges. I'm going to hand things over to Mr. Andime now."

"Thank you for sharing your story, Chef Tony Birns. Ladies and Gentlemen, we have reached the conclusion of our slide show. The time has come for judging. Chef Birns, Chef Baker, and Chef Lee are champing at the bit, pardon the pun, to start taste-testing."

In the kitchen, Sherry and the other cooks cheered, with the exception of the lanky contestant with tortoiseshell glasses. Jamie Sox wrung out his slender hands over and over until Sherry thought he might rub the skin right off. He adjusted his glasses and began pacing over the three-foot-wide area behind his cooking station. Two steps, about-face, two steps, about-face. When Jamie finally stopped, he threw his hands up to the top of his head. "Can we just get this over with, please? Let's go, let's go, let's go!"

Jamie's repeated approach and retreat made Sherry feel claustrophobic in their tight confines. From one extreme to another. From Marla's chill demeanor to Jamie's overwrought state. It was like a side-by-side comparison of a vanilla wafer and chipotle chili cheese dog.

"Mr. Andime, may I add one more thing? I would personally like to invite the members of our audience, the cook-off staff, and our talented contestants to use the discount coupon you found on your seat and come eat at my restaurant, Chef Lee's Splayd and Spork, located in beautiful Stamford, Connecticut. Contestants, you will find yours in your OrgaNicks gift basket. Our specialty is 'universal fusion!'"

Kenny laughed through his nose. "Sounds more like 'useless con-fusion.'"

"Why are you so ornery?" Sherry's question fell on deaf ears. Kenny just shifted in his seat. "Well, I think the restaurant coupon is a great idea. I can't wait to use mine."

"Thank you, Chef Lee. Contestants, would you please line up with the two plates of food you have constructed. Remember to bring one to the judges' table and one to the display table. Please keep your contest aprons on until directed otherwise," a female voice announced through the speakers.

"It's go time!" Kenny leaped out of his seat.

Sherry secured a serving of her prepared recipe in each hand and stood ready for further instructions. A wave of thick sour air wafted through her nostrils. She swallowed hard to suppress something acidic rising in her throat. She glanced at Jamie, who was doubled over just off her right elbow.

Jamie straightened up with a groan. "Can anyone help me carry my plates? I've got a mess here."

Sherry turned to offer assistance, but when she pivoted, she was met with a scene messier than a napkinless Sloppy Joe dinner.

"I don't believe what I'm seeing." Kenny side-stepped the pool of vomit. "Dude, be a man and carry your own stuff. Do you see the rest of us losing our lunches?"

Jamie removed his glasses and wiped them with the hem of his contestant apron. "I didn't mean to. It just happened again."

A man in a brilliant white coat embroidered with the name Chef Anthony Birns appeared at Sherry's side. Sherry corrected her slumping posture and forced a smile. "Chef Birns, we were just listening to your fascinating talk. Be careful of the mess on the floor." Sherry curled down the sides of her mouth as the acrid smell assaulted her senses.

"My first chance to get to the men's room all morning." A bead of sweat trickled down the chef's temple. Sherry resisted the urge to put down her plates and dab his face with a napkin.

Chef Birns walked past Sherry and laid a kitchen towel over the mess at Jamie's feet. "Whew." The chef recoiled. He inspected his hands before wiping them down the sides of his pants. He studied the cook's nametag. "I'm sorry, Mr. Sox. You have to carry your plates yourself. The contest rules state no one besides the contestant themselves and their assigned helpers is permitted to touch the plates. It's necessary to avoid any tampering or accidental mishaps."

"I agree, Chef," said Kenny. "The contestant should know the rules, shouldn't he?"

Sherry rolled her eyes.

Nick Andime reentered the kitchen. "Chef Birns, we need you. Where are you going?"

"Nature calls. Be right back."

Nick clapped his hands three times. "Okay, people, time to move out. Watch your step, please, as you pass Mr. Sox's table. One plate to the display table and one plate to your assistant, who will see that it gets to the judges' table."

Chapter 3

"Okay, kids, put on your best beauty-pageant smile. Time to make our entrance." Kenny led the line of six cooks into the auditorium.

Sherry wore a broad grin, bolstered by the audience's hearty round of applause. She and the other cooks made their way to their reserved front-row seats.

"Do you mind if I sit next to my sister?" Sherry asked.

"Family first." Kenny acquiesced and moved down a seat.

"I might have found his soft underbelly." Sherry sat and turned her attention toward the woman on stage.

"Ladies and gentlemen, again let me remind you, I am Brynne Stark, spelled with a 'K,' although, I'm hoping to drop the last letter soon. I'm your official OrgaNicks Cook-Off hostess. Who has seen my appearances on National Public Broadcasting's TV show *Kitchen Heat*? My segments were titled 'Table Manners with Brynne.'"

A gray-haired woman in the audience cheered.

"Thank you. I love you, too." Brynne grinned and fluffed her hair with a shake of her head.

Sherry swore Brynne mouthed "thanks, Mom," before continuing.

"I just witnessed some of the most talented home cooks in the United States broil, bake, and fry their hearts out. Having been in beauty pageants most of my childhood, I know how harrowing contests can be.

"The judges will now begin tasting the contestants' food. It's a blind judging, meaning the judges only see a number associated with a plate, not a name. Runners will bring the prepared plates in one by one in no particular order.

"While the important task of picking a winner is going on, let's meet the cooks who have just joined us. Contestants, please rise when I call your name. First up is Sherry Frazzelle."

Sherry winced when Brynne mispronounced her last name as "frazzle." "It's Frazzelle, rhymes with 'la belly.'" Sherry stood and gave the audience a wave.

Brynne waited for Sherry to take her seat before continuing. "Amber Sherman."

Sherry glanced down the row of seats at Amber. She hadn't come across the woman with the pale auburn hair in any other contest, but she had shared a pleasant conversation with her before the cook-off began.

Brynne watched Amber rise and lower herself before referring back to the sheet of paper in her hands. "Diana Stroyer."

"She's a tough cookie," Kenny whispered to Sherry. "She's won a ton of contests. But word is she's the Queen of Mean Cuisine when it comes to contestant sportsmanship."

Marla leaned across Sherry. "Kenny, would you please shush?"

Kenny's mouth was left hanging open.

Sherry muffled a nervous snicker by putting her hand over her mouth, but a high-pitched squeal managed to sneak out. Marla swatted her sister's knee.

Brynne cleared her throat. "Kenny Dewitt. Am I pronouncing your last name correctly? Is it De-Witt or Dew-itt?"

Kenny stood amidst laughter and applause. "Hey, guys! You know Kenny can do it!" He raised his arms as if signaling a touchdown. "Over there is my posse. They traveled all the way from Cali to cheer me on!"

"Thank you, Kenny. Please have a seat." Brynne paused until the laughter died down. "Jamie Sox." Brynne drew in a dramatic breath before repeating herself. "Jamie Sox."

"Mr. Vomit," Marla whispered. It was Sherry's turn to give a knee swat.

Sherry saw Diana, who was seated next to Jamie, jab him with her elbow.

"Present." Jamie removed the iPhone earbuds.

Again, the audience erupted in laughter. Jamie sunk back down in his chair and pocketed his listening device.

Brynne waved her paper and brought it down to her side. "And Marla Barras."

Marla stood up, waved, then flopped back down.

"You've met our outstanding judges, Chef Tony Birns, Chef Brock Lee, and Chef Olivia Baker."

Brynne pointed to the trio seated on stage. "Ladies and gentlemen, feast your eyes on the task at hand."

Sherry sat up a bit straighter and began flexing her ankles. As she waited for the judging to be completed, Sherry's senses were working in overdrive, trying to sort out the aromas of savory spices, roasted meats, and complex sauces that thickened the air in the school's auditorium. The lighting in the room was dim, except for center stage, which was illuminated by overhead spotlights. The judges' arm gesturing, finger wagging, and head bobbing mesmerized Sherry. The room was abuzz with passionate debate. She overheard audience opinions being dished out like coleslaw at a barbecue. Her racing thoughts were questions desperate for answers. *Which dish is more visually appealing? Which recipe title best describes the most delicious entrée? Is my pork dish succulent? Will the pizza have a balance of flavors? Who deserves to win the title of "Best Recipe?"*

Sherry was also busy tracking Brynne Stark, as she strutted around the judges' table, monitoring their deliberations. Balanced on silver high heels, Brynne hustled to and fro between the chefs. Her light brown hair, accented with brassy highlights, brushed across her shoulders with each step. Her drop earrings reflected the spotlights, creating an aura of sparkly dots around her. After circling the table, Brynne raised the microphone to her red lips. The audience hushed.

"OrgaNicks Foods, the cook-off sponsor, would like to again thank the home chefs who made it to the final round of this competition. As the saying goes, 'If you can't stand the heat, get out of the contest kitchen.' These cooks turned up the heat and

left the kitchen only when their very best was
achieved. The competition today was dog eat dog.
It was a food fight for the ages. One that will reward
the last man or woman standing with ten thousand
dollars." Dramatic pause. "Who will claim the title
of OrgaNicks Supreme Home Chef?" Brynne lowered the microphone and stepped into the shadows.

Sherry's arm hairs began to spring up. Her skin
prickled and her palms chilled, as they grew damp.
Recognizing the signs of an impending panic attack,
Sherry drew in a deep breath and released it to the
count of one-one thousand, two-one thousand.
Much to her relief, her sprinting heartbeat steadied
to a jog.

The deliberation lasted until the head judge,
Chef Tony Birns, gave a nod. Following the chef's
line of sight, Sherry located Nick Andime, made visible by the shiny luster of his synthetic-fiber suit
coat. The lights throughout the auditorium brightened. Sherry was forced to blink the brightness
away before her eyes adjusted. Nick gave Brynne
the signal to address the crowd. She flipped her
head forward, sending her hair cascading over itself,
and then snapped her head back. Her hair, now
more airy than a perfect popover, created a striking
frame around her porcelain-skinned face. The only
blemish Sherry could see on the woman's clear skin
was the distinct mole just below the corner of her
eye. Brynne centered herself under the stage lights
and opened her mouth to begin her narrative.

"Wait, wait, time out!" Mac clambered toward the
base of the stage with his cameras. "I need to frame
the shot."

In unison, Sherry and the other five contestants blew out their breaths.

After the photographer took his position, Brynne pointed to the first plate on the judges' table, checked her notes, and read, "In front of the judges sit six food masterpieces created by our cook-off finalists. The first plate is Cherry Glazed Short Ribs and Couscous.

"Please don't stand, sir," Brynne warned. "But ladies and gentlemen of the audience, please feel free to applaud."

Kenny Dewitt, having already lifted his backside off his chair, plunked back down and scowled.

"Next, we have Chutney Glazed and Farro Stuffed Pork Tenderloin." Brynne swept her arm in its direction.

From her seat, Sherry smiled at the visual presentation of her plated food. She rubbed her perspiring palms on her pant legs. They left a moist smudge.

"This plate is Chicago Style Bison Sausage and Greens Pizza on Whole Grain Crust. The next plate is Cheesy Chicken and Grits. Here we have Cowboy Pork Chops with Black Bean Compote, and finally, New England Seafood Flatbread." Brynne released a breathy sigh between recipe titles. "The judges were unaware of who made which dish as they were being sampled."

Brynne waited for the applause to die down before she handed the microphone over to Chef Brock Lee. Someone in the audience let out an unfiltered howl, while another projected a piercing whoop. Sherry made an attempt to locate the noisy

audience members, but each face she saw was as
intoxicated with the excitement in the room as the
next.

Chef Lee wiped his weary eyes with his sleeve.
"So, once again, thank you all for being here and
making the inaugural OrgaNicks Cook-Off such a
success. Remember, OrgaNicks motto is 'Bugs Have
Mothers Too—Eat OrgaNicks.'"

The audience unleashed another round of applause.

"Imagine you are one of these six men and women
who have a chance at ten thousand dollars. How
would you feel right now? By the way, thank you,
Hillsboro High School, for providing our venue."

"Go Fighting Sea Urchins!" bellowed Mac, from
his perch just below the stage.

His cheer resulted in half the audience raising
their hands and wiggling fingers skyward in honor
of the school's official mascot, the spiny sea urchin.

"Well, I see we have a partisan crowd." Chef Lee
handed the microphone to Chef Tony Birns.

To Sherry, it appeared as if Chef Lee whispered
something to his colleague. After which, Chef Birns
ran his index finger across his front teeth to dis-
lodge some greenery.

Sherry elbowed Marla. *Now there's a friend for you.*

Chef Birns stood. The room hushed. He
plunged back down, appearing to lack stability.
Sherry sat up as tall as possible in her chair to assess
the situation. Chef Birns put his head in his hands.

The simultaneous exclamation, "huh?" blanketed
the audience. Sherry turned toward Kenny to say

something, but her thoughts were too muddled to continue.

"Is this part of the show?" Kenny ran his fingers through his lamb-chop sideburns. "What's going on? Come on already!"

On his second attempt, the chef was successful at standing. He placed one hand on the table for stabilization. He took a labored breath, unbuttoned his shirt collar, and cleared his throat. "So, without further ado, I would like to announce the ten-thousand-dollar winner of this year's Orga-Nicks Cook-Off." Chef Birns spoke sluggishly. He coughed between words.

Chef Lee pounded his colleague on the back, as if he were preparing veal for scallopini.

The urgency in Chef Birns' voice was palpable. "Sorry 'bout that. It was a very close competition, but the dish the judges feel best represents the theme and essence of the contest is the: Chh, sorry, the Chhh, again sorry, the Chhhh . . ."

Chef Tony Birns' legs collapsed. His head plummeted face-first into the Seafood Flatbread Pizza. Crustaceans and tomato sauce flew in all directions. The sight of the gray pallor of the chef's exposed skin bathed in the rosy sauce made Sherry's stomach lurch. The audience shrieked. Some leapt up from their seats. Chair legs creaked and scraped. Someone on stage barked instructions. The noise level became deafening.

"What's happening?" Sherry tried to see beyond the milling crowd. "Is he okay?"

"Maybe the pizza gave him a heart attack." Kenny slumped in his seat.

"Man down," yelled Mac, who looked over his camera viewfinder but kept the camera aimed at the chef.

"Help! Can someone help?" cried Chef Baker.

"Is anyone a doctor out there?" Chef Lee called out.

"Sherry, you know CPR." Marla leaned across Kenny to poke Sherry. "Get up there!"

"I took that course ten years ago." Sherry's face blanched. Her heart rate accelerated. She searched Marla's eyes for reassurance but only saw distress. An adrenaline rush propelled Sherry forward toward the stage.

Once at the fallen chef's side, Sherry explained, "I have CPR training. Can you turn him over for me, please?"

Chef Lee repositioned the stout body of Chef Birns from belly down to faceup. Sherry made a fist and encased it with her other hand. She hummed the Bee Gees' hit song "Stayin' Alive" to get her compression rhythm correct, as she had learned in class. After a short time, she realized the chest compressions weren't successful and her arm muscles were throbbing from exhaustion. She used her filthy apron to wipe food off his mouth. She stifled an involuntary gag reflex and closed her eyes. Just as she leaned in to begin rescue breathing, the EMTs arrived.

"Thank you, ma'am. We'll take it from here." A medic, who Sherry wasn't sure was more than sixteen, set his medical equipment next to the body.

Sherry shut off the song loop playing in her brain. She hoisted herself from her crouched position on legs stiff from clenching her muscles too hard.

Chef Birns was placed on a gurney and rolled out to a waiting ambulance while Sherry watched in horror. She was left standing idle next to Mac, who was wiping tomato sauce off his cameras.

"You gave it your best shot, but to put it in terms this audience can appreciate, I think you can stick a fork in him—he's done."

Staggering on weak knees, Sherry made her way back to her seat. A few people gave her a consoling pat on the back as she passed by.

When she arrived at her seat, Marla enveloped Sherry with a hug. "Sherry, you've got guts. You tried your best."

"If it weren't for your push, I'd never have had the courage to go up there. I'm a little ashamed of myself." Sherry hung her head.

"It was all you," said Marla, "and don't forget it."

"Ladies and gentlemen," Brynne broadcast from the side of the auditorium. "Due to circumstances beyond anyone's control, the conclusion of the cook-off will now be postponed to a later date, yet to be determined." Behind Brynne, Nick Andime appeared to give her a push forward. Brynne lifted what appeared to be a script up to her face with great effort, as if it weighed a ton. "When you get home, please 'like' the OrgaNicks Foods Facebook page, and you will gain access to all the information needed to learn the outcome of the contest as it becomes available. We are hoping to get to two hundred additional 'likes' by the end of the day with your help." Brynne aimed a smile toward the scattering crowd. "Thank you for coming and enjoy your complimentary recipe card collection. You'll find the gift box under your seats. Please exit to the rear of the building. I would also like to invite you to follow me on Twitter @BrynneStark after the cook-off concludes." Brynne clicked off the microphone, turned, and walked away.

"Did anyone notice that before he collapsed, the chef might have said Cherry Glazed Short Ribs and Couscous? I think he named Cherry Glazed Short Ribs and Couscous as the winner! I heard him say a word started with Chhh. My recipe starts with Chhh!"

Sherry shook her head. "Kenny, we may never know for sure."

"I hope he's okay. Nice job, kid." Kenny added.

As the audience dispersed, Sherry and the other cook-off contestants were left milling about anxious for guidance. They only relaxed when a police officer approached and told them they were free to go after they completed a brief round of questioning.

Chapter
4

Sherry dragged her tired legs up the front porch steps. Two other women remained at the first step. Once at the door, Sherry was glad to be sheltered from the summer sun by the cedar-shingled over-hang. She set down the gift basket she'd received at the cook-off and the newspaper she picked up from the end of the driveway.

Sherry held up her key ring and groaned. "How did I grab the set with no house key? I need to remind Charlie again to return his copy, so I can attach it. You wait here while I run around back and sneak in through the unlocked patio door."

After a few moments the reclaimed wood front door opened. "Come in, ladies. Make yourselves at home."

Sherry's guests entered the modest saltbox house. Marla, the last one in, closed the door behind her and set down her overnight bag. "You almost forgot these." She handed her sister her gift basket and the newspaper. "Let me tell you again how much

I love your house. So quaint, so New England. The show house of Augustin, Connecticut."

Sherry removed her shoes and squared them up with the doormat. "Thanks, Mar. But that's a bit of an exaggeration, don't you think? Watch out for my sleeping guard dog over by the steps. He's hard of hearing, so he won't wake up until he catches our scent. Not even this commotion will wake him." Sherry searched her sister's eyes. "I'm sorry you got in too late to stay over last night, but Dad's sofa wasn't too uncomfortable, was it?"

"I don't even remember. After he picked me up at the airport, I zonked out in the car. Let's just say, I may have had one too many glasses of my special calming elixir during the flight. As soon as I saw thunderstorms in the forecast, I loaded up my flask before I left Oklahoma."

"What if you had to make a life-or-death decision during the flight? You couldn't even find the plane's emergency exit if you were so out of it."

"That's the difference between you and me. You like to be in control as much as possible, and I might be a little more laid back." Marla kicked off her shoes one by one. They landed next to Sherry's after somersaulting in the air several times.

"Nice shot, Mar. You haven't lost a bit of your soccer skills. Amber, you can either take off your shoes or keep them on. Whatever you're most comfortable with."

Amber parked her overnighter next to Marla's. She followed the sisters' lead and placed her shoes by the door.

"Yikes, my stink could wake the dead."

"Marla! What a thing to say." Sherry clicked her tongue on the roof of her mouth.

Marla inclined her head toward her shoulder. "My God, I'm sorry. You know when someone says really dumb things at inappropriate times? You're looking at the worst offender. Maybe you can speak to that, Amber."

"It's actually a form of social anxiety," Amber said.

"Watch out, Sherry. Having a therapist as a houseguest could be a gift or a curse," laughed Marla.

"Actually, ladies, I'm a marriage and family counselor to be specific."

"Well, let the record show, Amber Sherman barely knows us and she has already diagnosed you as the anxious one. All my life 'anxious' was my label. Who knew?" Sherry gripped her basket brimming with plastic-wrapped OrgaNicks boxes and jars. "Grab your gift baskets because the best place to put them is on the kitchen counter. I don't think you'll forget them there when you leave."

"P.U., I smell like spoiled meat drenched in sour milk." Marla nudged Sherry aside to observe her appearance in the front hall mirror. "Yikes, I don't look too great either."

Marla tiptoed over to the stairs where Sherry's dog was curled up.

"I would be very quiet, Mar. You know what they say about letting sleeping dogs lie." Sherry put her finger up to her lips.

Marla passed the dog without incident. Sherry followed behind. She kneeled down and gave her Jack

Russell terrier a pat on the head. The dog thumped his stubby tail, even before opening his eyes.

"He's so sweet!" Amber squatted to pet the dog. "I bet he's happy to have you home. What a solid sleeper."

As if on cue, Chutney rose and began snarling. Amber and her gift basket toppled over like a four-tier cake assembled by a novice baker.

"Chutney, no!" Sherry restrained her furry bundle of security by his collar. No longer growling, the dog's nose began twitching as he sniffed the alluring aromas wafting from the women's clothes.

"I've known her dog for years, and he still wants to nip my ankles when I first come in the door." Marla tipped forward, pulled up a pant leg, and showcased her bare ankle. "Training would probably help."

"Sorry. I guess you really should let sleeping dogs lie." Sherry curled up her lips. "He'll relax in a minute. His protective instinct is strong because I'm usually here alone."

"Chutney is Sherry's child, basically, and he gets away with murder."

"Marla, again!" Sherry slapped her forehead.

"Ugh, sorry. Bad choice of words." Marla threw up her hands.

"I feel so bad about the judge losing his life at the cook-off." Sherry lowered her eyes. "The police told us the medics never revived him. But I still don't see why they had to detain us all after the event. I just wanted to get out of there. It was a death, not a crime. The general questions they asked could've been answered by reading the contest brochure. I'm not sure my answers made too much sense, anyway. Police make me nervous, and I've never even broken the law. Not even gotten a traffic ticket."

"It was awful," agreed Amber. "Just think how the morning started compared to how it ended. I was so excited to be in my first recipe contest. It was pretty thrilling to come in with no idea what to expect. Now, thinking back, the block of time between arriving at the high school and the police questioning seems kind of hazy. In my mind, the whole experience has a terrible dark shadow hanging over it. I'm having a hard time processing what happened."

The ladies continued on to the kitchen, where they set down their baskets on the counter.

As soon as the baskets were out of her guests' hands, Sherry headed out of the kitchen. "Let me show you where to put your suitcases."

Amber and Marla returned to the front hall to gather up their suitcases. The floor vibrated with a dull hum as Amber rolled hers toward Sherry. "I'm really relieved you invited me to stay over tonight, Sherry. I wasn't thrilled with the idea of riding the train back to Maine and going to my empty house. I know I'm going to have nightmares about seeing Chef Birns sprawled out, covered in my seafood sauce." Amber parked her luggage by the stairs and studied her forearms. "Gives me goose bumps."

Marla rolled up behind Amber. "It wasn't a great ending to the morning."

"The chef seemed in good health up until his last breath, as far as I could tell." Sherry put one foot on a step before noticing a dog hair. She collected it in her hand. "What do you guys think killed him?"

"I didn't hear anyone say anything definitive

about the cause. I'm no doctor, but my guess is years of rich food can't be great for you if you don't balance it with healthier stuff." Marla extended her belly and ran her hands up and down it.

Sherry wrinkled her brow and picked up another dog hair off the first step. "I agree. I guess it was just his time. Amber, I was relieved you took me up on my invite."

"Yep, you rescued me for sure." Amber drummed her fingers on the handle of her suitcase.

"Happy to have you." Sherry grabbed her sister's arm. "Usually I never let Marla go home without a two-night minimum stay, but this time she just can't."

"Are we going upstairs or are we just watching you clean them?" Marla took a half step forward.

"Sorry. Let me show you where you'll be sleeping." Sherry led the way up the stairs.

"Amber, I'll put you in the blue room. You just have to pardon the mountain of clothes. The last time Charlie, my almost ex-husband, was here, he promised to finish removing the last of his stuff."

Sherry caught a glimpse of Marla's furrowed eyebrows. "He promised he'd do it soon."

"I didn't say a word." Marla winked at her sister.

When the ladies entered the blue bedroom, Marla let out a gasp. Amber laughed. The sight before her mimicked an end-of-season blowout sale at the Mother Lode of Men's Attire Warehouse store. Stacks of men's shirts, pants, blazers, shorts, dress shoes, and sneakers in varying styles and colors lay around the room.

"Are you sure he's moved out?" Marla sat down on the queen-size bed.

"It's none of my business and I don't need to know any details of your private life, but maybe it isn't a good time for you to put me up." Amber's gaze jumped from pile to pile.

Sherry's face flushed. She sat down next to her sister. "It's the best time. I'll give you a quick recap of my situation. I met Charlie Frazzelle when I was finishing college and he was a senior in high school. Scandalous at the time, as we had a five-year age difference, but it was all very innocent at first. I was his organization tutor. He was the top of his graduating class, but his parents felt he had very poor organizational skills and would have trouble with time management in college. After the summer tutoring session, which was all business I might add, we kept in touch. Fast forward to his law-school graduation party where he extended me an invitation. We were inseparable after that until we married. Unfortunately, he pretty quickly realized he wanted to be single again and only married to his career. Our marriage was like a steak cooked on low temperature. It didn't sizzle. We tried to make it work for five years, and by 'we' I mean 'I,' but as they say, it takes two people to make a marriage work and only one for a divorce."

"A new life phase can be a tough thing, especially if it chose you and not the other way around." Amber patted a stack of shirts. "You can't just shut off feelings you've had for a long time in an instant."

Marla put her arm around Sherry.

Sherry fell silent for a moment before wriggling

out from under Marla's arm. "I'm not taking no for an answer. You're staying. You may be just what the doctor ordered."

"Okay, thank you so much. Maybe you could consider seeing this phase of your life as an opportunity to try something new." Amber raised her hands, palm side up. "Your competitive cooking is certainly a great place to start. Keep your options open, and you'll be shocked at what comes your way."

Sherry smiled. "I'm trying."

"If you don't mind, I'm just going to change out of my dirty things." Amber unzipped her suitcase and began searching through it. "I think this shirt I cooked in has a representative from all categories of the food pyramid on it, and it's beginning to ferment."

"All right. Come down when you're done." Sherry shut the bedroom door. "This way, Mar." Sherry led the way down the short hallway to a second guest bedroom. "I'm putting you in the green room."

"Best room in the house," said Marla.

When they entered, Marla wrapped her sister in an impressive bear hug.

Sherry's arms fell limp from the force of the embrace. "What's that for?"

"Just because I'm not always the best at letting you know I appreciate you."

Sherry left her sister and proceeded to her bedroom, where she changed out of her soiled clothes. She rummaged through her neatly organized drawers, found the light-green section, and grabbed a comfortable and bright summer outfit. Sherry caught her reflection in the full-length mirror. She saw a tall woman in her early thirties—thirty-five *is* "early," some would say—who still managed to wear shorts and a T-shirt with dignity. She liked the way summer colors drew out the otherwise muted highlights in her mousy brown bob-cut hair.

"Not bad. Could use a shower, but maybe later." Sherry twisted her torso to see the front then back of her arms. "I'll never have arm muscles like Marla's. She got all the good genes."

As she left her bedroom, Sherry straightened the photo of herself, Marla, their brother Pep, her mother, and her father taken on her fourteenth birthday. It captured one of their last group shots as an unbroken family. She picked up the photo next to it. It was a photo of her pretty mother, forever frozen in time. The matriarch of the family was flexing her impressive bicep in mock triumph after completing a mini-marathon. It was less than a year after that photo that Sherry's mother, who was so full of vitality and always in constant motion, passed away from an undetected heart ailment. That event put the brakes on Sherry's carefree childhood and catapulted it in to one overburdened with responsibility. As the eldest child it was up to her to fill the void left by her mother's premature death. Her father was busy earning a living, so she managed all other aspects of family life to ensure her younger siblings were happy and fulfilled.

"I'll be downstairs." Sherry descended the steps to the kitchen.

After she'd changed her clothes, Marla came downstairs. "I feel so much more comfortable." Marla's wheat-colored hair was pulled back in a ponytail. She wore blue jeans fitted one size too small, causing her stomach to bulge over the top of her pants, like proofing bread dough overflowing its container. Her short-sleeve chambray shirt with shiny snap closures completed the country ensemble. Her bare feet were calloused and as white as cauliflower from years of sneaker and boot coverage. One of her toenails was black from a lingering injury.

Amber joined them soon, dressed in a beige linen skirt and a short-sleeved cotton polo shirt. Her spotless white sandals framed her fresh pedicure. Amber's hair was well managed, its neatness reinforced with a recent application of styling mousse. Amber and Marla joined Sherry at the round kitchen table. Sherry was refolding cloth napkins she had brought out of storage.

"You girls clean up so nice!" said Amber. "How do you stay so trim with all the cooking you do? Isn't there a saying about 'never trust a skinny cook'?"

"Yep, Sherry is a stalk of asparagus personified. Comes from constantly burning calories. One hint about Sherry's daily routine, she never sits idle. For example, do you really think those napkins needed refolding?"

"Thanks for sharing." Sherry's tone was crisp. "This is how I relax after a tough morning."

"Don't worry about those napkins. We're not going to notice if they have a wrinkle. As for me, I'm not in the shape I used to be in." Marla grabbed her protruding belly and jiggled it. "I'm more like an eggplant personified. But I'm as strong as Limburger cheese." She reenacted the pose Sherry had just seen in the photo of her mother upstairs by flexing her bicep.

Sherry shivered. "Ugh. Stinky. I think you should come up with a better metaphor." She shook her head, trying to rid the memory of the cheese's unpleasant aroma from her nose.

"I was a soccer player growing up, and now I coach high school soccer," added Marla. "I think my body remembers my muscles from years ago and hasn't given up hope I'll start working out again. They're just hidden under a layer or two of insulation."

Sherry tucked her hair behind her ears. It was barely long enough to stay put and soon rebellious strands sprang free. "You can't believe how many soccer games I watched growing up."

"You didn't come to many games. Don't even try to say you did! You just dropped me off and picked me up most of the time." Marla softened her tone. "Sherry did a lot of mom duty after we lost our mother. She walked me to nearly all soccer practices before she could drive, then when she got her license, she was basically my captive chauffeur until I could drive."

"You're in great shape, Amber," said Sherry. "Have any secret workout tips you'd like to share?"

"Thanks! I did recently lose one hundred and ninety pounds." Amber cocked her head to the side.

"Really? Amazing!" Sherry raised her hands and spread her fingers wide.

"Wow, how'd you accomplish that?" asked Marla.

"Bad joke. My husband left me. I signed my divorce decree about ten months ago! I do feel a lot lighter though."

"I'm sorry." Marla's voice softened. "By the way,

is 'sorry' the right thing to say? You don't sound sorry. You sound relieved but a little sad."

"It was a sour ending to a sweet beginning," explained Amber. "We were two young professionals in Boston. We started out with a lot in common, but after seven years of marriage, it was becoming clear we made better business partners than spouses. His after-hours playtime with his gorgeous secretary definitely sealed the deal. Luckily, we were too busy to have kids, so there wasn't much to bicker about during the settlement."

Marla's eyes widened. "Let me tell you one of our dad's pearls of wisdom. 'Sometimes life is like a loaded diaper. If it begins to stink, change it.'"

"Thanks for the visual." Sherry laughed before turning her attention back to Amber. "Why did you move to Maine? Boston's a great town."

"Boston had too many associations with my old life." Amber shifted in her seat. "As I mentioned before, I was, actually—technically, still am—a marriage and family counselor. I noticed a severe drop-off in clientele when my divorce was finalized, so I left town embarrassed. I'd failed at the one thing I was supposed to be an expert at. Moving to Maine felt like an adventurous move to parts unknown. I wanted to go somewhere where no one knew me. I wanted to regroup, renew, refresh."

"I'd call that very adventurous," remarked Marla. "I can relate because when I made the move with my new husband to wild Oklahoma, after spending most of my life here in Augustin, it was quite a shock. I didn't know one single person except my new husband. He had to drag me there kicking and screaming."

"Come on." Sherry curled up the edge of her mouth. "You love kicking and screaming in one way or another. She was the rowdy one in the family."

"You two have quite a dynamic." Amber wrinkled her forehead. "Very interesting. Did you know birth order is a reliable way to predict future successes and failures?"

"I'm the oldest. There's a brother Pep, short for Joseppi, between us, so Marla is the baby. I hope you're going to say the oldest is destined for greater things."

Amber laughed. "I can't make any guarantees, but you're well on your way. How often do you two see one another?"

"I'll take this one." Marla tapped her fingers on the table. "Maybe only three or four times a year, but we talk on the phone, e-mail, and text a lot. I'll be the first to say, distance makes the heart grow fonder. I think Sherry needed a good long break from my brother and me after having us forced down her throat for years and years. Besides, she had to get her own life kick-started."

Sherry released a huff. "Let's get the spotlight off of me. I was thinking, Amber. You were a marriage counselor while your own marriage was crumbling." Sherry fiddled with her spot on her left ring finger where she used to wear a gold and diamond wedding band. "I mean, listening to your clients' problems all day long then, after work, facing your own. That's reason enough to want to run away. Did it help to relocate?"

"For a split second, but fast forward six months from when I had the bright idea to unpack my bags in a cabin in Maine. I couldn't wait to get the hell out of the frozen tundra! I mean the winters there are barbaric! I got so sick of my own company, I put a towel over the bathroom mirror so I'd stop talking to my reflection."

"Makes sense because all the crazy psychos in the news live alone in a cabin in the woods." Marla twirled her index finger around her temple. "Man is not a solitary creature. Being your own best friend comes with a price."

"I used to go to the grocery store just so I could hold a conversation with the check-out lady. Once, I swear, she saw me coming, switched off her 'this line's open' light, and ducked under her cash register. When I saw an ad in a magazine for the Orga-Nicks Cook-Off, with its promise of human interaction and the incentive of traveling south, I couldn't get cooking fast enough. I willed those judges to make me a finalist!"

"I wish it had had a better outcome. Such an awful ending!" Sherry shook her head.

"Really tragic," agreed Amber.

"Poor guy," added Marla.

Sherry sat in silence for a moment before pushing her chair back and heading toward a cabinet. "Can I offer anyone some relaxing tea?"

"Just what we need because it's too early for happy hour." Marla stood up and joined her sister. "Why were you so nervous today during the competition? You need to relax a little and enjoy the moment."

"I just wanted to do a good job. My adrenaline

starts raging, and I get a little wired. Not everyone can be as chill as you!"

"You had a really good chance of winning, I think. Your recipe was great." Marla handed a mug to Amber. "Sherry gets anxious easily. Instead of hoping for the best she has a tendency to prepare for the worst. Have any advice for her?"

"Amber's not here to fix our family." Sherry wagged her finger at Marla. "And by the way, that's exactly what did happen today. How much worse could it have gotten?" Sherry's question was left unanswered, interrupted by the teakettle whistle. She filled each mug with boiling water and a tea bag.

While the tea steeped, Sherry gave Amber a quick tour of the rest of the house.

"Such a charming house." Amber said.

"Thanks. When Charlie and I moved to this house, we started full throttle on building this into our dream home. We got pretty far before we agreed we couldn't make a lifetime together work, so he moved out and my dad moved in for a short time. Dad owns a local hooked-rug store, Oliveri's Ruggery, and I work there part-time. He helped finish the house before moving to his own townhouse. I may have driven him out, too, but he's too polite to admit it. I might be a bit particular in my ways."

Marla coughed and then cleared her throat.

"Here's my favorite room." Sherry let her arms flow out to her sides.

"You did a great job on the kitchen," said Amber. "These green granite counters are gorgeous! And these wood cabinets go so well with the earthy backsplash tiles."

"Sometimes I think I would trade it all in for a

second chance at my marriage." Sherry's wide-eyed gaze met her sister's. "But then reality sets in, and I realize the marriage ship has sailed. So it's the future that needs a remodel now. Dad made a comment the other day about how my life currently is a pizza for one and I just have to pick the right toppings."

"Dads are the best." Amber put her clasped hands over her heart.

"Okay, enough wallowing in my life mess," Sherry announced. "Anyone want a section of the newspaper? I wouldn't mind taking a few minutes to relax. Let's go out on the patio. Grab your mugs." Sherry led Amber and Marla outside to the bluestone terrace. Secured under her arm was the day's newspaper.

"I'll take the sports section." Marla plopped down on a cushioned lawn chair.

"No argument here." Sherry settled in to the lounge chair beside Marla. "I'll take the Home and Garden section, unless you want it, Amber."

"Front page for me." Amber reclined on another lounge chair.

"Yesterday in the paper I saw a print ad for cook-off audience tickets. I would think the article about what happened would come out tomorrow. Wonder what they'll report."

Amber scanned the headlines. "Wow, did you hear the food giant Visible Roots Produce is being sued for knowingly selling packaged salads with insect larvae in them?"

"Yuck!"

"Not a good news day for food companies," Marla added.

Sherry peeked over the top of her newspaper section. "Amber, I was thinking, after today, you may be put off by cook-offs, but there's one coming up featuring honey. Marla and I have made it a goal to try and get into the finals, and it would be great if you could be there, too. Maybe while you're staying here we could all work on some entries, if there's time?"

"I'll think about it," sighed Amber.

Chapter
5

"Sherry, wake up." Marla thumped her sister on the head as if she were testing a melon for ripeness. "I think someone's knocking at the door."

"Wow, I really zonked out." Sherry shook her head to awaken her brain. "Sorry 'bout that. I guess I was wiped out from the cook-off."

Marla pulled Sherry to her feet. "You were snoring."

"And drooling a bit." Amber struggled to get out of her lounge chair.

As Sherry wiped the corners of her mouth, Chutney began barking.

"I'm not expecting anyone." Sherry reentered the house from the patio and peered out the window beside her front door. She was met with the silhouette of a slightly crouched man in a suit. Another man, carrying a computer tablet, stood a step behind. Sherry unlocked the door and opened it a few inches, keeping one foot at the base of the doorframe.

The man wearing a crumpled hat wedged his

head sideways through the sliver of space the partially open door provided. "Good afternoon. I'm Detective Ray Bease. I'm the Hillsboro Police Department detective assigned to investigate the death that occurred at the OrgaNicks Cook-Off earlier today. And this is my assistant, Detective Cody Diamond."

Sherry widened the door opening.

"Here are our credentials. Please inspect them thoroughly." Detective Bease presented his badge and paperwork to Sherry. She took what he offered and shuffled through the collection.

"Is one of you Sherry Frazzelle?" the Detective asked.

"Yes, I am. My last name's pronounced Fra-sell-E, not frazzle. Please, come in,"

"Hold on. Let me just double-check those." Marla snatched the identification documents out of Sherry's hands. "You can never be too careful."

"She's right, ma'am. You can never be too careful," Detective Diamond added.

"Seems legit, Sherry." Marla looked up from the documents with a slight smirk. "Ray Bease. Really?"

Detective Diamond put his hand up to his mouth to conceal a smile. With his other hand, he swept his highlighted bangs out of his eyes.

"Not Bease, as in honey bees. It's pronounced Bease, rhymes with grease. As in elbow grease." The man eyebrows folded in on themselves. "If we could have a brief moment of your time, we have a few questions to ask. Is now a convenient time?"

"Please, come in, Detective Bease." Sherry glanced at the detective's dusty shoes. Her mouth twisted into a pucker. "If you'd like to take your shoes off, please do."

"No, thanks."

"Let's go sit in the kitchen." Sherry's arm twitched when she saw the flakes of dirt Detective Bease's shoes shed with each step he took. She suppressed the urge to run and get her portable vacuum cleaner. "This is my sister, Marla Barras, and our friend Amber Sherman. We were all contestants at the cook-off today. Please have a seat." Sherry waved the group into the kitchen and pointed out the chairs at the round table.

"Can I get anyone a glass of lemonade?"

"No, thank you," said Detective Bease. "We won't be here long."

"Yes, please, ma'am," Detective Diamond said. "I could never resist my mom's lemonade. You kind of remind me of her."

"I'll take one, too," said Marla.

"Me three, please," said Amber.

Sherry always kept a pitcher of lemonade in her refrigerator in case someone stopped by. She constructed a tray of glasses and rushed it to the table.

When Sherry returned to the table, the detectives were making a lengthy visual scan of her kitchen and dining room from their seats. Detective Diamond had set up a computer on the table. Sherry sat with a rigid posture, uncertain about the men she had invited in.

"I'm here to ask you, Ms. Frazzelle, if you have any details to add to the statements you gave the police at the scene this morning?" Detective Bease took a gold-trimmed pen out of his coat pocket. Detective Diamond handed his partner a spiral notepad. Bease began clicking the pen's retractor button manically.

Sherry's eyes were drawn to the detective's pen. She could make out the inscription "Connecticut: The Nutmeg State." "I like your pen."

"Thanks. I'm hoping to collect one from all fifty states." The detective stopped fidgeting with his pen, and the silence thickened.

"Back to your question. Do the police always treat a death this way? Seems a bit excessive. Can't the death certificate give you all the answers you need? By the way, why are you only asking me?" Sherry pointed to Marla and Amber.

The detective resumed clicking his pen. "I wasn't aware anyone else from the scene would be here, frankly."

"Okay, well, as I told the police, I don't think I know of anything outside of the cooking we did. I only saw a man collapse while judging the recipe contest. That's about it." Sherry picked up a napkin and fanned herself. "The contestants only found out he died after the ambulance left. I had a feeling it wasn't good when I was giving him CPR, but I was hopeful the EMTs could revive him. Sorry, not too helpful."

Detective Diamond leaned over to his associate. "Sounds like a reluctant witness. Chapter Four of *The Effective Detective* deals with getting those kind to cooperate."

Detective Bease's pen became silent. "I don't think your textbook can teach you more effective skills than I can. Watch and learn, bookworm." He turned back to the women. "If you would just keep your eyes and ears open to any clues as to why someone would have such a problem with Chef Anthony Birns that it may have led to his murder, I would appreciate it."

"Murder! Wait! Are you saying it was murder?" asked Amber.

Sherry shivered.

"It doesn't seem he died of natural causes, but we'll know with certainty when the autopsy reports come back." Detective Bease unbuttoned his dirt-brown blazer and placed his hand inside, as if searching for something. As his coat flapped open, Sherry caught a glimpse of what looked like a pistol holster. She couldn't control a ripple of uneasiness as it traveled from shoulder to shoulder.

"Preliminary tests indicate he died from a reaction to an irritant in his throat, and for many reasons it doesn't appear accidental," Bease continued. "The medics knew immediately when they were attempting to revive him they were dealing with an unusual food substance in the lining of the victim's soft tissue. We know of no one else who had an adverse reaction to anything consumed during the cook-off. If it was accidental, there would have been many people affected on some level because so much food was shared."

"Unbelievable." Amber stood. "Who would kill him? I can't even believe I'm saying those words. And why?" She sat back down.

"My job is to answer those questions. Ironic, isn't it, for a chef who makes his living preparing and sampling perfectly executed, no pun intended, food to have ingested something toxic enough to kill him? Hmmm." Detective Bease began working his pen retractor button with a renewed intensity.

"But, until we know what or who ended his life, all leads must be considered."

"I'm shocked." Sherry squinted and wrinkled up her nose. "What's so scary is we witnessed a murder and didn't even know it."

Amber and Marla nodded.

"I was just thinking the clues detectives gather are kind of like ingredients in a recipe." Sherry used her hand and an imaginary pencil to write down words. "When you get them all put together in the proper way, the case is solved, and the recipe is complete." She raised her invisible pencil and waved it overhead.

"Something like that," said Detective Bease. "You solve a crime by combining clues, and you make a recipe by combining ingredients. Yep, good comparison."

"She's becoming a 'friendly' witness," added Detective Diamond. "Chapter Three."

Sherry sat up a little straighter, proud of her amateur analysis. She flashed a broad smile at the detectives.

Detective Bease appeared to blush. He reached over and took a sip of his partner's lemonade.

"Can we get back to the cook-off, please?" asked Marla. "And can you please stop clicking your pen?"

"Honestly, I don't know if I'd be able to help in any way. I just can't think of anything to add to the statements I already made." Sherry sighed.

"Let me try to jog your memory. Do you recall any arguments prior to or during the event?" asked Detective Diamond.

"Think of any chatter you may have overheard,

ma'am. Something that may seem out of the norm as you recall it," suggested Detective Bease.

"Don't hold your breath, Mr. Bease. My sister was a wreck most of the morning trying to get her recipe to come out perfectly. I bet she wasn't focused on anything but her tenderloin."

"Not true." Sherry wiped a smudge on Marla's lemonade glass with her napkin. "I was very tuned in to the whole cook-off scene. By the way, Detectives, I prefer not to be called ma'am."

Bease raised his head and fixed his gaze on Sherry. Her eyelid fluttered. She hoped he hadn't noticed.

"It's a term derived from Madame, which refers to a woman of high rank, such as royalty. The Queen of England, for example," explained Detective Diamond, before his partner could respond.

"Have you seen how old the Queen is?" Sherry shifted to the side of her hip. She examined Detective Bease for a moment. *You're no spring chicken yourself.* Her gaze shifted to the younger detective. *Okay, I admit I may be a good ten years older than you.*

"Yes, ma'a . . . I mean, okay. Let's see. Can any of you tell me a bit about the world of recipe contesting?" Detective Bease turned back a few pages in his notepad. "That's what you call it, correct?"

"Yes," answered Marla. "It's just what it sounds like. People submit recipes to an organized contest, they're judged, and the best one wins. There are recipe contests conducted over the Internet, where you submit your recipe through the sponsor's website, and others are promoted through publications, like a magazine. Some require you to participate in a live cooking competition like the OrgaNicks Cook-Off."

"Do the contests ever get contentious? For example, is there any animosity amongst contestants or between contestants and judges? Any ill will you have witnessed?" asked Detective Bease.

"Honestly, I'd dip my grandmother in egg wash and roll her in panko breadcrumbs for a chance at a ten-thousand-dollar grand prize. That's what was at stake in the OrgaNicks Cook-off." Marla accented her reply with an exaggerated Midwestern twang. "I'm just joshing you. But I will say, my sister taught me what little I know about cooking. I'd love to win, but if I don't, I hope she does or Amber. But we'll have to wait and see on this one, if there ever is a winner announcement. At the end of the day, only the cooking gods know what the outcome will be."

Sherry shifted her gaze from Marla to Detective Bease. "Some individuals I've met are more intense than others, but I've never seen feelings escalate to a level where someone could get hurt. Every once in a while, you come across a cook who's solely in it for the money. More often than not, they come away disappointed because very few people win big. I think the fast-cash dreamers are the ones who don't enter more than one contest because their hopes are quickly dashed. Frankly, anyone who falls into that group is probably not very talented anyway. You know, most of us really are just a nice bunch of people trying to win a prize for doing what we do at six o'clock night after night."

Detective Bease put down his pen and tapped his notepad with his index finger. "Okay, let me ask you this. What's your experience with the judges of these events? Do they make themselves available to the cooks? Any interaction between judges and cooks, I mean? Are the judges pleasant or in any way abrasive? Not all are cut out to be judged in a public forum, and if the judge is detached, patronizing, or maybe even cruel, I could see a motive emerging."

"We don't get much interaction with the judges. Contests are designed to keep contestants and judges apart." Sherry created a partition in front of her with her hands. "Sometimes the cooks never see them. We may find out their names ahead of the contest or maybe not until after it's over. I suppose contestants could hold grudges if they feel slighted, but you'd have to be pretty twisted to kill a guy for not liking your Stroganoff."

"Okay, let me move in a different direction then." Detective Bease picked up his pen and pointed it at Sherry. "I am curious how you all come up with these winning recipes."

"I'm sure each one of us has different means to the end result," said Amber. "I'm really new to the game, so I just cooked and cooked and tested and tested until I was somewhat satisfied with the results—enough to send the recipe into the contest."

"As a new contestant, how upset were you when you didn't win?" asked Detective Bease.

"Wait! I didn't *not* win." Amber balled her hand in a fist. "We still don't know who the winner was. Weren't you told that?"

Detective Diamond's chair screeched as he scooted forward in it. "We've only just begun our investigation. We don't have all the information. That's why we're here."

"Sorry." Amber unclenched her hand. "Chef Tony Birns died before he could get the winning recipe title out of his mouth. The contest results would be postponed, we were told."

"I imagine the other two judges know who won or, at the very least, Nick Andime, the head of Orga-Nicks, does." Sherry squinted to see if she could bring what was on Detective Diamond's computer screen into focus, but he raised his arm and blocked it. "I'm almost certain he was the one who whispered the winner's name in Chef Birns' ear. I know because I was watching him like a hawk trying to read his lips, but he was too discreet."

"Very interesting." Detective Bease's pen danced across his notepad. "The perpetrator couldn't have been angry about today's contest results because the death took place *before* the winner was announced."

"It could easily be that someone who'd been in a previous contest with the deceased judge was in today's cook-off. He's been a judge in other contests. That information was listed in the contest brochure under each chef's bio. I just can't believe anyone there would do such a thing." Sherry closed her eyes and shook her head.

"Let's move on." Detective Bease flipped the page on his notepad. "I'm curious about how the mechanics of a cook-off work. I've been to state fairs where there's a baking contest or a blue-ribbon best chili cook-off, and I've watched 'cook for cash' shows on the Oven Lovin' Network, but I didn't realize live cooking competitions had grown into such a nationwide phenomenon. If the prize were large enough, I'd think people might resort to devious means to win at all costs. If the judge was the obstacle between the contestant and a pile of cash, maybe things could turn deadly."

"I've seen underhanded forms of *bending* the rules." Sherry's voice took on a sarcastic tone. "For example, there is one notorious home cook who is known for *taking*, and I use the term loosely—"

"She really means 'stealing,'" Marla interjected.

"—a previously published recipe, simply changing the name, and entering it as her own creation. But you can't get away with shortcutting creativity very easily now because a simple search of the Internet reveals who the recipe belongs to."

"What a cheater! Have I ever met her?" Marla asked.

"Maybe, but I'll never tell." Sherry dropped her head to the side. "And then there was the contestant who definitely was married to a cookbook author. You know they have recipe testers on their payroll, so that's a no-no. You can't get away with much in the way of cheating these days. But a few people will try if the prize is big enough."

"But those creeps are just rule breakers. They aren't murderers." Detective Bease's tone was brittle. "Being denied a blue ribbon isn't a motive for murder."

"I hope not." Sherry gazed at the ceiling before looking the detective in the eyes. "See what I mean? I just don't think I can be of any help."

"Wow, and I thought soccer parents were badly behaved." Marla shook her head. "Put people in a competition with a prize and watch as all hell breaks loose."

"Why do you all keep entering these contests?" Detective Bease lowered his eyes to his notepad.

Sherry squinted as she considered her reply. "For one thing, I've been doing this for a good seven years. It really has become a big part of my life. I've met so many nice people from all walks of life and all areas of the country that I may never have had the chance to cross paths with if it weren't for this hobby of mine."

Without warning, Detective Bease rose from the table and snapped his notepad shut. He hunted in his pocket and pulled out his sunglasses. "Ladies, I have taken up enough of your time. Thank you so much for all the valuable information."

The younger detective scrambled to finish his typing as his elder partner moved toward the door. Diamond slammed his laptop shut and jumped out of his chair.

"I'll let you get back to your business." Detective Bease tipped his hat with one finger. "One more question. What was your experience with the contestant by the name of Jamie Sox? From all accounts, he was exhibiting extremely nervous behavior before and during the contest. I'd think some nerves are the norm, but statement after statement from those at the scene pinpointed his behavior as borderline bizarre. Would you agree?"

"If nerves equaled guilt, you better handcuff my sister right now." Marla gave her sister a gentle punch on the back of her arm.

Detective Bease raised the aviator sunglasses to get a better look at the sisters. Detective Diamond elbowed his partner.

"You did not just say that, Marla." Sherry rubbed

her smarting arm. "Yes, Jamie Sox was extremely nervous, flustered, and out of his element for sure. I'm not surprised. While we were waiting around to be questioned after the cook-off, he told me he was an actuary by profession. Those people don't like to leave anything up to chance. Unfortunately, there are so many unknowns in recipe contests you can't even begin to plan for."

"Like the oven today. It was definitely running hot, so what should have taken twenty minutes to cook took sixteen," said Marla. "With a big variable, if you're not checking your food often, you're definitely pulling charred nuggets out of the oven when the timer goes off.

"And the medium-size shrimp I specified in my ingredients list must have been fed steroids because they were jumbo, for sure. Kind of screwed up my timing," added Amber.

"Talk about risk management." Sherry pointed her index finger skyward. "Normally, you pay guys like Jamie to reduce risk to a minimum. His career was all about what a cooking competition is not. Uncertainty can freak a person out, but I'm not saying he's guilty of any crime. I'm just saying in my case I was nervous because I always anticipate things going wrong, whereas he was probably nervous because his orderly world became unhinged."

"Unhinged?" Detective Bease reopened his notepad and pulled out his pen.

"He caught my eye in the first place because I was getting worked up about being interviewed by Patti Mellit, the reporter, or Brynne Stark, the cook-off hostess. I've done interviews before, and you really have to watch what you say because when your words leave your mouth, you've signed off on them. It's fair game to reprint them a million times." Sherry stretched out her arms while trying to remember the original question. "So, anyway, when I had a free second, I watched the other contestants take their turns. When it was his turn to speak, unfortunately, things immediately went from bad to worse. I was on my way to the refrigerator when I was caught up in the interview melee. The first thing I noticed was Jamie's hand was as unsteady as tomato aspic in an earthquake. I think he was cooking sausages, and their splattered grease got on everything. The spatula he held kept slipping out of his grip, forcing him repeatedly to risk touching the sides of the sizzling pan in order to retrieve it. Did I mention his hand was jitterier than a turkey on the day before Thanksgiving? That's when Brynne went in for the interview. I remember thinking, 'this isn't going to end well.' Like driving past a wreck on the highway, I didn't want to look but couldn't look away." Sherry paused.

"Continue, please," Detective Bease said.

"Brynne greeted him and asked him a question, but I got the impression she either couldn't hear his reply or she wasn't happy with it because the next minute she plunged the microphone toward Jamie's mouth. That must have blocked his line of vision to his volcanic skillet. Next thing I knew he was screaming, 'Medic, medic.' A young man carrying a medical kit rushed to Jamie's side, muscling Brynne and Mac out of the way in the process."

"Interesting." Detective Bease closed his notepad. "Too bad you powered your device down too early, Diamond. I'll show you what you missed when we get back to the office. I see you all got to bring home a hefty sampling of OrgaNicks products." Bease pointed to the gift baskets on the counter.

"The sponsors usually share their products at these contests, which is a really nice perk and makes for good public relations." Sherry stood to walk the men out. "And we're always happy to receive free stuff!"

Detective Bease's pants pocket began buzzing. "Excuse me while I take this call."

The detective broke away from Sherry and headed to the front door. Diamond and Chutney shadowed Detective Bease. A short time later, the detectives returned, sideswiping the small dog with one of their feet. Chutney whimpered.

"Well, the lab reports are in. Cause of Death was a lethal irritant in the victim's throat. The speed with which the test results were returned speaks to the victim's high level of intolerance to whatever it was."

"An allergic reaction to an ingredient?" Sherry shrugged.

"Not exactly. The substance was something not found in the traditional food pyramid. Another fact was just brought to my attention. The last dish the deceased victim consumed was"—Detective Bease glanced at his scribbled notes—"Chutney Glazed and Farro Stuffed Pork Tenderloin."

Sherry gasped. She shook out her hands, which had suddenly grown ice cold. "Mine?"

"Wasn't the decision to hold off mentioning that?" Detective Diamond hissed at his partner.

Overhearing the comment, Sherry shuddered.

Her sister shook her head and put her index finger up to her lips.

"Mr. Andime and the other two judges all gave statements to the police at the scene corroborating the fact Ms. Frazzelle's food was the last thing Chef Birns, now deceased, was seen consuming."

Both men kept their eyes on Sherry. She rolled up her sleeves as high as they would go to soothe her prickling skin. Before Sherry could open her mouth to respond, her sister stepped forward.

"Well, it's ridiculous to even consider my sister had anything to do with the chef's death, Detective Bease, so sniff around somewhere else because you're on the wrong track here. Did you not hear her say she was the one who ran up onstage and performed CPR on the chef before the EMTs arrived?"

"I commend you, Ms. Frazzelle, but the investigation has a ways to go, and it's going to take an experienced veteran, such as myself, to sift through and interpret the facts leading to a conviction. I wouldn't recommend leaving town, Ms. Frazzelle, until the investigation is complete."

"I'm not going anywhere." Sherry studied her feet. "How could anyone even think I could intentionally cause someone else harm? I've spent my whole life safeguarding others' well-being."

"Let me stress, your cooperation would be appreciated, ma'am." Detective Diamond pulled a business card from his pocket. "And because you may have cooked the food that may have taken a life, any details you may have overlooked because you thought they weren't relevant are of utmost importance. Please record them and contact me immediately."

Sherry took the small card and clutched it in her hand. She watched with a blank stare as the detectives left her house.

"This can't be real. I mean, what just happened here? First the detectives were asking some questions, and next thing I know they drop a bombshell on me. They stopped short of calling me a suspect, but it's on their minds, definitely." Sherry's bottom lip began to quiver, and she wiped away a tear.

As the women walked back to the kitchen, Marla put her arm around her sister, while Amber rubbed Sherry's back in a circular motion. Marla inhaled slowly and blew out noisily. Sherry took the cue to do the same. The breathing regulation exercise relaxed her, as the meditation manuals she had studied promised. In her experience, the relief was as temporary as the euphoria she felt when she took a bite of chocolate cake.

"I can't think of anything I saw today that would help me." Sherry tapped her temple with her fist. "What am I going to do? All the food I cooked today was fine, except maybe the amount of salt I used. They're wrong. They have to be wrong."

"Sher, calm down." Marla lowered her head. "They just reported what they know, nothing more."

Chapter
6

"Sherry, do you have a favorite cookbook?"

Sherry sat across the living room from Amber in what had been her husband's favorite marshmallow-soft leather recliner. The warm rays of the late-afternoon sun gleamed through the picture window behind her. But even nature's warmth wasn't enough to take the chill out of Sherry's somber mindset.

"Good question. Let me think." Sherry could only visualize the bars of a prison cell, not the cover of a recipe book.

"The phase my life is in, one hundred percent, defines my recipe choices," said Amber. "For a long time, up until last year, I was all about *Fondue to Stew—For Two*. My ex-husband and I had all our favorites dog-eared. Some pages were barely legible because they were so glopped with splatters. Tickle Me Tacos and Racy Romance Risotto were two of our favorite recipes. Now it's *Only One Plate? Go On, Create! A gift from my lawyer."

"I love *From the Range to the Range, Grazing to

Braising and *Round-Up to Ground-Up—Ranch Cooking Basics*." Marla plumped the pillow behind her and raised her feet on the ottoman. "Although, I'm still not used to seeing tomorrow's dinner roaming around the pastures without a care in the world. But you can't beat my dinners for freshness."

Sherry puffed out her cheeks. "I guess for me it's my new *Empty-Nest Entrees—No More Kidding Around*."

"Last I checked, you're not an empty nester," said Marla.

"Kind of the same premise being single after cooking for two or more for years. Only my empty nest went from two adult birdies to one birdbrain. Doesn't Dad say, 'If you feather your nest with tar, you'll be paving your way to a dead end?'"

"I think I see what he means." Amber changed her position on the sofa, sitting up straighter. "Kind of."

"Well, it's something to that effect. You know, like . . . be careful what you wish for." Sherry raised her arms and stretched her stiffening muscles.

Marla lifted herself off the warm sofa and made her way across the room. She wedged her body next to her older sister's.

"Listen to me. Don't let those detectives put you in a funk. First of all, you gave marriage your best shot. Stuff happens. And second, you're a great cook. Your dish didn't kill anyone. There's more to the chef's death than anyone knows right now, so don't take their speculations personally."

"Listen to your little sis. She's wise beyond her years. You know the ingredients you used today were fine. You probably tasted them all as you were using them, and you don't look dead to me."

"It's just been a tough day." Sherry stretched her

arms overhead. "Things seem pretty out of control, and I'm feeling kind of useless."

A cell phone ringing interrupted the conversation. Sherry, Marla, and Amber all scrambled for their devices.

"Mine?" Marla checked her phone. "Nope, not mine."

"My ringtone." Amber looked at her phone. "Nope, not either."

"Surprise, surprise, it's mine." Sherry answered on the fourth ring. After the caller with the "blocked" number identified herself, Sherry mouthed the name "Brynne Stark" to the other ladies.

Marla whispered to Sherry, "Brynne Stark? From the cook-off?"

Sherry nodded.

A frantic gesture from Marla caught Sherry's eye. She was miming toward Sherry to put the phone on speaker mode. Sherry shook her head. Marla nodded yes. Sherry acquiesced, hit the speaker button, then put her finger to her lips to silence the room.

"She's there. See you later," were the first words Brynne uttered.

"I'm sorry, I don't think I heard you. Were you talking to me?" A thunderous wham on Brynne's end of the phone startled Sherry and her hand wavered. "Did you drop the phone?"

"No, no. Sorry, someone here was just leaving. Not sure why he had to close the door so hard. Anyway, I was told by Mr. Andime to reach out to you. You left your contest apron in the kitchen this morning. In all the post-cook-off hoopla, you neglected to take it home with you. Nick," Brynne paused, "excuse me, I mean Mr. Andime, was concerned all the aprons were left behind, and I'm contacting the participants to verify their preferred mailing address. Assuming all the other contestants are in transit returning to their hometowns, I called you first. I know you live the shortest distance away."

"I didn't realize I had left it. It doesn't seem very important now, considering the events of the day." Sherry made a sad face to the others. "Last I saw my apron, it was in pretty rough shape. Someone will need to put on a HAZMAT suit before they touch it."

"Hazards of the trade, right? You should be receiving it in the mail very shortly."

"Thank you, I think."

"You betcha." The twang in Brynne's voice reminded Sherry of her first taste of lemon curd. Notes of sweet and sour simultaneously.

"Sorry about the way the cook-off ended," Sherry added. "Mr. Andime must be pretty upset. And you must be, too, of course, and the entire cook-off team."

"I haven't spoken to him in depth, but you're right. It was tragic and untimely, don'tcha know. Poor chef was so talented, with so much living yet to do."

Sherry ran her fingers around the phone's protective casing. "When I talked to the police during questioning, Mr. Andime joined in our conversation. He told the police, in no uncertain terms, his company's products would never make anyone sick. Anyway, I've already had a visit from two detectives here at home, hoping to dig up more information about what went on at the cook-off. While they were here, one of them got a call confirming the chef's death as a homicide. Homicide. Wait until Mr. Andime hears that."

There was extended dead air on Brynne's end of the phone.

"Hello? Brynne? Are you still there?" Sherry studied the face of the phone to check whether the call had dropped.

"I'm here," said Brynne. "I know. I just hung up a call from a detective named Bease who's working on the case. I'm just in shock. Unbelievable. Who would take the chef's life?"

Sherry was silent while she considered what to say next. Marla scribbled a blurb on a scrap of paper and handed it over. Sherry read the message and bit her lip. "I feel bad asking, but was there any talk of announcing a winner in the future?"

"Good question. I know one thing for sure, it certainly won't be the dish that made Chef Birns sick. Hope they identify the person soon. He or *she* has a lot to explain, right?"

Sherry's throat constricted, and tiny bright spots danced across her vision. She rubbed her eyes to clear them. "I'm sure it wasn't any of the food the contestants prepared."

"I'd like to believe that," Brynne replied. "I hope they find out soon what really happened."

"Even with everything that went on this morning, I think you did a great job. Must have been tough to maintain your composure."

"Luckily, I've had years of training." The country flavor of Brynne's accent disappeared. "I grew up performing in school plays in Minnesota, taking singing lessons, doing summer theater. At sixteen, I had a booth at the Upper Peninsula State Fair, where, for one dollar, I performed a three-minute improv if you gave me a story line. I'm not sure if you and the other contestants were able to hear me tell the cook-off audience, but I did some TV spots recently. I guess you could say I'm doing whatever it takes to get my name out there to see where it gets me.

"Not to say I don't enjoy the smaller venues, like hosting the cook-off, but I'm sure you can imagine I do aspire to greater heights in my career. Mr. Andime was very kind to hire me, and I'm always appreciative of any job. It just takes being at the right place at the right time to hit the big time."

"Did you know Nick, I mean Mr. Andime, before he hired you?" Sherry's question was prompted by Marla's wild hand gestures in the background. "Ignore me if I'm prying." Sherry used her free hand to signal Marla to stop her distracting gestures.

"Well, it's no secret we dated briefly, but the age difference was challenging. Now his new job is very time-consuming, and I just want to focus on my work. It's easy to see things wouldn't have lasted long anyway. Frankly, I was surprised when he called to see if I was available to host the cook-off. He even hinted there was a good chance I might be tapped for a commercial featuring his products. I have very photogenic hands, and he says he likes the way I handle his packages."

"Wow." Sherry coughed when something caught in her throat. "Well, that's all very exciting, Brynne. I hope all your hard work pays off. Thanks for calling, and I'll keep a lookout for the apron. And again, sorry about the tragic end to the cook-off. Give our regards to Mr. Nick, uh, I mean Mr. Andime, when you talk to him next."

"Thank you, I will, if I see him, I mean. Bye."

"Wait, Brynne, don't you need my address?"

"Yep, you betcha."

Sherry gave Brynne her address and, with a push of a button, the call was ended. Sherry stared at the phone as she considered the conversation.

"What was that all about?" asked Marla. "You were talking to her like she was your oldest friend. And what an accent she was sporting. I don't remember her talking that way at the cook-off."

"Sounds like the upper Midwest to me, don'tcha know. While I had her on the phone, I just thought maybe there was a tidbit of information to be learned from her." Sherry raised one eyebrow. "I wasn't half bad at getting her to talk."

"And was there?" asked Amber. "Any new information?"

"Hard to say. I'm not really sure I'd know a clue if it hit me in the face. But if I'm going to clear my name, I better be a fast learner. I wonder if Brynne knows who won. She seems pretty tied to Mr. Andime, and he must know."

"I bet the name of the winner is a closely guarded secret," said Marla.

"I agree," said Amber. "Word would get out fast if more than a few people knew. You know the old saying—"

All three women recited simultaneously, "Too many cooks spoil the broth."

"Did you hear Brynne say my dish was the murder weapon?" Sherry groaned.

"What are you talking about? None of us did," said Marla. "Because she didn't say it. So just get those negative thoughts out of your head."

"If the investigators don't feel like looking any further beyond who cooked the chef's last meal, the one he ate moments before his death, well, I'm in big trouble." Sherry crossed her arms across her chest.

"The detectives are in no hurry to catch the wrong person. The investigation has only begun. You have to let it play out." Marla stared in her sister's eyes.

"The whole world's about to know my food was the last thing the poor man ate." Sherry began pacing the room. "I can't go to jail. Who will help Dad at the store? How would he manage? And what about me? I was just beginning to start thinking about my new life, doing my own thing, for better or worse, for the first time ever."

"Calm down, Sher. You're not going to jail." Marla's tone was unconvincing. "You're putting too much pressure on yourself. The investigators will sort things out soon enough. And, by the way, you aren't even happy to be working for Dad, so going to jail would at least get you out of a dead-end job."

"Marla, what a terrible thing to say. I'm perfectly happy working with, not for, Dad." Sherry spun around and faced her sister.

"How nice it is you're able to work with your father. What kind of store is it?"

"Thanks, Amber. It is nice. I work twenty hours a week at his ruggery. Oliveri's Ruggery. It's one of the oldest shops in Augustin. His father ran it and his father's uncle started it. Hooked rugs, hand-painted canvas, and hand-dyed wool. Just beautiful. People come in with an idea for the canvas or sometimes only with a color scheme they want to match, and we take it from there. I guess it may all fall to me after Dad retires, unless my brother jumps in sometime soon. Which I wouldn't mind at all, actually."

"How long have you worked with your dad?"

"I lost my job assisting Charlie in his law practice when we split up, so not really that long. Working for my dad pays the bills." Sherry checked her phone for the time. "Back to Brynne's reason for calling, I'm not really thrilled about the idea of an apron arriving with festering food fungus all over it after days in an envelope. If you think about it, it was kind of weird Brynne had to ask for my address. I know the contest has it on file."

"I really don't want my dirty apron back, except to use it to line the kids' rabbit hutch," said Marla. "I'm going to say 'no thanks' when she calls me."

"I'd like mine," said Amber.

"In the meantime, I need to keep busy, get my mind off things or I'll go crazy. What would you ladies like to do about dinner?" Sherry headed toward the kitchen.

Marla and Amber followed.

"Hey, Sher. I have an idea." Marla sidestepped Sherry and searched the depths of her sister's kitchen storage cabinet. She brought out a large mixing bowl. "Game on?"

"I don't think so. I'm not really in the mood. How about takeout?" Sherry opened a drawer and pulled out a handful of restaurant menus.

"What game are you talking about, Marla?" asked Amber.

"It's a traditional game the Oliveri family likes to call Recipe Piggyback." Sherry stared straight ahead and sighed. "We played it growing up."

"Come on. You can't break tradition. It'll make you feel better. Amber, in this game, you'll be playing the role of our brother. We forced him to participate when we were all together, so it's only right we force you."

"Okay, why not? It might be the last fun I have before they lock me up." Sherry put the menus back in the drawer and closed it firmly. "I'll get what we need while you explain the rules to Amber." Sherry shuffled across the kitchen to the storage cabinet.

"Okay, listen up." Marla spoke with a stern tone. "Rules of the game are the following: we take turns adding an ingredient to an empty bowl. We each get just two turns in the 'bowl add-in' phase. On your turn, you're basically piggybacking off what others have placed in the bowl before you. You do have the power to change the recipe with your addition. Then we get two turns adding to the preheated Dutch oven, the contents of which will be finished on the stove. So, to review, the bowl blend will be the topping, the Dutch oven contents will be the filling. It should all result in a yummy mystery dinner. Today's theme: casserole!"

Sherry placed a large bowl, spatula, spoonula, measuring cup, three mixing spoons, and a medium-size Dutch oven on the granite counter.

"Amber, here's the spice rack." Sherry pointed to the carousel filled with alphabetized small bottles.

"These two cupboards contain my dry goods. And you're familiar with the common household refrigerator, I'm sure."

Sherry carried the heavy pot to the stovetop, added olive oil, and turned the burner to low.

"After we finish adding ingredients in here, the lid goes on and it gets popped into the oven." Sherry put her fingers up to her lips and kissed their tips with a loud smack. "There's to be no conversation during the entire game." She put her index finger to her lips.

"Why not?" asked Amber.

"It makes it fun. You'll see," laughed Marla. "This game always makes me feel eight again. I didn't cook a thing until I was married, except for the times Sherry made us play this game!"

"You can only indicate it's the next person's turn with a hand gesture or some other signature move. You'll get the hang of it when we get rolling. There are no winners or losers. It's just a game of creativity but not necessarily cooperation. The important thing to remember is we're eating this for dinner, so don't try to poison us." Sherry put her hand across her mouth.

"Sherry!" Marla grabbed a wooden spoon and banged it on the counter.

"Oops, I can't believe those words just came out of my mouth!" Flustered, Sherry took a moment before resuming. "Any questions?"

"This sounds ridiculously fun." Amber clapped her hands. "Thanks for adopting me, Oliveri family."

"It's best if we draw names to decide our turn order," said Sherry. She put their names on pieces of paper into a bowl and drew for the order they'd cook in. "Okay, girls, let the game begin! Silence, please."

Sherry's name was drawn first. *I have no idea where to begin. This never happens to me in the kitchen. It's usually my happy place. My brain is fried.* Sherry ran her fingers across the spice rack. She shook her head. After opening the refrigerator, panic set in when the familiar inspiration for a great recipe eluded her.

Behind Sherry, Marla cleared her throat. Conceding to her indecision, Sherry shut her eyes, thrust her hand forward and grabbed the first thing her hand touched. It was a soft log of goat cheese. She crumbled it into the mixing bowl. When she was done, Sherry snapped her fingers, indicating it was Amber's turn.

Sherry ignored Amber's silent plea for guidance. Sherry pursed her lips and displayed a solemn poker face. Amber rolled her eyes and opened the refrigerator. After searching the shelves, she decided on a bowl of mashed sweet potatoes. She tasted it then spooned the fibrous flesh into the mixing bowl. Amber clapped her hands to summon Marla.

Chutney began barking.

"Oops, sorry boy." Sherry smoothed Chutney's raised fur. "Clapping gets him worked up."

"Shhh!" warned Marla.

Sherry gave an exaggerated stink eye to Marla as she approached the mixing bowl. Marla moved toward the spice rack. She held up pumpkin pie spice.

Marla's trying to create some drama. What's she trying to make with that flavor? It kind of limits the possibilities. I guess sweet potatoes go with pumpkin pie spice. But do I want it for dinner? I don't think so. Sherry was relieved when Marla placed the seasonal savory spice blend back on the rack. *She's just messing with me. Tricky girl. She knows I have other things on my mind.*

Instead, Marla picked up an Italian seasoning blend of basil, garlic powder, and oregano. She stirred some into the bowl and then dramatically pointed to Sherry to proceed with her second and final addition to the bowl mixture.

The ingredients in the bowl aren't really steering me in an obvious direction. I'm going to have to take control, get this recipe on track, and figure out where it's headed. A little like a murder investigation. Oh, Marla! You're a smart one! No wonder you wanted me to play this game.

Sherry strolled to the refrigerator, searched for a moment, and returned to the counter with a small bottle of maple syrup. She stirred some together with the goat cheese, mashed sweet potatoes, and Marla's choice of seasoning, then used her interpretation of a yoga warrior's pose to point to Amber to begin her turn. It was impossible for Sherry to stifle a giggle because her warrior pose was so unstable she fell over.

On her next turn, Amber added pats of butter. Marla finalized the blend with a conservative sprinkle of Himalayan pink sea salt she'd found tucked away in the spice rack with the other S's. Sherry cringed at the sight of the exotic salt being added because of its robust price tag, but after giving it a second thought, what was she really saving it for anyway? She pushed the full bowl off to the side.

Sherry opened the refrigerator and brought out diced pork belly. She placed it in the Dutch oven.

She clapped twice to give Amber the go-ahead to begin her turn.

Chutney began barking again.

"Sorry again, Chutney." Amber patted Chutney's head then went to the sink and washed her hands.

"Shhh!" Marla tempered her scolding with a smile.

Amber followed up Sherry's pork belly choice with a healthy handful of chopped shallots that she found in labeled containers in the refrigerator. The olive oil and rendering fat from the pork belly in the hot Dutch oven enlivened the shallots and they began to sizzle and dance. Marla diced a sweet red pepper and added it to the pot, which amped up the recipe's aromatics. On her final turn, Sherry cubed two chicken breasts and tossed the poultry in the pot to brown.

Started with nothing and now there's a clear vision.

Amber searched the storage cabinet and found a can of organic cream of mushroom soup and poured it over the chicken.

Marla found her final ingredient, white wine. She measured out one half of a cup then added it to the Dutch oven and turned up the heat. Marla took a swig of the bottle when she was done.

Sherry gasped in mock displeasure before grabbing the bottle from her sister and tipping back a swallow. *I can do this.*

"Can we talk now, please?" Amber interlaced her fingers and rocked them back and forth, as if begging.

"Yes." Sherry applauded. "Great teamwork, girls!

Let's just spoon the topping on and in the oven it goes."

"Winner, winner, casserole dinner!" said Amber. "That was fun!"

"Yep, I really needed to play a game." Sherry winked at her sister. "It's been a while since I've made a casserole to share. They were too big for just Charlie and me, let alone just me. But I'll get this living-alone thing down some day. Just have to believe in myself." Sherry tore off a paper towel and blotted the counter. "While the casserole is baking, want to see my garden?"

"Sure." Amber ran to the front hall to collect her shoes.

"Let me just finish wiping the counter." Sherry held the patio door open for the others. "Chutney and I will be right there."

Sherry shut the door, double-checked she was alone, and pulled the casserole from the oven. She removed the lid and drizzled olive oil on the sweet potatoes before sprinkling them with smoked paprika.

"Even the best recipes can be improved. It just needed the perfect finishing touch." Sherry put on her shoes but, before she could exit the back door, her cell phone rang. "Be right there, girls. I just need to answer this." She removed her shoes and raced back to find her phone. Charlie's name was flashing on the screen when she picked it up.

"Hey, Sher. Just calling for a cook-off update. I assume it's over, although I can't exactly remember what time it was set for. You know, I miss going to those things with you. I consoled you when you lost and helped you spend the prize money when you won."

"Hi, Charlie. Yes, the cook-off is over. It's a long story, but the winner hasn't been announced yet. It was an unusual event, to say the least. But I don't really have time to give details right now. I have Marla here and a new friend from the cook-off." Sherry squinted and let out a low groan. She knew what was coming.

"What's the friend's name?"

"I'm under no obligation to tell you, but it's Amber."

Either Charlie was standing in a windy area or he blew out a puff of air. "Amber sounds nice."

Nice because she's not a man. Actually, who am I kidding? He probably doesn't care if I'm dating yet or not.

"Okay, just checking in. I'll be by for my clothes soon."

"Would you please? I need that room for house-guests. I feel like you're leaving them here just to torture me." Sherry nodded once with her eyes shut. *There, I said it.* She balled up her free hand and summoned up a morsel of the anger she felt the day Charlie uttered the words, "I met with a lawyer today." Charlie's transitions from husband to villain to recent friend were a roller-coaster ride Sherry didn't buy a ticket for but rode, nonetheless.

"Of course. Whatever you say. Bye." His parting words were as smooth and alluring as crème fraîche. *Why was it so easy for him to be nice? Because he got what he wanted, that's why. And to top it all off, it's impossible to stay mad at this guy.*

Chapter 7

"It says right here the top three reasons for murder are, 'number one, crimes of passion,' you know, like a bad break-up or jealousy. 'Number two, money disputes' and 'number three, revenge.'"

Sherry trotted up to Amber. "Sorry, guys. That was Charlie on the phone. What you were reading sounded interesting. What else did I miss?"

"Must have been a quick conversation. Was it just a check-in?" Marla cocked her head to the side.

"There was a little more to it. He wanted the details of the cook-off. I told him I was busy right now and would get back to him soon. But that's not important. What you were reading is."

The ladies walked across the terrace and descended three slate steps toward the small, tidy backyard. Tall oaks and maples framed the well-manicured lawn and created dappled light throughout the space. A mulched border of low-growing perennials butted up against the edge of the lawn.

Marla picked up a stick and tossed it a few feet in front of her. "What's Charlie's deal?"

"No breaking news here." Sherry retrieved the stick Marla threw and placed it on the lawn's edge. "We're still friends, that's it."

"Well, I think you'll never move on unless you two make a clear cut. Like Dad always says, 'If your dreams are only about the past, your future will be a nightmare.'"

"I'd be interested in meeting your father one day," Amber commented. "He sounds sage."

"I have to make an appearance at work in the morning, so maybe you could come with me. Plus, you can use my car while I'm there for a few hours. Just don't forget to come back and give me a ride home. Now, let's get back to the motives for murder you were outlining."

Marla was massaging the blades of grass between her bare toes, and the sight sent a shudder down Sherry's spine.

"From what I heard you say, it sounds like the investigators need to learn more about Chef Tony Birns' relationships. Things like his financial dealings and who he may have crossed in a bad way."

The late-afternoon sun was squeezing out its last rays of warmth for the day as the three ladies approached Sherry's garden. Chutney loped along behind.

At the gate, Sherry kneeled down and picked up a piece of thick twine. "It finally gave out." She put the cord in the palm of her hand. "I asked Charlie to replace this before he moved out, but he thought it could wait. Guess it's time to stop delegating and start doing." She held the twine up, and it disintegrated further. "I'm not sure we can get the door open without the pull-cord connected to the latch."

"Let me try," offered Amber. "My fingers are like shish kebab skewers. Skinny and long. I think I can get in there."

Amber wiggled her slim index finger through the door's mesh screen. "Got it. Quick, pull before the spring fires."

With Amber's finger still lodged against the latch mechanism, Sherry opened the cedar post–framed door that provided the secure entrance to the fenced-in garden enclosure. The ladies entered while Chutney remained just outside the gate.

"The fence is the only safeguard against the woodland critters. Close the gate very slowly, or we'll be locked in here until the coyotes find us. I can't count on the fact Chutney knows how to run for help, like Lassie." Sherry guided the door as Amber removed her finger, leaving it slightly ajar.

"Who does the fun stuff, like weeding?" asked Amber.

"You're not going to find a weed in here." Marla pulled a minute plant with no resemblance to the others around it and tossed it skyward. "My sister plucks them as fast as they can seed themselves."

They walked on the soft wood chips between the raised garden beds. The path led them to the two small boxes in the rear. Sherry parked in front of the boxes that didn't contain any plants.

"During the Dawn of Time, when I was nine or ten, I planted my first garden. Remember, Marla?"

Marla's shoulder rose up and met her cheek. "I've heard stories."

"I think gardening definitely led to my cooking obsession. Marla and Pep were very patient with my cooking experiments featuring goodies from my little garden."

"We weren't always thrilled to eat it, though." Marla kicked some wood chips.

"You never told me that!" Sherry knelt and repositioned the wood chips Marla had kicked out of place.

"Well, you were a sensitive kid whose feelings got hurt really easily. Now you can handle the truth. Plus, Dad secretly rewarded us if we ate your weird stuff. He gave us a few extra goodies for dessert. It was our deal." Marla used her big toe to push more chips around.

"Dad's a sneaky devil."

"What kind of things did you do as a kid, Marla?" asked Amber.

"I can sum up my childhood in four words: soccer, sleep, eat, repeat." Marla kicked an invisible soccer ball. "Now I'm trying to play catch-up to Sherry's cooking accomplishments!"

"No one says you have to." Sherry crossed her arms. "Let me just be better at something."

"Sorry, but you know I love a good competition. Can't suppress the urge."

"You'll have to suppress it if you ever have kids of your own. You'll take away every ounce of fun in sports for them if you make it all about winning." Sherry forced a smile.

Marla puffed out her cheeks and blew. "The world is a tough place. Sports are a great lesson in learning to use your wiles to surpass the guy who's not trying as hard as you. Kids can't learn that early enough as far as I'm concerned. And besides, you're as competitive as they come. If you don't think cook-offs are a kind of sport, then you might as well admit a tomato isn't a fruit."

Sherry released a short hum. "These are my compost piles." Sherry pointed to the banana peels and coffee grounds contained in the two frames. "I try to be as organic as possible and not use commercial fertilizer."

"When you say you try to garden organically, is your garden actually certified or whatever you call it?" asked Amber.

"No. I use the word 'organic' in the broad theoretical sense in association with my gardening techniques. But I do try my best to stick to the guidelines for organic, because I don't mind a few bugs in my veggies. Spraying tons of chemicals on my plants to kill bugs is so bad for you and the animals around here.

"The compost pile I have over there"—Sherry pointed to the corner of her garden—"is made of non-organic produce and fruits I have tossed in. So that alone precludes my garden from being able to pass rigid inspection. But the seeds I use are definitely labeled certified organic, and I only buy non-genetically altered seeds and seedlings. I'm even a seed saver. Next year, my beans will be the next generation of this year's crop.

"Labeling products 'organic' is also a tricky business because it can be 'made with organic ingredients' or 'one hundred percent organic' and you hope they're always certified and approved the right way. OrgaNicks Foods, for example, must have rigorous standards they have to adhere to. I can't even imagine how many hoops you have to jump through to get the label on your product packaging. Sorry, am I lecturing?"

Marla fondled a plant leaf between her fingers. "Maybe a lit—"

"No, no! It's fascinating," interjected Amber.

"Ouch! Those pesky no-see-ums." Marla swatted her arm. "Sun starts setting, and they start biting."

Sherry took her sister's not-so-subtle hint as the cue to head back inside.

"Just got to make sure the gate is solidly shut." Sherry tested the latch and followed Marla and Amber back to the house.

Chutney brought up the rear.

Back in the house, Sherry offered Amber and Marla a glass of rosé. They sat in the living room while Sherry went back to the kitchen to check on the casserole. Sherry peeked inside the oven. Predictably, the casserole was tantalizingly fragrant. She lowered the oven temperature and removed the Dutch oven lid to let the topping brown. Sherry poured three glasses of wine and brought them out to the living room.

Just as she was taking a seat, Sherry's cell phone rang. She ran back to the kitchen and found her humming phone on the counter.

"Hello."

"Is this Sherry Frazzelle?"

"Yes, it is."

"Ms. Frazzelle, this is Stacy from the OrgaNicks Company. How are you doing today?"

Sherry's knees trembled for an instant. She walked over to the kitchen table and sat. "Fine, thank you."

"Ms. Frazzelle, we would like to invite you to

participate in a cooking demonstration at the Au Natural Market this Wednesday. We will also be inviting your sister, Marla Barras, if she's still in the vicinity. It would be three hours maximum, and especially because you are the Connecticut finalist, we would love it if you would say yes."

Sherry let silence wash over the conversation before she sputtered out her reply. "Well, sure. Okay. I'm sorry, though, my sister will be back at her home in Oklahoma by Wednesday. Amber Sherman is staying at my house. She was one of the finalists. Could she do it with me? You don't think it's too soon? I mean too soon following the death of one of the cook-off judges?"

"Mr. Andime strongly suggested it would help the community heal. Let me e-mail you the details. We have your e-mail on file, so by this evening, you should receive instructions. And yes, we would love Ms. Sherman to participate. Would you please share the instructions with her? There will be a third contestant there, too. And, of course, you will be preparing the recipes you made at the cook-off. We'll have all the ingredients for you, if you could just pick them up the day before."

Sherry swayed in her chair before righting herself. "Okay. Thank you. Bye." Sherry ended the call and made a notation on the phone's calendar. She rejoined the others in the living room.

"Well, that was a woman, Stacy, from OrgaNicks. It seems they want the two cook-off sisters to do a cooking demo of our recipes at the Au Natural Market on Wednesday."

Marla's face grew sullen. "No can do. I've got to get back to Oklahoma. Darn, I've never done a demo before. Aren't they glossing over the fact the cook-off was never really completed, not to mention, a man died at the event? Shouldn't there be some sort of mourning phase for the poor chef, at least until the investigation is complete?"

"I asked, 'Isn't it too soon?' and the lady seemed to backtrack and explained it wasn't in association with the cook-off. Just a public relations attempt to keep OrgaNicks in a good light with their consumers. If you think about it, it's probably a good idea so OrgaNicks isn't forever associated with a tragedy." Sherry took a sip of her rosé to wash down the words that left a slight bitter taste in her mouth.

"Interesting." Amber held up her glass before drinking. "Not sure this is an appropriate time to put product sales first, but then again, I'm not the CEO, thankfully."

"The thing is I offered you up in place of Marla." Sherry took another sip to fortify her statement before Amber could respond. "The lady indicated there would be another contestant from the cook-off involved, but she was speaking so quickly I didn't have a chance to ask her who. Can you stay a few extra days?"

"What? No. I mean, I'd love to stay, but I don't know about doing the demo. My recipe seems like ancient history, and I'm not sure I want to dig up the artifacts," said Amber. "The last I remember seeing it was when it was all over the deceased Chef's face. I'm still sick about the terrible image."

Sherry pressed on. "Demos have a very different vibe. It should actually be fun. Might be a good diversion for me, too. The demos I've done before were organized completely by the sponsor. We'll be working with the store's own chef in a location where the shoppers are able to sample dishes, ask questions, and get excited to cook the recipe later for themselves. It's a win-win for all because you get to practice cooking, the store sells the ingredients, and the hungry customers get fed for free! Most demos are very low key, and the shoppers are quite nice."

"Sherry, are you sure you don't want to do this because you're getting into the idea of finding some clues about the murderer's identity?" asked Marla. "Have you given any consideration to the notion that whoever killed the chef is after anyone associated with the cook-off? Could be a dangerous scenario if they show up at the store because it's an OrgaNicks demo."

"That's ridiculous. You've watched too many crime shows. What do you say, Amber? Are you in?" Sherry fanned her hands, as if coaxing a positive response from Amber.

"But if they wanted two sisters in the first place, I'm no substitute for the real thing! And I don't like what Marla is suggesting." Amber's eyes widened, and she took a large sip from her glass.

"Listen," said Marla. "Sibling rivalry makes for good PR, but really, the whole thing's about showing off their products. I'm sure it's safe, too. I was just kidding about the danger. Don't worry. You'll be perfect!"

Amber tipped back her wineglass and emptied it into her mouth. "Okay, sure. Why not? It's good practice if I'm going to try some more contests. So far, my experience as a newbie in my first cook-off was sketchy at best."

"You cook, you chat, they eat, and you're done. There's no prize, but it's a good experience. A couple of hours of your life, at the most." Sherry examined her new friend for any signs she might change her mind. "I'm just happy OrgaNicks asked me. Do you think they haven't heard about the chef's last bite being my dish?"

Marla shrugged.

"Anyway, OrgaNicks will be providing our ingredients. All we have to do is pick them up. Full instructions are being e-mailed to me by this evening. Now, how about another glass of wine?"

Sherry brought what remained of the bottle of rosé to the living room. As she poured the last splash into Marla's glass, Sherry's phone rang again from the kitchen. She picked it up on its final ring before it transferred to voice mail. "Hello?"

"Is this Sherry Frazzelle?"

Sherry looked at the unfamiliar number displayed on her phone. "Yes, may I ask who's calling?"

"Hi, Sherry. This is Patti Mellit. We met at the cook-off. As a matter of fact, I believe you were that unsuspecting woman I corralled into admiring my ancient high school award. I'm sorry if I took any time away from your cooking."

"No, no. Of course you didn't." Sherry clutched the phone tighter.

"Ms. Frazzelle, I'm so sorry about the tragedy at the cook-off today. The contestants must be shocked and devastated."

"Thank you. We feel so sorry for the chef and his family. You must be quite upset yourself."

"Of course. I didn't know him personally, but it's always unfair to lose such a young soul. He was a rising star in the culinary world."

Sherry repeated the phrase, "Rising star." The words left her lips in a whisper.

Sherry heard what sounded like papers being shuffled on Patti's end of the phone. "The reason I'm calling is I was working on an article about the cook-off. With that now indefinitely tabled, my editor would like to run an article on cooking competitions in its place. May I ask you a few questions, Ms. Frazzelle, as our local Augustin contestant?"

"Of course, and please, call me Sherry." Sherry picked up a sticky note and pen in case she had to take notes. "Would you mind if I put you on speaker while I write down the questions? I like to organize my thoughts so I don't make a fool of myself in print."

"Of course."

Sherry set the phone down, increased the volume, and placed pen to paper.

"I have three questions I'd like to ask you. On second thought, would it be all right if I e-mailed them to you so you could have some time to think through your answers? I just need your e-mail address."

"That's easy, sure. My e-mail is . . ." Sherry went silent when Marla marched into the room.

"Use mine," hissed Marla.

Sherry placed her hand over the phone and mouthed, "Why?"

"Just use mine."

Sherry lifted her hand. "The e-mail address is m underscore Barras at comp dot com.

From the living room, Amber giggled. "M Barras, that's great!"

"Never knew my name was so funny," whispered Marla.

"Got it," said Patti. "Take your time, although I'm under a time constraint so when I say take your time, I mean as soon as possible."

"Okay, nice talking to you." The inflection of Sherry's words was lighthearted, but that wasn't the way she felt.

"Off the record, I heard it was your dish that may have sickened the judge. What do you think about that?" asked Patti.

Sherry's insides were doused with an ice bath. Her throat constricted, and she was unable to stifle a gasp. "I'm not sure how to feel right now. But I'll get right on the questions when I receive them. Bye."

Sherry ended the call and laid her phone down on the coffee table. "How is this news getting around so fast? I feel like the walls are closing in on me. Marla, why did you want her to send the questions to your e-mail?"

"Just thought it might be best if you don't have personal e-mails about the cook-off details out in cyberspace for all to see. The Internet is a permanent public record, you know. Just being cautious because I imagine the investigators might check those kinds of things if you're under the slightest suspicion. Don't want to send out any undue false signals."

"So you're worried about me?" Sherry rubbed her moist palms on her cocktail napkin.

"I didn't exactly say those words, but I am concerned I'll faint if we don't eat dinner soon."

"Okay, let's get the casserole out of the oven." Sherry set down her glass with a piercing clink and went to the kitchen.

Amber, Marla, and Chutney trailed behind in close proximity.

Sherry spun on her heels. "Patti's got a lot of power with her written words. I'd better stay on her good side."

Chapter
8

Sherry carried the hot casserole to the table, set it down on a trivet, and raised the lid. The steaming aroma escaped, and the anticipation of the first taste escalated. Amber and Marla were waiting to be served while discussing the overall drinkability of French versus American rosé. French rosé triumphed.

Marla squealed when the casserole lid was lifted. "Sherry! If I didn't know any better, I'd say you broke the 'Recipe Piggyback' rules and added some extras on top."

"Maybe." Sherry bit her lower lip. "I just thought it needed a finishing touch."

"Amber," said Marla, "is there a clinical term for someone who can't let things happen on their own accord without putting in her two cents every time? If not, I'd like to suggest Sherry-itis."

"I don't want to get into specifics because we're new friends and I like you both a lot, but I will say, sometimes it's okay to give up some control if you can, Sherry. The world will continue turning. Your stress and anxiety levels will fall noticeably. End of session. Now, let's eat!"

Sherry absorbed Amber's words and tucked the suggestion away in her brain's "to be considered" compartment.

After eating commenced, it was agreed the casserole and the game that created it were, in their self-congratulatory words, "winners."

"The ex-boss of the house isn't here to tell me 'no,' so do you mind if I grab my laptop? I want to see whether Patti e-mailed the questions. If she did, we can read them over dinner." Sherry left the table and returned with her laptop. "When Charlie lived here, our rule was no electronics at the dinner table, but who cares now, right?"

Sherry didn't have to ask Marla what her e-mail password was because she had committed it to memory. She knew the chance of Marla having changed the secret word over the years was nil.

"Marla, you got the e-mail." Sherry opened Patti's message.

"Wait, you know my password?" Marla balled up her napkin and tossed it at Sherry.

"No secrets among sisters. Okay, first question: What inspired you to enter the OrgaNicks Cook-Off?" Sherry paused, took another bite, and contemplated the lusciousness of the maple sweet potatoes on top of the smoky chicken filling.

"Second question: Are you related to or familiar with anyone who works at OrgaNicks Foods?" Sherry paused before continuing. "Last question: Without naming names, were there any of your fellow competitors you feel would do almost anything to win?"

"Sounds like she's doing a little investigating of her own." Marla licked the prongs of her fork until they were clean. "Yum, this is good. What should we name this casserole?"

"How about New England Shepherd's Pie?" suggested Amber.

"I like the name. Let me think." Sherry raised her eyebrows. "How about Uber Tuber Stew?"

"Or Sultry Poultry Pottage?" added Marla.

"Outdone, as usual," Amber said. "I've got a lot to learn about the name game."

"Patti's first question is pretty straightforward." Sherry swallowed a mouthful of chicken. "Off the top of my head, I'd say I entered the contest because I prefer organic foods and I'd like to see OrgaNicks products do well, since they're somewhat local to me. Also, living close to the cook-off location was a bonus, so it was a no-brainer for me to enter. Marla and I worked on some recipes together. How great is it we were both chosen for the finals? All boring info but true.

"Let's see, second question: nope, I'm not related to anyone affiliated with OrgaNicks. Rules say you can't enter if you are."

"She also asked if you *knew* anyone who works there," added Marla. "Maybe she wants to know some inside information about the place?"

"Well, sorry, I don't." Sherry reread the e-mail. "And the third question is nearly impossible to answer without judging the other competitors' characters, so I can't provide her with any info on the other cooks either."

"Who thinks those are weird questions besides me?" asked Amber. "I mean she's kind of putting you in the hot seat. Think about it. The first question is fine. We're all inspired by something. But if you had answered 'yes' to the second, you'd be a rule breaker. If you shared any insight in question three on the other competitors, your character could be called into question for being judgmental. What's she getting at here, and why are you her target?"

"Not sure, but she's just going to have to be satisfied with my boring answers." Sherry finished replying to the e-mail with one hand while eating with the other. "At least she didn't ask me straight up if I had an alibi. Or maybe she should have asked if that's what she really wanted to know. My alibi is I was busy cooking my recipe, but that's out the window if the food I spent an hour preparing was what killed the chef."

"Hold on. Take it slow." Marla patted down the air with her hands.

"Okay. This is stressing me out." Sherry pushed the computer away. "Charlie was right. We shouldn't eat 'plugged in.'"

"I was thinking, remember that guy, Kenny Dewitt, who was trying to get under people's skin when we were cooking?" asked Marla. "I wouldn't put it past him to try to win at all costs. But is he murderous? I'm not so sure."

"He writes a food blog of some sort." Sherry put her fork down.

"Doesn't having a food blog make Kenny Dewitt a professional in the culinary world and not eligible for amateur recipe contests?" asked Amber. "I'm assuming he runs a revenue-generating website."

"There's a chance he blogs out of the goodness of his nonprofit heart, but the way he was hawking his site all morning, I think he was definitely soliciting advertisers and website traffic." Sherry pulled the computer back toward her. "I'm curious. I want to see if he has ads on the site, then we'll have a good idea what he's all about. Wasn't the blog titled something about Doody?"

"Not Doody. I think it was Dude," said Marla. "Food Dude or Foody Dude rings a bell."

"Let's search for all of the above." Sherry studied the computer screen.

Amber and Marla moved their chairs and their plates closer to get a better view.

"Got it! Kenny Dewitt, The Foody Dude." Sherry knocked the fork off her plate as she gestured with her hands.

"Wow, how old is this picture?" asked Marla.

Sherry examined the screen from edge to edge. There, on The Foody Dude's homepage, was a photo of a clean-cut young Californian wearing a UCLA T-shirt. He was standing curbside by a food truck. The cars parked on the street indicated it was taken at least ten years ago. His youthful physique was svelte, and his face was lit up with an inviting smile.

Sherry scanned the webpage. "Solid layout, inviting content, flashy photography, recipes, tips. Nice job, Kenny."

"No blah in his blog," Marla thumped her hand on the table.

"There definitely are ads and commercial links on the margins." Sherry read on. "Here we go. He has already written about the OrgaNicks Cook-Off. That was quick."

Amber wedged her head closer to the screen, blocking Sherry's view. "He says the event was stressful, challenging, and competitive. I agree." Amber nodded. She gasped and pointed to a paragraph. "Here he speculates on whether the chef's death was by natural causes or possibly something more sinister. I'm guessing there's a very good chance he wouldn't know for sure it's now being investigated as a murder. How could he? It just happened."

Amber continued reading verbatim. "'The cook-off contained all the ingredients of a good recipe for murder.' Hey, he's using your analogy, Sherry. He goes on to say, 'The setting at the Hillsboro High School provided enough suspense for a great who-done-it plot, and everyone who was there that day should be considered a suspect, if it was, indeed, a murder.' He adds, 'Gives new meaning to "too many cooks spoil the broth."'"

"Hey, he stole my other line, too, sort of." Marla started to waggle her finger then curled it in to her palm.

"Uh oh, you're not going to like this part, Sherry," cautioned Amber.

Sherry shut her eyes and lowered her head. "What is it?"

"I'm quoting here, 'Since when did pork tenderloin stuffed with farro become big news? Since it was the Last Supper for one of the country's finest chefs.'"

"What an SOB! I'm so angry right now! He's drawing damaging conclusions just to sensationalize the event and sell his blog!" Sherry pounded her fists on the table, sending her fork flying again. Her eyes welled up with tears. She dabbed her running nose with her napkin. "How do we know he didn't have a motive? Maybe he smuggled in something devious. What's his alibi?"

"You read my mind." Amber tapped her temple. "Maybe he's trying to deflect attention away from himself."

"A definite possibility." Marla drummed the edge of the table with her fingers. "Okay, Sherry, here's your chance. Were there are any red flags about Kenny, beyond goofing around at the cook-off?"

Sherry stepped away from the computer and took a short walk through the kitchen. "The thing is, I heard him say it was his first recipe contest, and he was a last-minute sub, so I'm thinking, if Kenny did it, he didn't have much time for pre-meditation. I suppose he could have had an issue with the chef and seen this event as an opportunity for revenge, but that seems far-fetched."

"Didn't you tell me that Kenny hit Brynne in the eye during his contestant interview?" Marla balled up her fist and punched the air. "Does he have anger issues?"

"I don't think so. It was an accident. At the same time Brynne and Mac were on their way to speak to him, I was going to my oven to check my tenderloin. Kenny seemed so excited they were coming he began dancing and waving his arms in the air, as if he were guiding a jumbo jet in for a landing. He nearly beaned me as I passed by. From what I saw, it looked more like Brynne retracted her mic so Kenny wouldn't grab it, and in the process, she clobbered herself with it. But kudos to her, she continued the interview despite the fact her makeup was running all over her face.

"Since I was caught between them and the oven, I was forced to wait it out. Brynne led with the fact Kenny was a last-minute substitute for a contestant who had to drop out. In response, Kenny had a tagline all ready to go." Sherry deepened her voice. " 'When the judges taste my short ribs, they'll fall off their chairs with delight. My short ribs are famous out west, and the east doesn't know what they've been missing. I'm here with the definitive answer to the question, *What's for dinner?*'" She heightened her tone. "He seemed so confident about his chances of winning."

"Way to spice things up, Kenny. Spice, get it?" Marla contorted her arms around her own back and patted herself.

"Good one." Sherry's eyes trained back on the computer screen. "Listen to this. He writes he had never even come across any of the three judges previously, just in case 'you, the reader, had any reason to presume The Foody Dude's involvement.'" Sherry sighed. "Well, there goes the air out of my soufflé. Seems like he's just trying to cash in on a situation he stumbled onto. Something his readers might find titillating."

"On the bright side, he's a good writer, though,

don't you think?" asked Amber. "I bet his readership will soar with this kind of scandalous content,
but I'm still not happy about what he's suggesting."

"How about we send him a blunt 'cease and
desist' personal message, seasoned and spiced with
what we know about his blatant rule breakage
during the cook-off." Sherry tapped her fork on
her plate for emphasis. "He's still a rotten egg for
throwing me in the fryer, and, let the record show,
I'm not convinced he's innocent!"

Sherry crafted a personal message to Kenny,
strongly encouraging him not to make injurious
claims he couldn't prove. She also reminded him of
the stated rules of the cooking contests and how the
numerous banner advertisements framing his website might make the cook-off sponsor think twice
about maintaining an association with The Foody
Dude, whose honor and integrity were surely in
question. To intentionally end on a lighter note, she
wrote she enjoyed meeting him, found his site fascinating to read, and wished him well in its success.

"Kill him with kindness." Amber smiled a toothy
grin.

"Sent. Mission accomplished. Quit program.
Shut down laptop." Sherry shut the lid of her computer. She finished her remaining bites of dinner
in silence.

"Girls, watch what a creature of habit my puppy
is." Sherry put her fork on her empty plate with a
clink.

Chutney rose from his relaxed position under
the table and scrambled for the front door. "He'll
just wait there for his final walk of the night while I

clean up. Creature of habit, owned by a creature of habit."

Amber and Marla scrubbed their plates and loaded them in the dishwasher. They then retired to the small television room off the living room.

"Ladies, I'm off to take Chutney out for one last tinkle. Turn on a show and put your feet up." Sherry hooked the nearly all-white dog up to his leash. "If I'm not back in ten minutes, send out a search party." She waited for a reply. "Did you hear me?"

"Okay, we heard you," called Marla. "Time starts . . . now."

As Sherry fingered the front door handle, an inexplicable ripple of adrenaline, or was it nerves, traveled up her spine. She had never before hesitated to walk her dog in her quiet neighborhood after dark and was surprised by her body's spontaneous reaction. As the door shut behind her, Sherry shortened the leash length to keep Chutney close. The full moon and the evening breeze played games with the shadows the surrounding trees cast. Bats darted overhead across the darkening sky. In the distance, an owl screeched as if its life was in peril. At least she hoped it was an owl making the eerie scream. Her arms, too, broke out in goose bumps, and she shuddered. She turned Chutney around as soon as he produced and cantered home, checking behind her every few feet.

For the remainder of the evening, the three ladies sat in front of the television, which was on mute, and talked about future possibilities to reunite, whether for fun or competition. Before retiring, Sherry helped Marla pack her suitcase in preparation for the taxi ride to the airport early the next morning.

Just as Amber and Marla were about to turn in, Sherry announced, "I'm sorry, but I can't resist checking to see if The Foody Dude responded to our message. Anyone want to join me downstairs?"

Sherry, Marla, and Amber, already in their night-clothes, raced down the stairs and, once again, gathered around the laptop.

"He did! Kenny PM'd me." Sherry clicked on the message. "'Hi, Sherry. I hang my head in shame. I should rename my blog The Foolish Dude. You're correct. I felt it was such an honor and great opportunity to be asked to be in the cook-off, even if it was two days before the event, and I couldn't turn down the offer to come east. I knew the whole time I wasn't rightfully eligible because of my profession.'"

"He's eating crow," said Marla. "And I'm not buying it."

"There's more. 'To be honest, Chef Birns pulled me aside and told me I wasn't a contender because of my food blog earnings. He indicated the judging panel would go through the motions of judging my dish, but it wasn't eligible to be a prizewinner. The sponsor felt it was too late to get a substitute, and the reputation of the cook-off would suffer if they left the sixth finalist spot unfilled.'"

"That's true." Amber lowered her voice to a near whisper. "I didn't think of that."

"There's a little bit more." Sherry scrolled down the page. "He goes on to say, 'Despite all the suspense and intrigue that went along with the cook-off, the whole cooking contest world is ridiculous. You people, who spend so much time and effort making up recipes just to have them stolen right from underneath your noses by Corporation X, should have your heads examined. You're just a herd of cows giving your milk away for free to folks who're too lazy to create recipes for their products. I'd even go so far as to say the sponsors put the "con" in contest. So, who's "Foolish" or even "Clueless" now? So, in conclusion, consider me a recovering contester. I am one-day contest-free and counting.'"

"Wow, I should have known he couldn't end on a pleasant note," said Marla.

"Well, actually he did." Sherry pointed to the words she was reading. "He concludes with, 'Best of luck in future cooking, Ms. Frazzelle. While I can't say I had a great experience at the cook-off, I can say I met many remarkable people. May your life's ingredients be exotic and flavorful and your completed recipes provide full sensory satisfaction. Take care.'"

"It doesn't bother you it was Chef Birns, deceased, who gave Kenny the news he was disqualified before the judging?" asked Marla.

"I see your point. But would Kenny get so worked up he felt the need to kill the messenger? After all, it wasn't the chef who made the contest rules. And how would Kenny suddenly be able to come up with some poisonous substance after getting the bad news? Does he carry whatever it was around with him, just in case he needs to, well, you know, kill someone?" Sherry mimicked choking while holding a death grip on her throat. "I don't think he did it."

"The world of competitive cooking is more complicated than I could have ever imagined," said Amber. "If my next cook-off is anything like this last one, I may have to reconsider my involvement." She headed upstairs.

Marla followed.

Sherry was left at the table to close down the laptop. Amber's final reflection of the evening magnified the unsettled feeling in Sherry's stomach. She tried to squelch it with the promise of a good night's sleep in her safe, comfortable bed.

Chapter 9

Returning from an early-morning dog walk, Sherry held her cell phone to her ear with one hand, while trying not to smash a buttery apple muffin in her leash hand. The newspaper she picked up at the end of her driveway was tucked under her arm.

"Okay. We'll see you this afternoon. Good-bye." Sherry unhooked Chutney's leash and laid her phone on the front-hall table. The muffin dropped to the floor. Chutney took no time cleaning up the edible debris.

"I'm in here," Amber called from the kitchen.

"Sounds like we'll have some visitors later," Sherry told Amber when she found her seated at the table. "I just got off the phone with the detective. He has more questions. I think they like to see my face in person to watch me squirm. Otherwise, I don't know why they can't ask me questions over the phone. Oh, and I should have bought three muffins. Thanks to my clumsiness and Chutney's appetite, this is all that's left of the one I just dropped."

Sherry tossed the crumbs in the trash. "I hope you enjoyed yours."

Amber curled up one side of her mouth and nodded.

"Take a look at this." Sherry handed her the newspaper. "There's an article about the cook-off right there on the front page. It's a big story for Hillsboro. Says the last time the town had a murder was six years ago. The article doesn't give any new information on the investigation. I guess because it's only been a day."

Amber scanned the article before raising her eyes to meet Sherry's gaze. "I would bet you've seen some crazy things go on at cooking contests."

Sherry thought for a moment. "Nothing too out of the ordinary. There are always accidental knife wounds, self-inflicted, of course. I've seen an older lady faint at her cook station, only to be revived and back cooking again within minutes, as if nothing had happened. I've cooked with contestants who had casts on their arms, one was in a wheelchair, and another was on crutches. We're a determined bunch. But no deaths, thank goodness. Until yesterday."

Sherry glanced at the wall clock. "I need to put in a few hours at work, which I usually do in the afternoon, but I'm going early today. Do you have any interest in going to the beach later? I'll need some fresh air by then. You can drop me off and use the car this morning if you'd like."

"Good plan. I think I'll decline the car and just take it easy around here until beach time."

Sherry nodded. "Sorry Marla flew out so early this morning. She could have provided you with some company. But you're probably happy to have some time to yourself. So, I'll see you in a few hours. Maybe tonight we can eat at the restaurant we got the discount coupons for. Chef Lee's restaurant in Stamford."

Amber raised her thumb skyward. "Sounds like a plan."

"Make yourself at home until I get back."

The doorbell resounded overhead as Sherry entered the Oliveri Ruggery. "Dad? Are you here?"

Erno Oliveri emerged from the back of the store. His loafers tapped a hasty beat as he made his way across the wooden showroom floor.

"Hi, sweetie. You didn't have to come in today. And I thought you preferred afternoon hours. Isn't Marla still at your house?" Erno stretched his arms toward his daughter.

"Hi, Dad." Sherry gave her father a hug before she tucked her purse behind the sales counter. She ran her fingers across a small area rug that sat rolled and bound with string on the counter, awaiting pickup. "I thought I'd get my hours in early today. Sadly, no Marla. If she were still here, I would've brought her. She flew out early this morning. Her cowboy needed her back on the ranch. I have a houseguest, though."

Erno put his hands on his hips. "Do tell."

"Her name is Amber Sherman, and I met her at the cook-off. She was one of the six finalists. When the event ended prematurely, I took her under my wing and offered her a place to stay. She's hanging out with Chutney this morning while I'm here. I came in early because I really want to get the batch of wool I dyed that beautiful sea foam green rolled so Mrs. Dumont's niece can get her dining room rug finished. Such a gorgeous garden theme she chose."

"Before you start, can I ask you something?"

"Sure, Dad. What is it?"

Erno clasped his hands across his waist. "I didn't wait for your cook-off recap. I discovered it from a different source."

Sherry made her way around the front of the sales counter, stubbing her sneakers on the floor while inspecting her hands. Once at her father's side, she studied the man who had been one of her closest confidants since her mother's passing. The sunlight that beamed through the store windows emphasized how the years had etched creases on his face. The furrow in his brow seemed more pronounced than she remembered. Maybe he hadn't slept well last night. Maybe he knew his daughter was in a sticky situation. Maybe she should have been the one to tell him the details of the cook-off.

"What did you hear?"

Erno lowered his gaze towards his shoes. "Is it true about the chef's death having something to do with your recipe? I'm no expert taste-tester, but I know you're one of the best cooks in the state of Connecticut, if not the whole country, and you have plenty of trophies to prove it. You're Augustin's pride and joy when it comes to home cooks. Half my customers say they'd trade their firstborn for your cooking skills. So what's the story?"

Sherry's eyes widened. She plunged her hands

in the pockets of her capris. "How did you hear about it?"

Erno raised his head. "From two sources, actually. First of all, it may be hard to believe, but your ancient Dad is a huge fan of a food blog named The Foody Dude. One of my customers introduced me to it, in fact. It mentioned the cook-off. And the second time I heard about it was when Charlie called me this morning, really early I might add, just to see if I knew any further details."

"There are no secrets anymore." Sherry shook her head. "Thank you, Bill Gates or whoever it was who made computers so ubiquitous. Anyway, Dad, I don't know who killed Chef Birns, but you can count on the fact it wasn't me."

Erno ran a hand through his wispy hair. "That's all I needed to hear. The Foody Dude is taking his insinuations a bit far. Have you talked to the police?"

"The investigation's happening in real time, as we speak. There's a pair of detectives heading it up, and I trust they'll figure things out quickly. But just in case, I've been thinking about doing some snooping around on my own. Can't hurt and may help."

"Sherry." Erno dragged her name out until it almost sounded like a song. "This isn't something to fool around with. Leave it to the experts. But let me offer some words of advice: If the wind blows from the south, spit north."

"Thanks, Dad. I'll remember. I've got to get rolling, literally. We'll revisit this topic when the facts present themselves." Sherry flexed her arms and marched toward the back of the store where the storage room was located.

Erno followed his daughter. "I'm running down the street to the hardware store for tacks. Back in a bit." Erno slipped out the back door.

The tinkling of the bell over the door alerted Sherry that someone had entered the store. She wiped the excess wool fiber off her hands and emerged from the back room, carrying a bag.

"Mrs. Dumont. So nice to see you. I have your niece's wool right here." Sherry pulled a ball of sea foam green wool from the bag. "Isn't it the most perfect color? I've included some extra balls because it's nearly impossible to get the dye batches exact, so just in case, I always make a surplus." Sherry put the ball of wool back in a paper bag and placed it on the well-worn wooden counter.

"Beautiful. If it weren't for my arthritis, I'd be making the rug myself. But I'm lucky to have a niece who has caught the rug-making bug. She's out in Ohio, and I'll hold it for her until her next visit. Gives us a great excuse to get together. You and Erno, sorry, your dad, do such a great job here. It's really special to have this store in town. The next nearest ruggery that sells hand-drawn canvases and special-order wool is in Maine. I hope the store will be around for ages." Mrs. Dumont handed Sherry her credit card. "Make sure to record the purchase under the name Alice Kerr. Your father keeps meticulous records of customer activity, and I want it credited to my niece."

"I'm glad you reminded me, thanks." Sherry rang Mrs. Dumont's niece's purchase up. "Dad's at the hardware store right now, and he'll be sorry he missed you." Sherry ran her thumb across the raised numbers on Mrs. Dumont's credit card that indicated she had been a cardholder since 1974 before returning it. The woman must be about Erno's age, she considered, give or take ten years.

"How was your cook-off, sweetie? I've seen something in the paper about it, but instead of reading your name as winner, as usual, the article was about one of the judges who died. I don't like the sound of that. You know I've been following your cooking successes since your first win, and I consider you Augustin's celebrity chef."

"It went well until the very end, but because of the accident"—Sherry spat the word out as if it were a watermelon seed—"the announcement of the winner has been postponed."

"Such a pity." Mrs. Dumont picked up her bag of wool. "I wanted to ask you a favor. I'm not getting any younger. I've made the decision to retire from the pickle business. If you know anyone who would like to be my apprentice for my final year at the Augustin Farmers' Market, I would so appreciate your expert recommendation. I want someone to inherit my business who has a passion for pickles. I trust, with your gardening and cooking skills, you would know a great pickler if you saw one."

"Of course, Mrs. Dumont. I'll keep my eyes open for the perfect pickler. Have a great day." Sherry watched the tiny bell swing with the door movement.

"Sherry, who did I miss?" Erno emerged from the back room cradling a small paper bag.

"Dad, you scared the life out of me." Sherry clutched her chest. "We need a bell for the back door, too, if you're going to be so stealthy with your entry. You just missed Mrs. Dumont. She was her elegant self, as always."

After four hours at the Ruggery, Sherry hugged her father good-bye and returned home. She packed a beach tote with towels, sunscreen, hats, and water. Sherry gave Chutney a conciliatory pat on the head, and she and Amber piled into the car.

The drive to the beach, while short in duration, showcased nature's finest greenery. The speed limit was restrictive because the narrow road was windy and bordered by majestic trees that hung precariously over the cars.

"These trees look like they've taken a beating over the years," observed Amber as a low-hanging tree branch brushed the roof of Sherry's car. "I'm always amazed at how resilient and adaptive they are, though. They take a punch, maybe lose a limb or two, and just carry on for another half century."

"I'm beginning to feel a lot of empathy for the old-timers." Sherry rolled her aching shoulders. "I feel a bit beaten up myself."

The parking lot was empty except for two other cars. They unpacked their beach supplies and began the trek toward the water. Once they found a location to their liking, Sherry smoothed a patch of sand out with her foot. "This is as good a spot as any. We seem to have the run of the place, which is the beauty of weekdays. They are blissfully quiet. Most screaming children are mercifully absent because they're in camp or otherwise occupied. Guess that sentiment doesn't bode well for my desire to have kids, right, Amber?"

"No rush, my friend. Take your time."

The ladies unfolded their beach chairs and positioned them facing the water. It wasn't long before Sherry began crossing and uncrossing her legs.

"I know we just got here, but is your stomach growling as much as mine?" Sherry rubbed her rumbling belly. "What is it about the hot sun and sea air that makes me so hungry? Ready to take a walk and find some lunch? Augustin's lunch shack is one of its rarest gems, and it's only a relatively short walk from here."

"I thought you'd never ask."

The two ladies walked along the beach toward the roadside eatery, a tiny takeout restaurant named Eliana's. Outside on a gravel terrace, four family-style picnic tables were filled with small groups enjoying their food.

"Right this way." Sherry opened the squeaky screen door and led Amber inside to the order desk. "They serve Greek, Italian, and even a little Mexican. It's the UN of menu choices."

Amber studied the handwritten chalkboard menu while Sherry waited for her turn to order.

"Greek salad sounds good, or maybe the Caesar salad with grilled shrimp." Amber continued reading the menu. "The Mexican roasted veggie wrap sounds really good."

"The drinks and desserts are in the fridge behind you," advised Sherry. "I have to tell you, the lady behind the counter is a little hard to understand."

A heavyset woman in ill-fitting pedal pushers and a floral short-sleeved shirt stood in line in front of Sherry and Amber. The woman placed her order and turned to step to the back of the room to await her food. En route, she grazed Amber with her ample bosom, knocking her back a step.

"Excuse me." The woman maneuvered her wide girth sideways before bumping into Sherry.

"Diana!" Sherry flashed a welcoming smile.

"I'm sorry, do we know each other?"

"I'm Sherry Frazzelle, and this is Amber Sherman. We were just in the cook-off with you. Yesterday? I hardly recognized you without a cooking apron on. Would you like to join us for lunch?"

"I, well . . ." Diana stumbled over her reply. ". . . Okay."

"Miss." The woman at the cash register called to Diana. "Your food is ready."

"If there's a table available, grab it." Sherry pointed to the picture window. She could see a group evacuating an outdoor table.

Diana headed out with her full tray of food.

"We'll be right out," Sherry called after Diana. She got no response.

"I'll have the Greek Chicken Wrap, please, and this brownie. Have you decided yet, Amber? I think you're up."

"It all looks so good. I don't think I can decide." Amber clutched her head with her hands.

"You no like eat when you think too hard." The woman belted out the words from behind the counter and scowled at Amber. "Olives, beautiful! Romaine, sweet! Your heart and eyes choose, head follows. There's no mystery here to solve."

"She means choose with your heart and eyes, don't overthink it," Sherry interpreted. "You know my father always says, 'If you drum with your heart, you'll never lose the beat.'"

"Okay. I think I understand what she means and your father, too. I'll have the Greek Salad with Grilled Chicken, please." Amber slumped over on the counter. "If I choose my second husband with as much consideration as I gave my lunch choice I'll stay married forever."

"Hope that didn't wipe you out." Sherry laughed and mopped Amber's brow with the back of her hand. "Can you believe Diana's here?"

"Wow, I'm surprised. I can't wait to talk to her about the cook-off. You mentioned she was the contestant to beat, the infamous Diana! She'll have an interesting perspective on things, don't you think?"

"You know, in the couple of times I've been in contests with Diana, I have never spoken to her beyond, 'Are you happy with your dish,' so I'm beyond thrilled to corner her for a nice long chat." Sherry put her palms together and held them in front of her face. "Her reputation precedes her as being arrogant and aloof with an impenetrable exterior, but I'm hoping you can't judge a cook by her cover."

"A new twist on an old saying," laughed Amber.

After Sherry and Amber were called to the pickup window, they collected their orders and paid their bills. They carried their Styrofoam containers of food out to the table where Diana was waiting. Amber slid down the picnic table's bench next to Diana. Sherry sat across from them.

"I wish restaurants would stop using Styrofoam containers," said Sherry. "I read they take five hundred years to break down, plus they contain toxic chemicals that leach out when hot food comes in contact with them. When they find their way to the water supply, the chemicals again begin to leak out and poison the marine life and the water. They also require a special recycling process, which is expensive. When and if they are recycled, it is only to turn them into those nasty packing peanuts we all love to hate. Ugh, hopefully they'll get on the bandwagon soon and stop using them. Anyway, I'll get off my soapbox."

"How do you know all this?" asked Diana.

"I worked in my husband's, I mean soon to be ex-husband's, law office for a few years, and he had a number of environmental cases pending. I was a researcher there."

"Hmmm."

Sherry stared as Diana separated the components of her Big Fat Greek Chef's Salad with her fork. She made neat piles of ingredients until her plate resembled a relief map. Sherry, entranced with Diana's unorthodox culinary work of art, tried desperately to catch Amber's eye but was unsuccessful.

Diana put down her fork. "You'd make a good detective since you can read and remember facts that well."

Sherry's cheeks tingled. "Thanks. Not sure it's my choice of profession, but good to know I have some skills in that area." Sherry cocked her head to the side and poked at her food. "I didn't think you lived around here, Diana. It's a shock to run into you. Did you plan on staying around the area for a while?"

"Not too long. It's so different here than in Montana. I tacked on two extra days to my trip to do some sightseeing. OrgaNicks is still paying for my flight, and actually it was cheaper to wait two days to fly home than to turn around in forty-eight hours. Do you two live nearby?"

"I live in Maine, but Sherry lives here and graciously offered to put me up for a few days," Amber said. "I'm at loose ends right now. Kind of on a journey of self-discovery after a divorce. I entered the cook-off on a whim and was so thrilled to be chosen for the finals."

As Amber spoke, Sherry realized that the more Amber shared, the less Diana seemed to be listening. Seeing Diana wasn't engaged in the subject matter, Sherry came up with, "I wonder which state is more northern, Maine or Montana?" in hopes of inspiring a lively debate.

Sherry waited for Diana's reply, which never came. The three ate in silence. Just as the frustration grew overwhelming, finally Sherry caught Amber's eye. "I give up," she mouthed.

Amber curled down the edges of her lips.

"Sherry, do you have a pharmacy you recommend?" Diana asked. "My hearing aid battery has no juice, and I can't hear a thing. It's pretty embarrassing trying to hold a conversation when I can only catch every other word."

"Well, what do you know," said Amber.

"If I can see your lips move, I can catch most of what you're saying. If I can't see them, I just guess. I got so tired of asking people to talk louder, I gave up a few years ago. Finally got a hearing aid last year, but now the darn thing's conking out."

"I was just saying I got divorced, and I'm trying to figure out my next move." Amber cupped her hands around her mouth to amplify her voice. The loud comment didn't go unnoticed by her neighboring diners.

"I'm just about to enter a new phase myself," Diana said. "My only child just got married and moved three states away. My situation leaves me with lots of spare time, so I'm thinking of going back to work. I was a middle school gym teacher for years before I adopted my daughter. I think it was the coach's whistle I blew during those years that damaged my hearing. Anyway, I don't really have to work because I win so much money with my recipes. But there's a lot more competition these days, so it's getting tougher."

"You're the best at cooking up winning recipes." Sherry was slow and deliberate in her delivery.

"I know," Diana agreed. "I hate losing more than anything, and I mean anything."

"So you'd do anything to win?" Sherry regretted the question because Diana began poking around her plate and didn't reply. Sherry winced when her shin was assaulted by Amber's sandaled foot. Sherry aimed an eye bulge at her assailant.

When Sherry was sure Diana was between bites, she asked, "Do you remember the male contestant with a ponytail from the cook-off?"

"I don't really notice other people while I'm cooking," said Diana. "Disrupts my focus. What about him?"

Sherry's foot searched for Amber's shin under the table but only found the bench leg. "He had a strong personality, to say the least."

"He wasn't the guy who threw up, was he?" Before Sherry could answer, Diana exclaimed, "The one who was missing a finger! Yep, I remember him. Kenny Dewitt. He's the one who told me, after I bumped into him once, maybe twice, I should cook less so I could slim down. He bragged about making a fortune if he published his book, *The Just Close Your Mouth Diet,* and I should be the first to buy it. He thought I'd laugh, but I just replied, 'Okay, how about you demonstrate your diet method right now and close yours?'"

"Good comeback." Amber offered a high five to Diana, but she was left hanging.

"He took it well. I respect it if you can dish it out and take it, too. No pun intended."

"Kenny Dewitt writes a blog, and we were reading his comments about the cook-off," added Amber. "He painted a picture of murder and intrigue when describing what went on."

"Did you say murder?" Diana launched some bacon bits through her teeth.

"Murder." Sherry winced as the sharp word tumbled off her tongue.

"Murder," Diana repeated. "Okay, here's the lowdown on Kenny Dewitt." Diana lowered her voice. "He's harmless. In case you didn't notice, he lost a finger. It was a kitchen accident during a screen test for a cooking show. His career began and ended in one day. No one wants a four-fingered cook on camera. Thus, the bitter attitude. Writing the blog is his way of venting. He's got a great following, and I'm now one of his readers, too, despite his nastiness to me."

"Explains a lot." Sherry leaned forward until her shirt sat in her food. "What are your thoughts on

Chef Birns' death? It was quite a bizarre occurrence, to say the least."

Diana dabbed her lips with a napkin. "I thought it was really sad the man died so young, but now you're telling me it was murder? How awful!"

Amber put her finger to her lips suggesting lowering the volume.

"That's what the investigation has revealed. Have you ever been in a contest where he was a judge?" Sherry shifted her rear end back farther on the bench.

"I've had both Chef Birns and Chef Baker judge me on separate occasions," said Diana. "One was the judge at the Big Beef Chow-down, and the other was the Egg-stravaganza Bonanza judge. I won both."

"I was actually in the Beef Chow-down with you. Do you remember me?" Sherry wiped her mouth with her napkin, hoping to provide Diana with a more representative image.

Diana studied Sherry's face. "Were you blonde then?"

"Well, as blonde as I am now, if that's what you mean, so yes, I was blonde then." Sherry ran her fingers across the knots the ocean wind created in her hair. "I just haven't had time for a root touch-up. I may also have a few gray hairs now, too."

"I can't really recall meeting you. I'm sorry. I thought this contest was the first time we'd competed against one another," said Diana. "You have to forgive me. There's always so much to do when I win, like press conferences and photo shoots. It becomes a whirlwind. It doesn't leave much time for socializing."

"I guess." Sherry inspected her fingernails. "The Beef Chow-down was pretty rough. I got a scathing face-to-face critique of my recipe from Chef Baker, and it took me a long time to recover. I thought if I ever saw her again, it would be too soon, but time heals, as they say, and it didn't even bother me to see her on the judging panel again."

"Good thing for you it wasn't Chef Baker who was murdered then or you'd be at the top of the suspect list since you have a bad history with her." Diana chuckled before she spooned more chopped salad into her mouth.

Sherry coughed up a lettuce leaf. She raised a napkin to her mouth to conceal it.

After she swallowed her mouthful, Diana continued. "Funny thing was, at the Egg-stravaganza, both chefs were there, but only Chef Birns was a judge. Anyway, let's just say the two chefs were more than acquaintances, even though at least one of them was rumored to be married. I came across them in an elevator before the contest started, and they had their ovens preheated, if you know what I mean. They were cooking up a little spicy fusion."

"Wow!" Sherry exclaimed, matching Amber's shocked expression.

"They were very cozy during the entire event," Diana said. "Fast forward to the OrgaNicks Cook-Off and suddenly I didn't get the impression they were cozy in the least. As a matter of fact, when I saw them during down times, they appeared to be playing 'hide and don't seek me' to avoid a face-to-face meeting.

"Chef Birns has been trying to establish himself for years as an executive chef, but the story is when he neared success he either had a falling-out with his business partner or, as in the case with Chef Brock Lee's new restaurant, egos clashed and money divided friends. Chef Birns lost out on being the head chef there, too. Chef Birns was a talent but may not have had his head on straight. He definitely had his issues."

"Must be such a difficult line of work," added Sherry. "Where does Olivia Baker work now?"

"Word is she's in a bit of a career lull at the moment," said Diana. "Unfortunately, she had a financial stake in Chef Birns' failed food truck. Maybe also in Chef Lee's new restaurant, and she has been trying to get herself out of debt ever since. I would think she would have reason to be angry with Chef Birns. Working with him has cost her some cash. This last judging stint was probably mostly about exposure for her and getting back in the game."

"I bet putting money in a restaurant venture is about as sound an investment as transferring your life savings to the Nigerian prince who e-mails requesting funds in exchange for future earnings," said Amber.

"I've got to be honest with you." Diana leaned in toward Sherry. "I know which recipe was the last Chef Birns ate before he got sick. I always keep track of the plates the judges are sampling, if I can, because I think the order in which the judges taste the recipes makes a difference in their ultimate choice. Last dish tasted is often the winner, in my opinion." Diana garnished her comment with a wink. "In this case, I'm not sure how beneficial it was for you. I bet you're hoping that nugget of info doesn't go public, especially now, since the death's been labeled 'murder.'"

Sherry's heart skipped a beat.

Diana tapped her plastic fork on her empty lunch container. She excused herself, butt-shimmied across the bench, and proceeded to the ladies' room.

"I think I'm having a panic attack." Sherry clutched the front of her shirt. She put her head down and sulked in silence until Diana returned.

"Okay, ladies, I've got to be hitting the road," Diana proclaimed. She collected her empty container and utensils and turned toward the garbage can and its neighboring recycling can.

Diana tossed her earth-destroying container in the garbage. "I'm on my way to visit my Uncle Grayson upstate. He's in a nursing home, and I haven't seen him in about five years. I hear he's the life of the party up there."

"Nice talking to you," said Amber. "I hope we meet up soon."

Sherry nodded and waved to Diana.

"Maybe." Diana turned and left.

Sherry watched the woman walk away. "That was incredible. Diana knew so much about the judges. She knew Chef Olivia Baker wasn't getting along with Chef Birns after what seemed to once be a romantic relationship. And that Chef Lee had to fire Chef Birns from his restaurant. She's yet another person who knew my pork dish was the last thing the chef ate. That list is growing rapidly. For someone hard of hearing, she seems like a pretty good listener. Well, we've learned Chef Birns had misfortunes in business and love, but he had his most unfortunate day of all as a contest judge."

Chapter
10

"Am I blind?" Sherry surveyed the sugary sand in all directions. "Amber, do you see my beach towel?"

"I only see this one." Amber held up the solid blue towel on her chair. "I specifically remember you had the other towel in your hands before we went to lunch. I was going to ask how you got Chutney's image imprinted on it. What a clever idea! You didn't leave it at the lunch place, did you?"

"I definitely didn't have it at lunch. I'm positive I folded it and left it on my chair here."

Losing things was one of Sherry's pet peeves. "A place for everything and everything in its place" was more of a mantra than a mere suggestion for her.

"I'd hate to think it was stolen, but my luck is in the crapper right now, so it probably was." With so few people around, it took no time for Sherry to take a complete inventory of the surroundings. Nothing resembling her favorite towel was evident on her short trip around the beach. She returned, empty arms dangling.

A check of the lost and found at the lifeguard

station revealed a summer season of lost towels, but not Sherry's. "I'm so sad."

The picturesque ride home took Sherry's mind off her missing towel until they arrived at her driveway. As she pulled her car around the side of the house, she caught a glimpse of a multicolored pile on her front porch. The ladies emptied the car of their beach items and approached the front door, arms full. Sherry was stunned at what lay before her. It was her towel laid out so Chutney's image was facing them. Sherry set down her cargo and picked up the towel for inspection.

She immediately dropped it in disgust. "What is that smell?"

When the towel hit the porch, a decaying fish carcass tumbled from it and broke into dozens of putrid bits. Sherry retched at the smell and recoiled at the sight.

"Amber, can you grab the key ring right there and let yourself in? If you wouldn't mind, just toss me a garbage bag from the kitchen. I'll take care of this disaster. I need to figure out how I can possibly clean my favorite towel. I hope I don't have to toss it out."

Sherry used a hose to spray the fish bits off the porch and down to ground level.

"Here's the garbage bag." Amber handed the plastic sack to Sherry.

When she was done cleaning up the porch, Sherry left the towel stuffed in the garbage bag on the side of the house.

Sherry secured the front door behind her after she entered. "How in the world did whomever it was who brought it here know where I live? Kind of scary."

"People in the neighborhood see you walking Chutney all the time, right? Maybe the towel caught a gust of wind and blew down the beach. Then, whoever found it knew you and wanted to return it. Does any of that sound somewhat plausible?"

"Amber, that doesn't explain the bonus sushi wrapped inside."

Before Sherry had time to give it more thought, there was a knock at the door. She peered out the sidelights and recognized the two men holding up their identification. Sherry opened the door as Amber joined her.

"Hello, Ms. Frazzelle, Ms. Sherman." Detective Bease fingered the rippled brim of his hat. "You remember Detective Diamond?"

The young detective, dressed in slim-fit khakis and a tailored dress shirt, acknowledged the women with a nod.

Detective Bease stepped in front of his statuesque partner. He flipped open his notepad and turned to a dog-eared page.

"You really should consider a tablet or laptop instead of paper and pen," Amber said.

"And an iron," Sherry added, under her breath, as she inspected the same crinkled suit pants he wore the day before.

"No, I'm all set with these." Detective Bease held up his note-taking implements. "My way of doing things works just fine for now."

"Boss says he has until the end of the summer to make the switch to digital." Detective Diamond avoided his partner's disapproving glare. "But I suspect they may have to pry the pen and paper out of his hands when time's up."

"Thank you for meeting us. I just wanted to relay some new information." Detective Bease adjusted his hat, which was as well-worn as Sherry's favorite oven mitt, and no less grimy. "We only have ten minutes."

"Would you prefer to come inside the house? The sun is getting pretty strong out here," Sherry offered.

"Do you smell something?" Detective Bease surveyed the front porch. "Like death warmed over."

"Did you say something?" Sherry scanned behind the detective and spotted a chunk of fish she must have missed.

"Nothing," said Detective Bease.

"Come in. We can sit in the kitchen." Sherry led the way to the kitchen. "Have a seat. I'm sorry, is he bothering you?" Sherry reached down to find Chutney's collar so she could relocate him away from Detective Bease's legs.

"No. I'm a dog person. I prefer them to humans, for the most part."

Sherry glanced at Amber with raised eyebrows.

"The reason we stopped by is to inform you the crime lab's report on Chef Birns' cause of death has been made official." Detective Bease gave a head bob in Detective Diamond's direction. Diamond set down his computer and handed Bease a stapled group of papers.

"'Anthony Scarpato Birns, Caucasian, male, age thirty-four, died of asphyxiation, the result of multiple needle-shaped calcium oxalate crystals, also known as raphides, embedded in the throat tissue.' His body's reaction to the foreign substance was severe, and the rapid swelling that occurred ended his ability to breathe. These crystals are found in the leaves of plants people decorate their houses with."

Sherry nodded. "I know what those are."

Detective Diamond typed as if the keys his fingers landed on were blazing hot.

"I'll continue." Detective Bease fidgeted in his chair.

"These crystals commonly cause a temporary burning sensation and erythema to those who regrettably swallow them. As you say you already know, Ms. Frazzelle, the crystals are basically lots of tiny razor-sharp needles. Plant leaves with these crystals naturally repel predators."

"Sorry, but erythema? Not sure what that is," said Amber.

"It's a technical term for redness and inflammation." Detective Diamond stood and walked to the small kitchen bookshelf. He ran his index fingers across a row of titles. "With all these gardening books, I'm not surprised you're familiar with plants capable of causing harm." He pulled a book out and held it up. "This book in particular, *Happy, Healthy Houseplants,* must be very useful for growing the perfect plant."

Amber leaned in tight to Sherry's ear. "Remember, their job is to collect information. Your job is to listen, stay positive, and give them the truth and not a word more."

"Well, I can assure you those raphides weren't in my recipe."

"Who mentioned anything about them being in your recipe?" Diamond asked.

Detective Bease turned the page of his notepad and continued writing. "But, Ms. Frazzelle, you *do* study plants, judging by your book collection."

Detective Diamond peered out the window over the kitchen sink. "Sure is a nice garden out back. Must be a lot of work."

"Thank you. It keeps me out of trouble."

A throat was cleared. Amber bumped Sherry's leg with her foot. Sherry couldn't take the words back if she tried. Diamond returned to the table.

"We just had lunch with another contestant we ran into, Diana Stroyer," said Amber. "Have you talked to her?"

Detective Bease flipped his notepad back a few pages. He ran his finger down the page.

"'D. Stroyer, Caucasian, female, age sixty-two, resides in Helena, Montana.'"

"Her name says it all," said Amber.

"'Never married, adopted daughter, retired gym teacher.'" Detective Diamond read from his screen.

"We did get statements from her and others involved with the cook-off, but any additional information you can share, by all means, go right ahead," said Detective Bease.

"We discussed the cook-off, and she had some interesting things to say about it," said Sherry. "She's been in previous contests, one with Chef Tony Birns and another with Chef Olivia Baker, both of which she won, may I add. She couldn't help but notice the two chefs were romantically involved at a previous contest. But she thought at yesterday's cook-off they definitely weren't together romantically. They were barely speaking, she thought. It was amazing how much she knew about them."

"Hmmm. Could you repeat that statement?" Detective Bease flipped the pages of his notepad.

"Don't worry. I got it," said the younger detective.

Sherry reconsidered the information she was providing. "Amber, can I see you over here for a moment?" Sherry rose and shuffled her way to the microwave.

Amber rushed to her side.

"What if I'm getting Diana in trouble? She may have not been the contest's nominee for Miss Congeniality, but that in and of itself is no crime. There are questions about the woman's wealth of knowledge, but jumping to false conclusions can be as damaging as adding lemon juice to a cream sauce. Kenny Dewitt did it to me, and it was very painful."

"Ms. Frazzelle," Detective Bease called from the table. "I don't have much time."

Sherry and Amber returned to their seats. Sherry's eyes trained on the pen Detective Bease was holding. It sported a tiny lobster near the top. Must be from Massachusetts.

"I see in my notes you're a relationship therapist, Ms. Sherman. Being a student of human behavior, you must know sometimes people can be vengeful if they feel judged unfairly, and Ms. Stroyer certainly willingly put herself in a vulnerable position many times over the years, as Ms. Frazzelle seems to be suggesting. The saying, 'you can't win 'em all' is just that, a saying. In fact, if you think you should win 'em all, you may become enraged if you don't, you know, if your ego takes over."

"Interesting theory, but if you're talking about Diana, she went so far as to admit she earns so much with her winnings she doesn't even have to work at another job," said Amber. "She isn't the most personable woman around, but frankly, she's so self-involved, I wouldn't think she'd even be bothered by anyone else's opinion of her or her food."

"Ms. Frazzelle, do you win as often as Ms. Stroyer does?" asked Detective Diamond.

"I try, but no, I don't. Not even close."

Diamond's computer keys ticked and clicked as he recorded the conversation.

"Well, Ms. Frazzelle, all we have to go on at this very moment is the chef died after eating food your hands created," stated Detective Bease. "Do you have anything else to add?"

Sherry froze. Her thumping heart battered her chest. Her scalp tingled. She reached up and buried her fingers in her hair. Words collided in her brain but never made the journey to her mouth.

"She'd like to add you should be working harder to find the killer. You're wasting your time even considering Sherry," said Amber. "This lady right here is an upstanding citizen and a loving daughter and sister. That's all you need to know." Amber drummed a furious beat on the table. "Don't make baseless accusations. It's not professional, and, in my opinion, borders on harassment."

"I admire your defense of your friend, Ms. Sherman, but I assure you, facts are facts. No one is accusing anyone of a crime, but I want Ms. Frazzelle to be aware of where the investigation is currently because she is front and center on our radar." Detective Bease's expression softened as his eyes lingered on Sherry.

Sherry hardened her return glare and sent the detective's eyes darting in the direction of his partner. Sherry thought she detected a rosy tinge bloom on Bease's cheeks.

"You know, yesterday we also spoke briefly to Brynne Stark, the cook-off hostess," added Sherry.

"Where did you see her?" Detective Bease sat up a little straighter, bumping Chutney in the process. Chutney nestled closer to the detective's feet. Sherry scooted Chutney away with a wave of her hand.

Detective Bease intercepted Sherry's hand. "He's fine."

"You two do get around," said Detective Diamond.

"She and I spoke on the phone. She was contacting all the contestants to alert them they'd be receiving their cook-off aprons in the mail because no one thought to bring them home. They're a common gift from the sponsor," said Sherry. "Anyway, we got to talking about different things." Sherry paused. "Did you know she had a relationship with Mr. Andime, the OrgaNicks CEO, for a while?" She waited for a reply, then wondered if the detectives thought the statement rhetorical because they remained silent. They weren't going to divulge whether they knew or not.

Detective Diamond broke the silence. "Just to be clear, 'she' being Brynne Stark."

"Yep. I mentioned you two had been by for more questioning, and then I told her about the death being investigated as a crime. I realized by her reaction I shouldn't be the one to spread such shocking news around. I couldn't tell if she already knew."

"We've spoken to her, but I cannot elaborate further. Did you record that, Diamond? My pen seems to be out of ink." Bease shook his pen as if it was on fire then stowed it in his pocket. "Good-bye, old friend."

"Of course." Detective Diamond's head was buried in his laptop.

"Did Ms. Stark call you too, Ms. Sherman?" asked Detective Bease.

"No, actually she didn't. I'm sure she will soon. The contest organizers have my cell phone number, so I'm sure they'll call in the next day or so. I really want an apron. I'm inspired to start a collection like Sherry's."

"Did Ms. Stark say she's calling all the contestants?" Bease asked Sherry.

"Definitely." Sherry bobbed her head. The tone of their questions was becoming as challenging as avoiding lumps while making a roux.

"Okay, well, I'd like to know when the others have heard from her."

"I can only speak for myself," said Amber.

"Got to keep moving." Detective Bease stood and collected his hat and notepad. Stepping around Chutney as if the dog was a poisonous snake, the detective fell backward when he grazed his canine admirer's paw. His chair toppled over. As it went down, it banged into Sherry's small work desk, sending an open cookbook flying.

Detective Diamond launched himself off his chair, righted the overturned seat, and retrieved the fallen cookbook. He studied the cover for a moment.

"Do you mind if I ask your advice on how to cook a chicken breast for dinner tonight? My last attempt at cooking for myself was more like a science project gone awry than an edible meal."

Sherry stayed silent, surprised by the question.

"You have so many cookbooks. I guess being a skilled cook comes with studying the craft." Detective Diamond flipped the book over and back again.

Sherry pondered the poultry preparation possibilities. "Easiest would be to poach it in chicken broth, garlic, herbs and a little olive oil. Just cover the chicken halfway with the liquid, garlic and two of your favorite herbs. Basil and thyme are great. Add about two tablespoons olive oil, cover, and simmer on low for about twelve minutes. It's really moist and juicy."

"Satisfied? She's a good cook." Detective Bease walked toward the front door.

Sherry cracked a weak smile.

"Did you ladies go to the beach today?" asked Detective Diamond as he passed their beach equipment near the front hall closet on his way to the door.

"You don't miss a thing," said Amber. "Yes, we did."

"Did you go fishing? Smells like you did." Diamond wrinkled up his nose.

"Well, actually, see the garbage bag just over there?" Sherry asked as she pointed through the open door. "In there is a towel that was involved in a fishy mishap."

"Almost lost it today, and it's Sherry's favorite," said Amber.

"You might want to lose it now. Whew!" Detective Diamond raised his forearm to cover his nose.

"I left it on the beach with all our stuff while we went to eat lunch, and it wasn't there when we returned. Miraculously, it was on my front porch when we got back."

"I don't like the sound of that." Detective Bease turned his back to the women and spoke to his partner before turning back. "I would like to bring your towel to the lab, as a precaution, and have it analyzed."

"Why? It's not a big deal." Sherry shrugged. "But fine, it's over there on the side of the porch all bagged up. I'd like it back though, clean, preferably."

"Hmmm." Detective Bease held the door for his partner. He yanked it shut behind him as he left. Through the window, Sherry watched Bease pick up the malodorous bag with the care of a baker taking a chocolate soufflé out of the oven.

Chapter
11

"We're making great time." Sherry's car flowed down the parkway at the posted speed limit. "Where are all the cars? It's rush hour! I've never had such good luck." Next thing she knew, Sherry was forced to brake when traffic came to an excruciatingly slow crawl.

"I broke my own rule of never mentioning good traffic luck." Sherry rolled up the sleeves on her turquoise linen shirt. She gripped the wheel in frustration and checked the dashboard clock. "Well, my thirty-minute trip estimate wasn't even close. Try an hour and a quarter. I'm sorry about that."

"In Maine, there isn't much of a rush hour," Amber commented, as the car turned into the Splayd and Spork Restaurant parking lot. "Unless you're stuck behind a logging truck, a moose crossing, or a snowplow, you can pretty much get from point A to point B without seeing another car or even using your brakes. Of course, any two points are really far apart! Quite a change from my Boston commute."

"Wow, this place is full to the brim." Sherry maneuvered the car into the first available parking slot. It was a good distance from the entrance. "I didn't even think to make a reservation. Strike two!"

"What is a splayd anyway?" Amber asked as they walked into the restaurant. "I thought it was a verb not a noun."

"Funny you should ask because I only found out when I read Chef Brock Lee's bio in the cook-off brochure," laughed Sherry. "A splayd is an eating utensil combining the functions of spoon, knife, and fork. I guess the chef's into combo utensils because obviously a spork is a spoon-fork. Apparently, the restaurant's name was inspired by his fusion viewpoint toward cooking."

"Do you think the food is served on plowls—a plate and bowl combined?"

"We'll find out soon."

Sherry and Amber entered the restaurant and walked up to the hostess stand. They were greeted by a pretty young woman flashing a welcoming smile but were told there was a forty-five-minute wait for a table. As an option, the hostess offered them a seat at the bar.

"We'll sit at the bar," Sherry told the hostess. "As long as we can order food."

"Of course." The hostess led Sherry and Amber to the bar. "The waitress will be right over with menus and place settings."

Sherry placed her wrap on the empty stool next to Amber. "Amber, do you mind if I run to the ladies' room? I'd say come with me, but I don't want to lose these seats. I'll be quick."

"No problem," Amber said.

Sherry patted Amber on the back and headed to the back of the restaurant. Past the bar, Sherry noticed a woman swathed in an oversized floral scarf at a dining table against the wall. A second scarf was draped around her head, partially obscuring her facial features. Something about the woman's exposed eyes, nose, and mouth seemed vaguely familiar to Sherry. Trying to not stare, but needing a closer look, Sherry charted a path that led her by the woman's table.

"I'm sorry, but have we met? You seem so familiar." Sherry positioned herself just beyond the woman's table.

The woman raised her head from one of two entrée plates she was examining. "Of course. We were at the OrgaNicks Cook-Off together." She seemed to study Sherry's face with the intensity with which she had been studying the food on her plates. "Yes, you are the cook-off contestant from Connecticut, Sherry Frazzelle, correct?" The woman lowered her voice, making it difficult for Sherry to hear her. "I'm Patti Mellit. How are you?"

"I talked to you at the event and on the phone. I hope my answers to the questions you e-mailed were of some use."

"They were perfect, Sherry." Patti laid down her fork. "Thanks for responding so quickly."

"By the way, the pronunciation of my last name rhymes with la belly, but most people pronounce it frazzle. At this point you'd think I wouldn't care how people say it, but I do."

Patti seemed to not understand the gist of Sherry's words over the restaurant din because she made no effort to acknowledge the comment.

"Anyway," Sherry forged on, "I'm here with Amber

Sherman. You probably remember her. She was the contestant from Maine."

Patti swept her scarves to the side and nodded.

"I'd ask you to join us, but you are much further along in your meal," Sherry raised her voice and enunciated each syllable with dramatic pauses separating each word. "We just got here and haven't even read the menu yet. Also, we're seated at the bar so we don't have a table.

"Thanks for the thought. I prefer to eat alone when I'm working." Patti swatted a scarf that had cascaded into her food. "Maybe next time."

Sherry took a step closer and crouched down.

"Among other things, I'm a restaurant reviewer." Patti gestured toward her disguise. "I always prefer to do it incognito so I don't get any special treatment. These aren't a fashion statement. They serve to disguise me, hopefully."

Sherry laughed and felt a twinge of pain. Her back was beginning to ache from hunching over Patti's table.

"I like to have a broad sampling of the menu, but it's tricky because so many plates on the table often attracts attention. Do me a favor and let me know how your dishes are, if you wouldn't mind. Also, keep your eyes peeled for Chef Brock Lee if you pass the kitchen. He isn't always on the premises, but tonight you're in luck. He's here. The food is always a notch better if the executive chef is in the house."

Before leaving Patti's table, Sherry whispered in Patti's scarved ear, "You may want to hide those." She pointed to the press credentials slung across Patti's purse in plain sight. Sherry continued on to the ladies' room. Passing the closed kitchen door, she peeked inside its small glass window in hopes of catching a glimpse of Chef Lee. She was mesmerized by the industrious hubbub of the busy kitchen, but there was no sign of the restaurant's executive chef.

After a relieving trip to the ladies' room, Sherry headed back to join Amber. She proceeded down the dark corridor, nearly colliding with two figures, one dressed in a chef's coat and the other a woman in jeans and a polo shirt. The woman was wiping her eyes and blowing her nose. Sherry shuddered when she read the name on the man's coat.

"Chef Lee, Chef Baker!" Sherry regretted the enthusiasm of her greeting when she saw the miserable expression on Olivia Baker's face.

She softened her voice. "I'm Sherry Frazzelle. I was in yesterday's cook-off. I want to say how sorry I am about the passing of your colleague. Such a tragedy. Amber Sherman and I are here tonight taking up your offer to visit your beautiful restaurant."

"Those damn cook-off coupons you insisted we hand out will bankrupt you."

Sherry rocked back on her heels.

"Olivia, please. Thank you, Ms. Frazzelle. We are happy to welcome you to the restaurant." Chef Lee glanced at Chef Baker.

Sherry cleared her throat. "I'm not sure if you've heard, but Chef Birns' death has been ruled murder by the investigators. The authorities are now on full alert to find the killer." She studied the two chefs' reactions, just as she had seen Detective Bease do when he broke the news to her.

"We were just discussing the situation, coincidentally." Chef Lee held a stone-faced expression. "You're confirming our worst fears. We knew him for a long time. We all grew up around here. We gravitated toward each other from high school on because we all loved to cook, and it didn't make you popular with the cool kids like it does today. It helped having someone like you when other kids were putting you down for being different. We were quite the trio. When Olivia and I were planning our wedding, Tony was going to be in the wedding party. We were really close friends."

Olivia pressed her finger to the corner of her eye. It was wet when she removed it.

"I'm confused. I didn't know you two were married! Wow, what a well-kept secret. I read the chefs' bios from cover to cover, and I swear that wasn't mentioned."

"Let me jump in here now," said Olivia. "Brock and I were engaged, but we didn't get any further than the planning stage. Water under the bridge now. But our professional lives will forever be bound together."

The chefs gave each other a sideways glance, the meaning of which Sherry couldn't interpret.

"It was quite devastating to lose Tony." Olivia blinked back a glistening tear. "He will be sorely missed. Speaking for myself, I'm baffled over the whole thing. If you'll excuse me, I was on my way out."

"Do you remember me from the Beef Chow-down

a few years ago?" Sherry couldn't resist asking before Olivia could escape.

"Ah yes, my first judging stint. Let's see, Diana Stroyer's Deconstructed Beef Wellington is my fondest memory of the Chow-down. I can still taste its deep, succulent goodness as we speak. But I'm sorry, I have no idea what you made."

"I can't recall either." Sherry studied the palms of her hands. "Nothing memorable, obviously."

"By the way, you see the interestingly dressed woman eating alone at the table near the wall?" Olivia pointed into the darkness. "She's Patti Mellit, the journalist who covered the cook-off. I had an interview with her and was hoping to see the article come out, but I heard she had to postpone or possibly cancel it.

"She must be reviewing the restaurant because the staff noticed how much she ordered and gave Brock a heads-up. She also tipped her hand when she used that ridiculous 'discount' coupon on herself, twice. Somebody should tell her all those mismatched scarves wrapping her up make her look more like the remnants of a Seven Layer Dip than a reporter."

Sherry was shocked at Olivia's animosity.

"Relax, Olivia." Chef Lee patted her forearm. "Patti Mellit's first review of Tony's cooking when he began working here wasn't favorable, only a half fork rating, but sometimes it's just the spark to ignite a restaurant to catch fire. Problem was, keeping Tony's life on track was like trying to make a successful risotto in a hurry. Good things take time to develop properly. Too many rash decisions kept him from success." He lifted Olivia's chin with his fingers. "Ms. Mellit's review can't be blamed for his downfall."

"We'll see how you feel when her latest review of this place comes out in print," said Olivia. "I've never read a review by her that wasn't harsh. She shoots from the hip and doesn't mind who she wounds."

Olivia returned the pat to Chef Lee before leaving. Sherry noted Chef Lee's gaze followed her until she was out of sight.

"I should get back to work. If I'm able to get out of the kitchen again tonight, I'll come check on you to make sure all is well. Please enjoy!" Chef Lee walked away.

Sherry returned to her waiting friend. She grimaced when she checked her watch and realized how long she had been gone.

"I'm glad you're back. I was about to sell your seat to the highest bidder! Was there rush-hour traffic on the way to the bathroom? Maybe a moose crossing?"

"Okay, I deserve the reprimand you're dishing out. I'm so sorry. I'll explain."

"I ordered you a wine, by the way. I've already finished my first, so you're a glass behind. And I even know what I want to order."

Sherry skimmed the menu and then ordered fish and beef tenderloin to share. They would start their meal with a locally grown beet, walnut, and goat cheese salad.

"The reason my bathroom break took so long was I saw Patti Mellit at a table. Remember she's the reporter who was covering the cook-off and also the one who called me. What a fun job Patti has.

Eating, taking notes, then eating some more. Being paid to eat is a dream of mine. She invited us to stop by her table on our way out because she wants to know how our food was. So we have to focus when we eat and think like we're mini-reviewers! She was the first interesting character I ran into."

"First? There were more?"

"Outside the kitchen I ran into Chefs Baker and Lee. They were having a tête-à-tête in the dark hallway right outside the bathroom," said Sherry. "Olivia Baker wasn't in a great mood. Something was going on, and I got the impression it had to do with Patti Mellit being here to review the restaurant. In passing they mentioned the two of them were once engaged—Chef Baker and Chef Lee—and they mentioned Chef Birns was their high school pal. That trio is complicated, to say the least."

"It must be really rough on them to lose their friend so suddenly," said Amber. "Kind of amazing they're even here tonight, don't you think?"

"People grieve in mysterious ways."

"You were right to take your time. It sure was quite the informative bathroom trip."

Their waitress placed the balsamic, orange blossom honey, and olive oil dressed ruby root salad down in front of Sherry. Sherry picked up a fork and jabbed the plate's contents. Taking the task of food reviewer very seriously, she contemplated each chew at length.

"How's this for a review so far: The fresh beet salad saturated my tongue with its vibrant red nectar, allowing the sweetness to linger longer on my palate," began Amber, "and the earthy goat cheese adorning the greens was Baahh-u-tiful."

"I think a lamb makes a noise like that. A goat would be more like beh-heh-heh-u-tiful, I'm not even sure I'd know the difference if I heard them both together. Where's Marla, the animal expert, when I need her?"

The ladies let out hearty giggles, stoked by the Pinot Grigio.

"Look at you," exclaimed Sherry. "You're a vampire."

Amber checked her reflection in her silver knife and laughed. "Beets will do that to you." Amber bared her blood red stained teeth.

"We probably need more training before we go after Patti's job," admitted Sherry. "But it's fun to try to describe what we're eating. It would be really easy to embellish the truth if you got carried away. Patti's famous for not holding back on criticism when she's not happy with the food or service or both. She has a huge following because she tells it like it is."

After enjoying a sobering cappuccino and paying the bill, Sherry suggested stopping by Patti's table to give her their reviews. They reached it only to find it occupied by a young couple.

"Darn," exclaimed Sherry, as they left the building. "You'd think with all that food she ordered Patti would be here for hours. I had my entrée review all ready to run by her. It goes something like this: 'The perfectly cooked tenderloin caressed my taste buds with its juicy goodness. The succulent broiled salmon that swam in a luscious lemon caper sauce made me blush with excitement.' Good, right?"

"Patti asked for a restaurant review, not food porn," laughed Amber.

In the parking lot, with her thumb poised on her car keys' unlock button, Sherry paused. "After thinking about it, I'm not sure I'm cut out for Patti's job. Seeing how her reviews affected the chefs tonight, she might end up with more enemies than friends. I'm too much of a people pleaser."

When they arrived back at Sherry's, a man was waiting in front of Sherry's house.

"Sherry, do you know the man on your porch? Who comes a-calling at ten at night?" Amber asked in a panic.

"Don't worry. He's no threat." Sherry walked up behind the man who was a head taller than her. He had the face of a young man, skin as smooth as a fresh picked peach. A few premature gray flecks in his well-trimmed beard betrayed his age. "May I help you, Charlie?"

"I was in the neighborhood and thought I'd say hi. When you didn't answer, I got worried, so I thought I'd hang out a bit to make sure you got home safely." Charlie's sleeves were rolled up, and his gold watch that glimmered in the moonlight caught Sherry's eye.

"Charlie, you could have called. Despite rumors to the contrary, I don't just sit at home alone when the sun goes down." Sherry examined Charlie's face for a reaction, but like the good lawyer he was, he was expressionless. "This is my friend Amber Sherman. She's staying with me for a few days. We were in the cook-off together."

"Nice to meet you." Charlie extended a hand. "Was she your date tonight?"

"I guess you could say that." Sherry held out her arms. "What are you holding?"

"I found this leaning on the door." Charlie passed Sherry a padded envelope.

"Thanks, Charlie, it's late. Was there anything else you wanted?"

"No. Have a good night, ladies."

"Would you mind giving me back the house key? I've almost locked myself out a few times now when I grabbed the set of car keys with no house key."

"Sure." Charlie took his key set out of his pants pocket. "Bye, old friend." He unhooked a brass key from the ring, fondled it for a moment and handed it to Sherry. "Good night, ladies." He turned and disappeared into the darkness.

"Don't ask. I know I should have asked for the key back the day he left. I admit I had the tiniest glimmer of hope he'd change his mind and come crawling back." Sherry shook her head.

Once inside, Sherry tossed the key in a bowl on the front hall table. She ripped open the unmarked envelope and pulled out its contents. "Sure arrived fast," she remarked in amazement. "Didn't I just talk to Brynne?"

She unfolded an apron only to realize this particular apron had a distinct difference from the one she wore at the cook-off. The OrgaNicks Cook-Off logo, which was about the size of a five-inch dessert plate, had a menacing black circle and a diagonal slash through it, the universal sign for *NO*.

"Someone took the time to alter this apron and deliver it, presumably by hand. The envelope has no stamp or return address, and Charlie didn't see who delivered it." Sherry flipped the envelope over to check both sides. "But whoever delivered it knew where I lived, even though the envelope wasn't addressed. Just my name."

"Do you think it was the same person who brought your beach towel back?" asked Amber. "It doesn't make sense Brynne would send you this crazy thing, but it sure is quite a coincidence. So who else would send it?"

"Let's hold the whole package for the detectives to see if maybe there are fingerprints on it, or is that just something they do in the movies?" When she spoke the words, she didn't recognize the sound of her quivering voice.

"You know, Sherry, you've been asking people a lot of questions. Do you think this is some sort of warning to back off?"

"Back off from what? I've only asked a few people questions. Patti Mellit, Chef Lee, Chef Baker, Brynne Stark, Diana Stroyer. I think that's the complete list. And I'm not sure I've learned a thing from any one of them that the investigators don't already know. If it's a warning, I'd like to know what they think I know, because I don't know." Sherry threw up her hands.

"I understand what you're saying, I think," Amber said.

Sherry put the apron and its envelope in the kitchen, out of her line of sight. A wave of nausea swept through her stomach reminiscent of the first time she smelled the intense stench of fish Nam Pla sauce reeks of.

Chapter
12

"How'd you sleep, Sherry?" Amber poured herself a mug of deep-roasted coffee.

"Just okay. Listen to this dream I had." Sherry took a sip of her steaming brew. "I went shopping for cooking aprons, and when I got to the store, it dawned on me I already had way too many, so I turned to get out of there but the glass doors were locked. Chutney was on the outside of the glass doors. I was calling and calling to him, but he couldn't hear me. Then he disappeared. Charlie strolled casually by the doors but didn't react when I signaled him to get me out. He just went on his merry way. Me, stuck on the inside, him free as a bird on the outside. I was going to have to figure out my escape all by myself and that put me in a panic. I woke up in a full flop sweat. Rough night. Did you sleep okay?"

"I tossed and turned all night." Amber cradled her mug with both hands. "I do remember a dream I had just before I woke up. I was in a cook-off where the requirements were you had to capture a live animal and cook it, and I refused to do it. Our blogger friend, The Foody Dude, was in it, too, and he brought a takeout meal to submit as his recipe entry. The whole thing was crazy!"

"Wow, must have been the after-dinner cappuccino talking. Sometimes one last jolt of caffeine before bed doesn't sit well with me." Sherry retrieved her cell phone and placed a call.

"Detective Bease?"

"Bease here."

"This is Sherry Frazzelle. You gave me your number in case I needed to contact you."

"Go on."

"I wanted to mention a cooking apron was delivered here. Nothing too strange about that except it had a bit of a warning attached to it."

During her five-year marriage, Sherry had talked to her husband countless times while he was multitasking and she'd grown adept at sensing when he wasn't fully engaged. She recognized Detective Bease was doing the same on the other end of the line. Sherry also heard a muffled voice other than the detective's. Possibly Detective Diamond, but she couldn't be sure.

"Warning? An apron with a warning? How does that work? Please explain."

"The apron had the OrgaNicks logo on it just like the cook-off aprons, but this one had a big dark circle around it and slash through it. Picture a no parking sign with the big capital letter 'P' inside a circle and a thick diagonal line through it. Definitely not something you'd want to cook a comfort meal in." Sherry hoped the detective could visualize the apron from her description. "I think you should see it."

Sherry heard what she could only interpret as a grumble through the phone.

"Ms. Frazzelle, you did the right thing by calling me. My schedule is tight today, but I could pick it up tomorrow."

"Actually, I'd rather not wait that long. I'd like to get this thing out of my house. I don't like the karma that surrounds it. Amber Sherman and I are going over to the OrgaNicks headquarters this afternoon to pick up our recipe ingredients for a demo we were asked to do. Is there any way we can drop it off with you while we're out? I'm not exactly sure how close you are to Augustin."

"I'll be in Hillsboro at the OrgaNicks facility this afternoon to meet with Mr. Andime. Maybe we can coordinate our appointments. What time will you be there?"

"Two."

"There must be a visitors' parking lot where we can meet up at around, say, one forty-five?"

"That works. We'll look for you there. Thank you very much."

Sherry heard the muffled voice again but couldn't decipher any words. The tone seemed urgent though.

"Ms. Frazzelle, was there anything else?"

"That's it. See you later." Sherry disconnected the call. She faced her phone screen toward Amber. "I got a text from my sister while I was talking to the detective. Marla wants to Skype and show us a recipe she's working on for the next contest. I'll tell her we'll be ready in fifteen minutes."

"Great, I'd like to see how you sisters operate

when you're in recipe invention mode," Amber said, as she took a seat at the kitchen table. "It's so early, though. She's already cooking up a storm at this time of the day?"

Sherry nodded. She set up her laptop on the table and waited for Marla to dial her up.

"Hi, gals! Here I am, bright and early," sang Marla, before stepping in front of the camera. "You know I get up before the sun out here. It's one hour younger here, too. So bear with my appearance. I haven't primped yet. It's about the food, so don't judge the cook."

Sherry shook her head at her sister's attempt at wit.

"As you can see, I've already been cooking furiously." Marla aimed her computer's camera at her cluttered dining room table. Ingredients, utensils, and serving platters filled the screen. Behind Marla's table was a window that framed the early-morning Midwest sun. A field of what appeared to be golden wheat was swaying in the breeze through the open pane of glass.

"Beautiful day out there," said Amber. "Your ranch is lovely."

"Thanks. There's always so much to do, which is why I get started before dawn. Otherwise, there's no time for my silly hobbies."

In the center of the table, Marla had staged two plates of food side by side. They seemed to be prepared with similar ingredients but each was arranged quite differently.

"Let me zoom in a bit. I can tell you're distracted by too much background, but you both are proving you have great observational skills." Marla moved the laptop closer to the plates of food. "Here I have two versions of Moroccan Spiced Stuffed Chicken Roll-ups with Pistachio Honey Couscous. I'd like your honest opinions on which plate would photograph best for the Sweet Bee Honey Recipe Contest. Let the debate begin."

Sherry and Amber studied the vibrant colors and textures presented before them.

"Good job on both. I defer to the expert." Amber pointed to Sherry.

Sherry's eyes darted from plate to plate. "The student has become the master. You don't need my opinion. They're both great."

"Come on, Sherry. I couldn't have come this far without your input. Don't be afraid to let me have it."

"I just wanted to hear you admit that." Sherry sported a broad smile. "Hold on."

Sherry grasped Amber and spun her around one hundred eighty degrees so their backs were to the computer's camera.

"She does this to me every time," whispered Sherry. "She gets a head start on a contest before I can even think about it, and then I'm under pressure to match her. I'd rather not know what she's entering so she doesn't have any impact on my entry. Why does she have to do the things I do, only better? I'm a step behind, as usual."

The women rotated back around to face the computer.

"We unanimously choose the plate on our right, which I believe is your left."

"Reason being?" asked Marla.

"Well, since honey is the contest's theme, we like

the way the chicken roll-up glimmers with its honey glaze." Sherry pointed to the plate on the left. "Also the couscous screams glorious honey pistachio flavor! The other plate is nice, but it's not as show-stopping. Our only other suggestion is to remove half of the garnish on the plate. The proportions seem out of balance. What is the garnish? Cilantro?"

"You have a good eye." Marla waved a bunch of leafy cilantro.

"I'm a food geek, and don't you forget it." Sherry garnished the word "don't" with a tone as sharp as cheddar cheese. "Mar, it's a winner for sure! By the way, I like the way you're using the OrgaNicks couscous from our gift bags. I see the box on the counter behind the plates."

"Very perceptive. You're a natural detective, I'm telling you. Thanks, girls, for all your great advice. I've got to get going, but any time I can return the favor, let me know!" Marla signed off.

Feeling the inspiration, Sherry and Amber began to brainstorm what recipes they might enter into the honey contest. Sherry reviewed the contest rules because she knew no two contests were the same when it came down to the fine print. "Okay, here we go. The cook-off for the honey contest will involve only five finalists. The smaller the number the harder it is getting your recipe chosen to compete, but I love the challenge. Wouldn't it be fun if you, Marla, and I all got in the finals?"

"You and Marla have a good chance. Me, not so much."

"Can't hurt to try. As my dad says, 'The only thing you get sitting on the bench is a splinter.'

Let's go out to the garden and see if we can get some inspiration from what's ready to be picked."

Amber and Chutney followed Sherry out the back of the house to the garden gate. "Stay right here, boy. He loves his sentry duty."

Chutney parked his small body just out of reach of the swinging gate. Once inside the protective fencing, Sherry followed Amber as they walked around the raised garden boxes. Amber stopped at the herb plants. She bent over and inhaled their fragrances.

"You have cilantro and parsley. Can we bring in some of each because I think I have an idea for something?" She tore off a small bunch of the brilliant green leaves with ruffled edges. She pinched off some leaves from the neighboring basil plant, also.

"Grab me some cilantro, too. I have a cilantro pesto in mind. Cilantro's pungent, but I won't use too much. I like to temper its strong flavor with parsley. Some people don't take kindly to cilantro, so I don't want to overpower the dish. I really like your idea of only cooking up sections of a new recipe to see what works. Otherwise, recipe testing can get pricey if you remake the full recipe a bunch of times."

"Do you think Marla would mind if I also did a take on couscous?" asked Amber. "Honey goes so well with it."

"Well, I certainly hope not because I was thinking of hopping on the couscous wagon also! As long as we're all heading in different directions flavor-wise, it's not a problem. I'm going to bring in a hot pepper because sweet heat is a great

combo. Actually, on second thought, maybe I'll go
down the taco road and leave couscous to you two.
The jalapeños are ripe." Sherry strolled over to the
box containing a potpourri of peppers. She picked
two brilliant green jalapeños about the size of her
big toe.

Back indoors, Sherry and Amber laid their
bounty across the kitchen counter.

"Lemon pesto sweetened with honey on lamb
chops. Now that sounds delicious." Amber clasped
her hands over her head in triumph.

"Honey jalapeño salsa and shrimp tacos. That
doesn't sound half bad either." Sherry high-fived
Amber. "We're on a roll."

Sherry's phone rang. Sherry read the caller ID
and sang out, "It's my Dad." She accepted the call.
"Hi, Dad! Are you missing me at the store? I'll be in
soon. Amber and I are just brainstorming recipes
here. Marla inspired us to think about our next
cook-off. How's it going?" Sherry put the phone on
speaker. "Say hi to Amber."

"Hi, Mr. Oliveri. You've raised a great cook here.
I'm hoping to get to the Ruggery before I leave
Augustin."

"I hope you do and please call me Erno."

"Short for Ernest," Sherry whispered. "Dad, I'm
going to bring you some cook-off goodies I got in a
gift basket. I'll see you in about a half hour. I'm
coming in early."

"See you then, sweetie. Bye, Amber."

Sherry put her cell phone in her purse's side
pocket after checking the time on the screen. "I'll
put in my four hours and be back around lunch.
Want to give me a lift?"

"No thanks. Chutney and I will do some culinary experimentation right here. If all the stars are aligned, it could be your lunch when you return. Then we'll head over to OrgaNicks."

Sherry located her OrgaNicks gift bag, which was still in its unpacked state. She wriggled a squeeze bottle of OrgaNicks mustard and a box of brown rice out of the packing material they were lodged in. Products in hand, she walked over to her kitchen's cupboard and took out another box of organic brown rice. She always bought rice in the organic section because she had heard some suspicious things about chemicals rice might contain, namely arsenic. "By the way, do you have any idea if there are different types of organic certification seals on packages? The symbol on the OrgaNicks box is different from the one I'm used to seeing on the packages I buy."

Sherry placed the two rice packages side by side on the counter. "See, they definitely have different organic seals."

"I'm not an expert in organic certification, but it boils down to misrepresentation if a product is labeled something it's not. Only makes sense," said Amber. "But I'm sure there are many misleading food labels out there, so buyer beware!"

"For the premium you pay for an organic label, you want to get what you're paying for." Sherry placed the OrgaNicks rice and mustard in a shopping bag. "Dad will love these." She pulled her grocery list nearer and penciled a note on it to check out other product labels next time she shopped.

Chapter

13

"What a nice campus," commented Amber when they arrived at the OrgaNicks facility in Hillsboro. "Someone's spent a lot of time and money landscaping the grounds to perfection."

Sherry drove through the front gate to the security guard's shed. She rolled down her window. "Hi. Sherry Frazzelle and Amber Sherman are here to pick up our ingredients for a cooking demonstration."

"Says 'Frazzle,'" The man displayed a computer printout.

"Not 'frazzle,' it's pronounced 'Fra-sell-E.'" Sherry treated the syllables of her last name with as much care as she handled expensive saffron.

"I can hear you perfectly well, ma'am," said the guard. "No need to shout."

"There's the 'ma'am' label again." Sherry drummed her fingers on the steering wheel. "How does he know I'm not a Miss or Ms.? Actually, I'm a bit of both."

While Sherry and Amber waited, the guard flipped through a pad of paper.

"Ah, yes. Amber Sherman, you're on the list. You both are all set. Just follow the signs to the distribution dock, and Paulina will meet you there. I'll give her the heads-up you've arrived. Takes her about fifteen minutes to collect and bring your items out."

"You know what's not fair?" asked Sherry as they pulled the car away from the guard shack. "The male equivalent of 'ma'am' is 'sir.' I know because I researched it. To me, 'sir' sounds so respectful and upstanding and 'ma'am' sounds like I have one foot in the grave."

"It's more of a gender thing, not a judgmental age thing, Sherry. Besides, you're only in your thirties, still very young."

"I really bring out the therapist in you, and I'm not sorry."

With a few minutes to spare, Sherry made an impromptu decision to take an abbreviated driving tour of the corporate grounds. The detour took them by a two-story brick house with a historic designation plaque to the side of the front door.

"I love those date plaques." Sherry slowed the car to a near stop. "Makes me so curious about who lived there and what their life was like. It was built in seventeen eighty-nine. Amazing. Someone's taking really good care of the building. It's in great shape. Sign says 'Corporate Offices.' Must be where the Big Boss works."

Sherry pulled her SUV over to the side of the road so as not to block the delivery truck blasting its horn behind them. No sooner had Sherry considered the location of Nick Andime's office than

Devon Delaney

she saw Nick and Patti Mellit leaving the building.
The duo was heading toward the small parking lot
in the back of the building.

"Look who's here." Sherry nudged Amber.

Nick and Patti walked at a crisp pace while appearing to carry on a heated discussion. Sherry
slumped down in her seat to avoid being seen.

"Pull in over there." Amber pointed to an adja-
cent parking lot.

The two drove at a snail's pace over the next
twenty feet. Sherry peered out the tiny opening
under the steering wheel. She parked the car far
enough away to avoid detection but close enough
to witness the action. In front of them, a scene was
being played out that included hand gestures,
raised voices, and facial scowls.

"I can't hear anything. Roll down your window,"
directed Amber.

Sherry still wasn't able to hear more than sen-
tence fragments, even after lowering the windows
completely.

"None of your business . . . that article . . .
opportunist . . ."

Nick and Patti seemed to be doing an equally
strong job of fortifying their points, often speaking
over one another.

After a short time, Patti got in a car, revved the
motor, rolled down her window, and called out,
"Blood is *not always* thicker than water." She drove
away, leaving Nick shaking his head.

He returned to the office building.

"What was that all about?" asked Amber.

"No idea." Sherry unfurled her rounded spine

like pop-can dough after it'd been whacked on the edge of a counter. "There's a lot going on between them, without a doubt. We better get going, though. Otherwise we're going to be late meeting with Paulina."

On her way around the campus a second time, Sherry noticed a large warehouse behind the administrative building. In front of the warehouse was a large "Restricted Area—No Admittance Without Proper Clearance and Identification" sign plastered across the entrance.

Sherry slowed the car to a crawl again and studied the words. "Hmmm, what would need 'restricting' at a place like this?"

"Maybe secret organic blends no company has marketed yet," said Amber. "I'm sure competition is getting cutthroat between companies in this branch of the food industry."

"True. Makes sense."

"There he is!" Amber pointed toward Detective Ray Bease. "Pull in right here."

Sherry steered her car toward the open parking spot next to the detective's car.

He flagged them down with his hat. "Hello, ladies. What have you got for me?"

Sherry got out of her car and moved around to the back, where she lifted the hatchback. She pulled out the large bag containing the altered cook-off apron and the envelope it arrived in. She handed it to the detective. He, in turn, handed the package to Detective Diamond, who had sidled up to him.

"Is there any chance your fingerprints are on

file in any police database, Ms. Frazzelle?" Diamond asked.

"Well, as a matter of fact, yes." Sherry turned her hands over and eyeballed the tips of her fingers. "My fingerprints are definitely on file. I was a teacher for many years. During the hiring process, you must be fingerprinted at your local police precinct. It's the law."

"Okay." Diamond's punctuated the two letters with aggression.

Detective Bease used a softer delivery. "In the meantime, the towel situation and the delivery of the tainted apron to your home should be considered a warning."

"Or, on the other hand," Detective Diamond said, in a near whisper, "could the towel and apron have been planted, you know, to lead the investigation in a different direction."

"That's not what happened. I'm not guil . . . not a murd . . ." Sherry bit the inside of her cheek.

"Ms. Frazzelle, take it easy," said Detective Bease. "Just keep your eyes and ears open, and things will fall into place."

"One way or another," added Detective Diamond.

Sherry raised her chin high.

"Another thing. I spoke again with Mac Stiles, who was the photographer at the cook-off," Detective Bease said. "I'm sure you remember him. His job was to accompany the hostess, Brynne Stark, during her contestant interviews, while documenting the event."

"He would be a tough one to forget," said Amber. "He was quite a character."

"I brought his photographs from the event." Detective Bease turned and began to rummage through the backseat of his car. He brought out a box labeled OrgaNicks Cook-Off—Official Photos. "I'd like to get you two to thumb through these at your earliest convenience. Spend time analyzing each one, and just make note if you see anything out of the ordinary. Compare what you experienced that morning versus what Mr. Stiles captured on camera. Let me remind you it's in your best interest to notice the subtleties."

"If you need any tips, I was at the top of my class at spotting details others missed." Detective Diamond lowered his sunglasses from the top of his head to shade his eyes and placed his hands on his hips.

The detective shuffled through the box and removed a photo. He set the box down on the hood of his car and held up the picture. "It's about seeing what's *not* there, mostly. Don't let your book learning restrict your mind with rules and guidelines. Instinct for observation can't be taught. Watch and learn." Detective Bease moved closer to Sherry. "Ms. Frazzelle. There's a background and foreground of each shot, not just the central subject—study the tiniest of details. Don't take anything at face value. And, I'd prefer it to be done by tomorrow, please." He replaced the photo in the box.

Sherry took a mental note of the request for immediacy. The faster, the better.

Detective Bease handed the box to Sherry. "You cooks are used to working under time restrictions. Don't want the fresh ingredients to grow stale and useless." He nodded to the ladies and, without a farewell, turned and left.

Sherry's gaze never left Detective Bease until he entered the corporate building. She turned her attention to his partner. "Aren't you going with him?'

"I have a spreadsheet to complete. By the way, the recipe for chicken worked out perfectly. Reminded me a bit of my mom's cooking. I even went rogue and added some noodles to the dish. Let the record show, I don't always go by the book." Toting the package he was given, Detective Diamond let himself in the passenger side of his partner's car and slammed the door.

At the cavernous OrgaNicks warehouse, Sherry and Amber collected all their pre-packed ingredients. Their refrigerated items were also bundled in well-marked bags.

"This is making me a little nervous," said Amber as they carried their parcels back to the car. "What if I burn my flatbread or overcook the seafood tomorrow? People defer to us to be the recipe experts, and if I screw up my New England Seafood Flatbread, I'm letting a lot of people down, like the store customers, the OrgaNicks reps and, possibly, all of New England."

Sherry lost her grip on her packages. "Now you're making me nervous." She regrouped before they tumbled to the ground. "This demo is supposed to be fun!"

As Sherry approached her car, she noticed Detective Bease's car was still in the neighboring parking spot. Detective Diamond's silhouette was visible through the car window.

"Wonder how the meeting's going." Amber climbed into the passenger seat of Sherry's car.

Instead of getting in the car with her, Sherry went around to Amber's side of the car.

"I'm going to have a peek inside that building, Amber." Sherry smacked the car with her hand. "Wait for me here. If I'm not back in ten minutes, call my cell."

Sherry jogged toward the building designated "Off Limits." She crossed the "Restricted Area" warning sign. Sherry tiptoed down the sidewalk to the building's front door and tried the handle. When it turned with ease, she took it as a sign she was meant to proceed. Once inside, she scanned overhead but could see no obvious cameras or sensors that might alert others to her presence. She moved through one room without seeing anything unconventional. She pried open another door leading to a smaller room full of neatly stacked boxes.

Sherry made her way over to the boxes to investigate them. The packing label identified the contents as packaging material imprinted with the OrgaNicks logo. To the right of the first stack of boxes were larger containers sitting side by side on the floor. There was one box unsealed, which held empty jars and bottles. It didn't seem there was anything unusual, certainly nothing appearing "top secret." Sherry moved deeper into the room.

The vast space echoed her footsteps with an eerie hollow reverberation. Sherry swiveled her head every few seconds to ensure she was still alone. Just to her left lay an empty conveyor belt and a reserve of filled food containers. To the right was an assortment of papers; next to those was an industrial-size printer.

Sherry took a few lumbering steps closer to the printer. Suddenly feeling as if she were walking through thick tapioca pudding, she willed herself forward on heavy legs. Her ears were pounding with the irregular thumping of her labored heart-beat.

Within range of close inspection, she saw a batch of small round label stickers. She also noticed the garbage bin next to the printer contained discarded printing misfits. Sherry pulled out two of the blue and yellow labels with her ice-cold hand—"USDA Certified Organic"—then she stuffed one in her pocket.

"May I see what's in your hand, ma'am?"

Sherry swiveled about and came face-to-face with a uniformed man. He stretched out his arm to receive the remaining paper.

"Ugh, I am not a *ma'am.*" Sherry sounded more aggravated than startled.

"Come with me please, ma'am. Our president would like to have a word with you in his office." The man dressed in uniform clutched Sherry's arm just below the elbow. She retracted her arm from his grip and crossed it in front of her so he couldn't touch it again.

The man led Sherry out of the warehouse, down the walkway, and across the parking lot to the historic administrative building. As they approached the entrance, a young woman was also entering the building.

The security guard held the door open for her. "Ladies first, Miss."

Sherry turned to her escort, double-checked his identification badge, and addressed him with a shrill voice she hadn't produced since she dropped her meat mallet on her toe last winter. "Mike! Why is she a 'Miss' and I'm a 'ma'am'?"

"Can't say I know the reason why, but that's just the way I see the situation."

Sherry and Mike took two seats in the waiting room outside Nick Andime's office. While they were waiting in silence, Sherry read the office sign. "Nick L. Andime. Now that's a name."

Mike furrowed his brow.

Just as Sherry was going to pursue the subject, her cell phone rang.

"Hi, Amber. Yes, you did see me being escorted into the administrative offices. By the way, how old do you think I look?"

In the quiet room, Amber's concerned voice projected through Sherry's phone speaker. "Why are you asking me? Are you using code words because you're being held against your will?"

The security guard shook his head and smirked.

"No, no. I'm fine."

Amber sighed. "It's a good thing Detective Diamond has your number on file or I would have never been able to contact you. You never gave it to me. He wasn't thrilled sharing it—kept telling me something about the stated rules in chapter twenty-two of his manual."

"I'm okay." Sherry tapped her toes. "How long will we be here, Mike? My friend's waiting for me."

"We will wait right here while Mr. Andime finishes up his current meeting."

"Be there soon, Amber. Sorry for the delay." She pocketed her cell phone. "Amber's going to have a field day telling me, 'I told you so.'"

Sherry gritted her teeth and willed her agitated stomach to settle as they waited. Next to her, Mike sat staring straight ahead. Sherry was tempted to brush an unidentifiable foreign clump off the sleeve of his nubby, olive green blazer but clasped her hands together instead. She remembered the scratchy feel of his shirt cuff on her bare arm when he guided her out of the warehouse, and she was sure the coat was no softer. Some people have no taste for comfort, she thought.

A moment later, Detective Bease came out of the office, escorted by Nick Andime.

"Thank you for your time, Mr."—The detective choked on his words when he spotted Sherry seated in the waiting room. He put his fist to his mouth and coughed—"Mr. Andime." Detective Bease continued out the door without acknowledging Sherry.

"Yes, Mike, thanks for bringing our guest." Nick directed his gaze at Sherry. "Hello, Ms. Frazzelle. You are Sherry Frazzelle, correct?"

Sherry nodded. She was pleased he pronounced her name correctly.

"So nice to see you again. I see you've already met my security guard, Mike."

Sherry swallowed as a sour taste rose from her throat. "I remember him from the cook-off. He was the ID checker."

"Sir, you directed me to bring you any violate . . . I mean, visitors, who may have wandered into the Number Three Warehouse and that's where she was found," said Mike.

"Thank you. You've done the right thing. I'll take it from here." Nick pointed toward the door.

Mike excused himself and left the room.

"Come into my office, Ms. Frazzelle." Nick led Sherry to a chair facing his. "Please have a seat." He walked around his desk and sat. "As I recall, you're one of three talented home cooks who will be demonstrating their OrgaNicks product recipes tomorrow at The Au Natural Market. Is this accurate?"

Sherry's heart was pounding out of her chest. She was sure Nick could hear it, too. She felt like a naughty adolescent being called out by elders after getting caught with a hand in the cookie jar. She drew in her breath and held it for seven seconds, then released it. Her heart rate slowed, but the exhalation tickled her nose, and she began sneezing. Nick handed her a tissue from a box he pulled out of his desk drawer.

"Thank you." Sherry fondled the thin tissue. She was satisfied the sneezing fit broke the tension, but she knew the elephant was still in the room. "Yes, I'm here picking up my ingredients. I must have gotten lost on my way. I'm sorry if I caused any problems."

"Not at all. We just didn't want you to get hurt in the process. I was told, though, you had indeed already picked up your foodstuffs. Do you require any more assistance, for example, locating those bags that don't seem to be with you?"

His expression challenged Sherry to reply.

"No, thank you. May I ask you, was that Patti Mellit I spotted leaving your office earlier? I just love her writing." As she spoke, Sherry thought she detected a slight grimace in Nick's facial expression, as if he had just bitten into a raw cranberry.

"Yes, she's my sister-in-law."

"I know. I admit I was quite surprised when she mentioned it at the cook-off."

"She mentioned it?"

"I was on my way back from the ladies' room and passed her looking at a trophy case. She apparently won an award as editor of the yearbook or school newspaper. Frankly, I was in a bit of a hurry and don't remember the full conversation."

"Patti may have peaked in high school if she's still holding that memory dear." Nick's eyebrows crawled together, with only a bulging vein separating them.

"Wait, that wasn't when she mentioned it." Was his vein going to keep growing until it burst? "I know when it was. After I returned to cooking, you and she were talking in front of my worktable. I couldn't help but overhear her call you her favorite brother-in-law. That was very nice to hear."

"She's married to my half-brother, Rafe. Patti's writing a short article on tomorrow's recipe demonstrations. Her article on the cook-off was incomplete, and her editor wanted something in its place. It's good for my business to get my brand's name out there in print. We're new in the field of organic food products, and I'd like to think we're on our way to being the best. Getting the good word out is my current mission. Anyway, back to your original question, yes, that was Patti. It was a surprise to me Patti showed up here, but she's never been inside my office, so I showed her around."

Despite the calm in his voice, Nick's fingers fidgeted like the legs of a lobster just before it's thrown in boiling water, resulting in the black Sharpie he held dislodging from his grip. Sherry watched it arc toward a large potted plant. Seizing the opportunity, Sherry bent over and retrieved the pen from the soil it lodged itself in. She neglected to return it to the desk, and Nick didn't appear to care.

"Looks like you're a plant lover. That's a beauty." Sherry gestured toward another plant next to his desk. It had distinctive leaves, dark green with beautiful ivory markings, the color of which reminded Sherry of the fresh cream she loved to put in her morning coffee.

"My secretary is always trying to spruce up my office. Plants make her happy, and the result is a contented work environment. I just hope she doesn't expect me to water it."

"Plants do make people happy. Well, I better be on my way. I'm sure I absentmindedly put the bags of food in my SUV already, so it should all be there. Will you be at the grocery store tomorrow?" Sherry forced the edges of her mouth to curl upward.

"Yes, I'll be there, and I'm very excited to have OrgaNicks showcased by you great home cooks. Don't let me down. See you tomorrow, and be careful not to lose your way going home. You may be directionally challenged."

Sherry stood on jelly legs, shook Nick's hand, and backed out of the office. She returned to her car to find Amber and Detective Bease involved in a conversation.

"Detective Bease, add this to your evidence collection." Sherry held up a tissue-wrapped bundle. "It's a pen from Nick Andime's desk, and it's sure to have his fingerprints on it."

"Ms. Frazzelle, I appreciate the fact you seem to be on a mission to gather what you believe might be helpful evidence, but it's bordering on interference at this point. I have no reason to suspect Nick Andime."

Sherry eyed Amber. Amber lowered her head. Sherry's cheeks burned.

Detective Bease took a step toward Sherry. "Ms. Frazzelle, your efforts don't go unnoticed, but you're taking undue risks snooping around the way you did today. You don't want a trespassing charge hanging over your head, among other things."

The detective's words twisted Sherry's gut like week-old sushi.

"Ms. Sherman told me she tried to stop you. Take your friend's advice next time. She's a smart cookie."

"Okay. Point taken." Sherry lowered her gaze, then turned toward Amber.

Amber mouthed, "Sorry."

"Amber and I have our photograph assignment. It'll have to wait until after the demo, though, so give us until dinner tomorrow, please."

Detective Bease extended his hand to receive the confiscated black pen from Sherry. He seemed leery of the crumpled tissue it was wrapped in.

After giving the bundle a prolonged once-over, he took it from Sherry.

"Sorry. It got smooshed in my pocket. No guarantees, but I don't think it's been used, much. But you must be used to handling unsavory items. Wait. See the label stuck on the tissue? Take that, too."

Detective Bease relayed the items to Detective Diamond. After doing so, it didn't go unnoticed when Bease pulled out a fraying handkerchief and wiped his hand repeatedly.

"What do you do with those things?" asked Amber.

"They'll go to the crime lab," said Bease. "But not before we make a visit to another contestant."

"Good luck," said Amber.

"No luck involved. Only skill and persistence."

Chapter 14

In the morning, Sherry brought out the box of photos she had received from Detective Bease. The prints were in chronological order, with a time stamp in the lower-right corner. Sherry laid them on the kitchen table in piles of ten.

"This is a good one of you, Sherry." Amber held up a photo. "Your focus on your food prep is laser-like."

"I was chopping parsley. Didn't want to lose a finger. Oops, no offense to Kenny with his missing finger. Hold on. Can I have another look?" Sherry took the photo out of Amber's hand and scrutinized it. "In that shot, Nick Andime and Patti Mellit are behind me. The look on Andime's face is the exact one he had when he told me in his office Patti was his sister-in-law yesterday. And also the same sour expression he wore when the two of them were arguing in the OrgaNicks parking lot. Judging by the look on his face, either he sucks on a lemon when he's with her or he's not too fond of her. Let's put that photo aside."

"Why? This is about Chef Birns, not two feuding in-laws."

"I'm beginning to wonder."

They continued flipping through the pictures and placing any of interest in select piles.

"Can you find the one of Jamie Sox holding his finished plates of food again, Amber? And the two right before it, where he's in the final stages of his plating. Check the time stamps so they're in the proper order. Let me run and get my reading glasses."

"Right here." Amber placed the requested shots side by side on the table.

Sherry donned her glasses. "Something in those pictures seems awfully familiar."

"I don't think Jamie would be too happy with this one, which caught the moment he threw up, nearly all over his food. Yuck."

"Okay, let's separate out that one, too." Sherry pinched the corner of the photo and moved it to the growing pile. "I'm putting them on top of my special interest pile, even though they're out of order."

Half an hour later, the task was wrapped up. Sherry brushed her palms together. "Okay, done and done. Cook-off photo review complete."

"I was just thinking, still no call about my cook-off apron," said Amber. "Aren't they going to send me one? I want to start my collection."

"I have no clue what's going on with those aprons. I guess we could call OrgaNicks and see if they know anything. I think *you* should call, though. I don't want to push my luck after yesterday's run-in."

"I will, right after the demo," said Amber. "Don't you think we should head out now? I'm excited to see this trendy gourmet all-natural food store."

"It's go time."

"Hi, we're here for the OrgaNicks recipe demonstration." Sherry stepped up to the store's customer-service counter. "We have all our supplies. We just need to know where to go."

The helpful man behind the counter responded by waving the ladies in the direction of the prepared-foods section. There they found their designated workstations. A third table was already set up with ingredients, dishes, and utensils.

"Hi, ladies."

Sherry did a double take when she saw Diana Stroyer in a striped maxi-dress.

"Diana. What a surprise! We were wondering who else was going to be here." Sherry hoped her face didn't betray the astonishment she was trying to conceal.

"Well, it wasn't actually supposed to be me, but Jamie Sox canceled, and it seems I was the next best thing," said Diana. "OrgaNicks switched my flight plans for the third time, and here I am."

"Great." Sherry dropped her bags on the table with a thud. She turned to Amber and whispered, "Ugh. Now I'm nervous. I'm such a novice in comparison to one of the all-time greats."

"You! What about me? I really am a novice." Amber sighed as she set down her ingredients.

"Let me help you two set up." Diana stepped out from behind her small table, revealing the full volume of her flowing garb. "I wasn't sure how long it would take me to get here from my uncle's home, so I arrived very early. I've walked around all the aisles twice and know where every overpriced and underwhelming item in the store is if you need something! Is it mandatory for the shoppers here to be dressed in yoga-wear? The clientele looks like they haven't eaten in weeks. I can't believe such skinny people have the strength to get their down-dog on or whatever that position is called. One day they'll appreciate the functionality of caftans and the fact that you can let it all hang out while wearing one." Diana twirled around once.

Sherry exploded with nervous laughter.

"Hello, I am Philipe L'Herb, Au Natural's head chef in residence," announced a doughy man wearing a towering chef's hat. "If you need anything, please ask." He lumbered away, glancing Diana's table with his stomach as he passed.

"Who was that?" Sherry asked.

"Isn't he adorable? I could just tickle his belly for hours." Diana wriggled her fingers in his departing direction before returning to her table.

"I do *not* want to see that. I couldn't help but notice Diana must have fixed her hearing aid. She seems to hear just fine today."

"I noticed, too," Amber said. "Sherry, I'm a little worried about all the prep steps I have. What if I'm too busy to field questions from anybody?"

"Once you start working, just pretend you're at home in your kitchen. You'll be fine. I promise. What can go wrong?"

When setup was complete, the three women stood idle near their tables, waiting for further instructions.

Chef L'Herb appeared again, studied the scene, and raised his eyebrows. "Home cooks are so quaint. My sainted mama was a home cook."

Sherry was amazed at the lengthy once-over Diana gave the chef before issuing him a challenge. "What wine pairing would go with a gamey bison sausage pizza, in case someone asks?"

"Madam, pizza is a peasant food, but it can be made dignified when combined with an artisan beer. The spirited bison element transforms the recipe into something worthy of pairing with Merlot. Its notes of dark cherry, chocolate, vanilla, and cinnamon will round out the dining experience." The chef wiped his hands on his apron then disappeared.

"I'm in love," said Diana. "Just between you and me, I knew the answer before I asked, of course, but I just wanted to hear him speak. If I had found someone that dreamy when I was younger I would have definitely considered taking the marriage plunge. But on second thought, after hearing both your stories, I'm kind of glad I didn't."

Sherry scrutinized Diana's ingredients. "Diana, didn't you make pork chops at the cook-off?"

"I did, but because I was given such short notice to sub for Jamie, the store wasn't able to reprint my recipe in the flyer in time. So, I'm making Jamie's recipe." Diana glanced at the print copy of the recipe, "'Chicago Style Bison Sausage and Greens Pizza on Whole Grain Crust.'"

"Have you made it before?" asked Sherry.

Diana didn't respond, but the nonplussed tip of

her head she gave Sherry belied the fact she had no fear conquering anything new.

"It actually reads like a very good recipe," Diana added. "The kid may have had a decent chance at the OrgaNicks event. Not the Grand Prize, but maybe second place."

Sherry didn't even have to ask whom Diana thought the Grand Prize winner should be. Sherry glanced at the time on her cell phone. "I'm just going to run to my car." She left her perfectly organized table and dashed out of the store's automatic doors. Instead of opening the car door, Sherry remained next to it and pulled her cell phone from her pocket. She found the number she needed in her contact list.

"Bease here."

"Hi, Detective Bease, this is Sherry Frazzelle."

"Ms. Frazzelle, what can I do for you?"

"I'm at the Au Natural Market about fifteen minutes south of Hillsboro, and we're just about to start a recipe demonstration. I wanted to mention there'd be a number of people here who were involved in the OrgaNicks Cook-Off. Things have already taken an interesting turn."

"Ms. Frazzelle, I'm very busy."

"Sherry! Five minutes! Come on!" yelled Amber across the parking lot.

Sherry held her hand up with index finger extended. "I've got to go. You should try to make it here."

"Ms. Frazzelle, this investigation is led by a team of professionals, I remind you. I cannot just follow

where the wind blows because you think I should."
Bease hung up.

Sherry returned her phone to her pocket and
ran back inside the store. It was nearing the noon
hour, the time the demonstration was to begin. The
three ladies took their positions behind their prep
tables. In front of them, each had a portable double
burner. Behind them there was one shared microwave
and two ovens supplied by the store. Sherry saw two
familiar faces approaching.

The woman in the linen pantsuit wrestled with
her carryall before placing it at her feet. "Sherry, so
nice to see you again. I'm here to write a story on
the cooking demonstration." Patti Mellit pointed to
the two men with her. "You remember Mac Stiles,
the photographer from the cook-off? He's here to
snap a few shots. And this is my husband, Rafe. He's
here to hustle a few free bites."

"Hi again. Good to see you, Mac." Sherry turned
her attention to Rafe. "And you must be the famous
Hillsboro High yearbook co-editor. Thanks for
coming."

"Ah, the good old days," Rafe laughed. "My career's
been on a slide ever since."

"The printed guide lists you, Amber Sherman,
and Jamie Sox as the cooks. I only see you and Ms.
Sherman." Patti waved the flyer in her hand.

"Jamie canceled, and Diana Stroyer stepped in at
the last minute." Sherry continued to re-organize
her already organized ingredients. "Diana's making
J▇▇e's recipe, though, so the recipe in the guide is
▇▇ct."

▇▇usc me one second, guys. I need a word with

Ms. Frazzelle." Patti steered Sherry a few steps away from the others with a gentle tug of her elbow.

Sherry studied the woman holding her arm.

"Sherry, you and I both know you're in trouble."

Sherry's eyes opened wide at the blunt proclamation.

"Listen, I'm a journalist not a detective, but you passed my character test with the answers to the questions I e-mailed you. No one who'd just committed a heinous murder would ever be so sweet, humble, and unassuming. Forgive me, but I used an old journalism trick to get a better perspective on who you really are. I have confidence you didn't poison the chef. I'm willing to stake my reputation on it, so listen up.

"Here's what I know. I'm not surprised Jamie Sox is a no-show." Patti lowered her voice. "He was having all sorts of problems at the OrgaNicks cook-off. My firm belief is that was he should've been disqualified because he let someone besides his assigned helper handle his ingredients during the final phase of his plating. I saw the whole thing as I was waiting for the contestant plates to be set out on the display table."

"What? No, that's not right! If anyone was up for disqualification it was Kenny Dewitt because he's a paid professional in the food industry."

"That's also the case, but Chef Birns apparently told the other judges just before deliberation he witnessed Jamie Sox breaking a rule," explained Patti. "The chef and I saw Nick hand Mr. Sox two bags of ingredients from the refrigerator. A big contest no-no. We approached Nick and Mr. Sox immediately to point out the indiscretion, but because Nick was involved and it's his contest, of course, the chef was given the word to let it blow over. Nonetheless, the contestant was horrified with his error."

Sherry made a mental note to review a few of Mac Stiles' photos a second time to check a few details.

"Just when I thought things couldn't get any more confusing," said Sherry. "But you're saying Jamie was never officially disqualified?"

"No, the judges were told to turn a blind eye, something they probably had trouble doing in good conscience. The final decision was Nick's, though. I think that's why he wanted Jamie Sox here at the demo today, kind of a 'sorry I messed things up for you' consolation prize. But the whole scenario smells fishy to me."

The irony of Patti's last statement wasn't lost on Sherry. Before Sherry could respond, she noticed a crowd was beginning to gather in front of Amber and Diana. "I'd better get back to work. People seem to be heading in this direction. Word must've traveled that free samples are available. Thanks, Patti."

When she raced back to her table, Amber had begun mixing ingredients. Diana had yet to start constructing her pizza. The woman was intently studying the written recipe in front of her. Mac and Patti approached the prep tables just as Sherry placed her tenderloin on the cutting board. Diana leaned across Sherry's table to get Mac's attention.

"Mac, would you happen to have a close-up of Jamie Sox's uncooked pizza from the day of the cook-off? I'd be very interested to see how he arranged his toppings. I think I owe him getting the appearance of the dish as close as possible to the way he wanted it."

"Mac to the rescue. I still have all the cook-off shots on my other camera. Detective Bease told me not to erase any for now. It would've been nice of him to offer me some Benjamins for the equipment he put a freeze on, but no way, Ray."

Mac lifted the camera from his equipment bag. "This one right here has the photos. Let me find it for you." Mac clicked the arrow keys on his view-finder. "Give me a few minutes."

Mac stepped to the side of the table while shop-pers circled the cooks like great white sharks around a school of anchovies. After a few minutes, Mac strutted up to the front of the crowd. "Important in-formation coming through. Move aside." Mac dis-played his camera playback for Diana to see.

"Perfect, thanks!" said Diana.

People began jostling for position in front of the cooks. On the table between the shoppers and the cooks was a placard that read, "Questions are encouraged."

"Excuse me." A young woman in a revealing workout top with a toddler on her cellulite-free hip waved her muscular arm up from the middle of the crowd. "I'm trying to go meatless. What could I sub-stitute for the bison sausage in your pizza?"

Sherry slowed the pace of her knife work so she could hear Diana's reply.

"There are meatless sausage crumbles you could use," Diana didn't hesitate to reply, "but add some smoked paprika, cumin, cayenne, and thyme to the sausage to give it a more gamey flavor."

A white-haired man holding a small boy's hand shouted a question at Amber. "Does your seafood stain tables?"

"I'm sorry?" Amber spoke to Sherry rather than the man.

Sherry couldn't think of any advice to offer.

"No, it shouldn't stain tables."

The young boy with a backward baseball cap whined, "No, Grandpa. I wanted you to ask if it's sustainable."

The crowd chuckled.

Amber giggled. "Yes. Of course it is. No ecosystem was compromised in the making of my recipe."

"Good job, Amber," Sherry called out.

Step by step, the dishes came together, and Sherry's assembled dish was the first to go in the oven.

"Soon it's pizza time," Diana sang. "Does anyone have a pair of oven mitts I can borrow?" Sherry handed Diana hers as Diana chanted her cook's prayer.

"Let's give thanks for the quality food I prepare,

"Well-done in a world of mediocrity is quite rare."

"Looks so delicious." Sherry surprised herself with her enthusiasm.

Diana bowed her head. "Visual appeal is just one component of a winning recipe, but thank you."

The audience clapped when Diana carried her pizza to the oven, caftan billowing as she moved. Sherry hustled to open the oven door for her. Diana shoveled the pizza from the paddle into the preheated oven then turned and curtsied. Sherry returned to her table, accompanied by Diana.

"Is there a particular way to cut a pizza?" The inquiring woman was dressed in form-fitting tennis attire, and Sherry was sure pizza seldom touched the slender woman's lips.

"You know some Chicago-style pizza is cut into squares, 'party-style.'" Diana etched a quotes sign in the air with her pizza cutter. "Today I could stick to traditional wedges, but I'd like to be accurate." Diana turned to Sherry and Amber. "Do you ladies remember how the pizza was cut at the cook-off?"

Both Sherry and Amber shook their heads, "No."

"I'm guessing we need Mac again. Let me grab him and see if he has your answer." Sherry threw down her cleaning towel and skirted around the tables.

"His pics will also help me figure out what garnish to use," Diana called out after Sherry.

Sherry found Mac fishing in a bowl of cheese cube samples at the back of the crowd. "We need a shot of Jamie Sox's pizza after it was baked, so Diana can see how he sliced and garnished it." Sherry studied the cheese cubes. "Don't you ever think about how many grubby hands have been in that bowl before yours?"

"Never." Mac wiped his fingers on his shirt and picked up the camera equipment at his feet.

Mac followed Sherry back to Diana's table, where they caught the tail end of a dissertation on garnishes.

"I know lots of people think garnish is just for show, but I'm definitely of the mind it should complement and harmonize with the flavors of the dish.

You're not just accenting with a touch of color on the plate. Garnish should make sense with the entire recipe. One of the subtle herbs used in the pizza sauce would serve as a logical garnish.

"There were even green herbs in the bison sausage," Diana concluded. "Think of garnish as having the same purpose as a Walmart greeter. It welcomes you in an unassuming way to the dish, while subliminally setting the tone of your entire dining experience."

Sherry whispered in Diana's ear. "Mac has the photos you wanted. He's coming."

"Right here." Mac bumped his way through the milling crowd to get to the front of Diana's table.

"Perfect. I'm curious how he cut his slices. Never mind about the garnish, though." Diana picked up a copy of Jamie's printed recipe and pointed to the bottom of the ingredients list. "He doesn't have any listed. I would've included one, but that's just me. A recipe without garnish is like a guard dog without a bark. Incomplete."

"No. Jamie Sox's pizza definitely had a garnish." Patti Mellit held up a glossy piece of paper from the side of Diana's table. "Check this out. It's even in the photo in the store flyer."

"Mac sees a garnish, too." Mac showed Diana two photos from his camera's viewfinder.

"Can I see?" After lengthy consideration, Sherry added, "Wonder if anyone noticed Jamie didn't use the same garnish on the plate sent to the judges versus his plate on the display table." *Do I have that photo at home? Note to self: pull that photo.*

"Well, there's none listed in his written recipe, and if it wasn't, it shouldn't be in his finished dish," stated Diana. "A rookie mistake on Mr. Sox's part. Enough said."

The oven timer behind the cooks rang out. Sherry handed Diana her oven mitts and watched as she pulled the bubbly pizza out of the oven and relayed it to her cutting board.

"Guess I won't be needing this." Diana tossed a plastic bag of herbs off her table. It touched down in front of Sherry. "Oops, sorry."

"Delicious!" a spandex-clad woman raved at the sight of Diana's pizza. "I'll definitely have my personal chef make this for my family."

The oven timer rang again, signaling Sherry's dish was done. She donned her oven mitts and chanted her cook's prayer before removing her dish from the oven.

"Thanks for the food we're about to share,

"There's love in all the delicious layers."

Much to her delight, her tangy, luscious Chutney Glazed and Farro Stuffed Pork Tenderloin had the appearance of perfection. The glistening chutney glaze bubbled with gingery goodness. The split pork tenderloin was stuffed with organic farro and wilted baby spinach. Sherry's trained eye recognized the meat had retained the majority of its juices, ensuring inner moistness, while releasing just enough of its rich drippings in the roasting pan to be spooned over the slices.

Sherry pulled her aromatic pork out of the cramped oven. The internal meat thermometer read 165 degrees. It was cooked to her liking, medium rare. She let the meat rest for seven minutes before she cut it at an angle. Her growing audience seemed to be buzzing with what Sherry hoped was escalating anticipation of a taste. One woman in particular had been at her table from the demonstration's onset. She stood at the ready to receive a tasting plate. The woman, even while being bumped and jostled, wasn't going to give up her prime spot at the front of the tasting line for anything.

Sherry placed the meat on paper plates, leaving the majority of the pork on a serving platter for display purposes. Patti was waiting by Sherry's station with notepad in hand. Before Sherry could set the first filled plate down on the table, the woman at the head of the line grabbed it and speared a bite with a fork she held at the ready. She hummed as she chewed. The woman had yet to swallow when Patti asked for her comments.

An instant later, the woman bent over at the waist and began dry heaving while shivering violently.

"We need a doctor over here!" Patti called out to her husband, "Rafe, can you help us?"

Sherry rushed to the side of the ailing woman. She searched the crowd for Patti, hoping she still had an ally. When she found her, their gazes met briefly before Patti turned her head. Rafe hustled over and aided his wife as they guided the woman to the store's customer service center for further assistance. As the woman was whisked away, Sherry moved her dish off the table and behind the ovens so she could evaluate the problem.

"Madame." Chef L'Herb waddled over to Sherry. "Was the pork cooked to the proper temperature?"

"Yes, Chef. I was very careful to get it cooked through to one hundred sixty-five degrees."

The chef replied, "Humph."

Sherry bit her bottom lip when she spotted Detective Bease and Detective Diamond push through the crowd of gawkers.

"What's going on?"

"My dish made a lady ill. I don't know what happened." Sherry put down her carving knife. "I can't let anyone else try a bite. Ugh, I broke my own rule of always being the first to taste my dish when it comes out of the oven, you know, to adjust the seasonings. But because the crowd was restless, I served it without trying it. It could have been me doubled over in pain!"

"Ms. Frazzelle." Nick Andime, accompanied by Mike, the security guard from the OrgaNicks facility, wedged himself between the detectives and Sherry. "Sorry I'm late. I heard a bit about the woman who became sick."

"It's awful, I'm so sorry," said Sherry. She pushed her plates of tenderloin to the back of the table and covered them with dishtowels.

"I think you shouldn't take it personally," said Nick. "The customer may have come in to the store under the weather. While we sort things out, would you mind just helping Ms. Sherman and Ms. Stroyer with their recipes? We'll clear your area, just as a precaution. I'll go check on the woman, but I'm positive it was a coincidence. She'll be fine. Follow me, Mike."

On his way out, Nick peered back. "Keep cooking, ladies. We have mouths to feed."

Sherry shimmied over to Amber's table. The detectives shifted their location, shadowing Sherry.

Amber had just removed her Seafood Flatbread from the oven. "I'm going to slice this up. I think it looks okay, but I'm really nervous."

"I thought mine was okay, too, but I was very wrong." Sherry shuddered and, like a contagious yawn, Amber followed suit and shuddered.

Amber sectioned off a slice of saucy flatbread while Sherry crossed her fingers. Sherry willed herself to keep a cheerful dialogue going with the audience while watching for any signs Amber's shrimp and scallops topping might be toxic.

"I doubled my recipe," Amber said. "I hope I haven't cooked up double trouble."

Amber took a bite. Sherry clenched her teeth as she concentrated on Amber's facial expression.

"Pretty good." Amber wiped the excess red sauce off her lips with her apron. "Anyone want a slice?"

Cheering ensued. Sherry picked up plates with shaky hands for Amber to fill, then passed them out. Detective Bease circled to the back of the table. Seeing him, Sherry let the plates fall on to the table from her hand and ran full speed toward him.

"Can't you see someone is out to discredit me?" Sherry's eyes pleaded for understanding. "I can't be having this much bad luck. It's just impossible. If it was a deliberate act today, whoever it was knew exactly how and where to hit me the hardest."

"You have quite a substantial list of odd incidents happening to you, Ms. Frazzelle." Bease squinted. "Did you happen to know the woman who got sick?"

"Of course not. I've never seen her." Sherry's voice quivered as it raised an octave.

"I'll take your food back to the lab and the results can tell us more," said Detective Bease. "Diamond, gather a sample."

As the midday demonstration neared its end, Nick came over to the cooks to let them know OrgaNicks deemed the demonstration mostly a success, despite the hiccup. Patti, Rafe, and Mac accompanied him. For their time, the cooks were presented with another gift basket filled with OrgaNicks goodies.

"Thanks, ladies," Patti said as she and Rafe exited.

Mac hoisted his cameras to his chest and waved farewell.

"Mac, before you leave, could you e-mail me a copy of the photo you took of Chef L'Herb and me?" Diana asked. "He's such a cutie. You girls want a copy?"

Sherry, in her exhausted state, relented. "Sure. Why wouldn't I want a permanent reminder of another one of the worst days of my life?"

"Sherry, unfortunately your food was gone by the time we searched for a sample to bring back to the crime lab." Detective Bease picked up Sherry's gift basket and waited for her to finish folding her apron. "No trace of it, whatsoever. The ingredients on your table check out fine. We have no way of identifying what caused the woman's discomfort. Thankfully, she did seem to recover and has since disappeared before I could get her professionally examined, but the whole scenario is troubling, to say the least. As for your disappearing food, it's not an advisable move if someone is tampering with evidence."

"Sherry, I think you handled it so gracefully." Amber removed her apron and put it in her basket. "I know you're technically not a 'pro,' but you sure acted like one today."

Despite the kind words, Sherry was left with a lingering unrest in the depths of her stomach. A question sizzled on her brain like a strip steak on a blazing fajita platter: What's really going on here? She wrung her hands out to shake off the clamminess and yelled, "Stop!" The trick that worked for her in the past worked again. Her negative thoughts retreated and she was back in the present moment.

"Sherry?" Amber halted in her tracks.

"Ms. Frazzelle, I was just helping you carry your gift basket. No need to shout at me." Detective Bease's free hand plunged inside his coat.

Sherry saw the strap of the detective's shoulder holster when his coat flapped open. The skin on the back of her neck prickled with discomfort. "Sorry. I'm fine. Just ignore me."

The detective relaxed his arm and dropped it to his side. He took two steps toward Sherry. He ran his fingers through his hair and looked her straight in the eyes. "Ms. Frazzelle, things are getting complicated. My advice would be to keep a distance from anyone or anything associated with the cook-off until further notice."

Sherry's eyes darted toward Amber.

"Ms. Sherman excluded." Detective Bease turned and marched away but not before adding, "Reminder, I need those photos back, ASAP."

Chapter
15

"Amber, remind me again why doing yoga is better for me than giving in to the tuna melt craving I'm having? It's your last afternoon here and this is how you want to spend it?" As Sherry neared the Namaste All Day yoga studio, she caught her reflection in the building's tall window. Sherry tugged at her compression capris to loosen the wedgie they were giving her.

"Body, mind, and spirit," chanted Amber. "Body, mind, and spirit. Each of those needs attention and replenishment periodically, and yoga is just the answer. Remember, our goal at this stage of our lives is to keep calm, keep growing and move forward. No backslides. All positives. Tuna can wait."

Sherry slammed into a wall of ninety-degree heat when she opened the studio doors. "Okay, you make it all sound worthwhile, but wow, does it have to be so hot in here? It's like an oven. I hope it's not me that's cooked by the time we're done."

"Did you know men who practice yoga are referred to as yōgis, and women are yoginis?" Amber asked.

"I'd prefer paninis and martinis, but I appreciate your wealth of information."

"Just trying to keep you in the know."

As the two ladies passed the other yoga students, Sherry noticed how protective they were of their chosen spots. If Sherry so much as glanced at empty floor space, someone would throw a mat or towel down to cover it. She followed Amber to the unpopulated area in the back of the room, taking care not to step on those who had sprawled out to begin preliminary stretches.

After Sherry unrolled her funky-smelling mat, she found herself staring headlong into a room-width mirror. It had always been a source of pride that her weight had been the same for years, but now her reflection introduced an undeniable revelation. Her shape had transformed. Muscle, once uplifted, was now as droopy as a popsicle in the August sun. In vegetable terms, she was still a scallion but the lower bulb was widening.

"The few times I did yoga, it wasn't this 'hot' yoga," said Sherry. "I'm glad we brought lots of water, because I think I've already lost a pint of bodily fluids just standing here. The smell in here brings back fond memories of Marla's sweaty sports clothes."

"Sherry! Don't make me laugh or people will think we aren't serious!"

When the class began, Sherry had trouble focusing on her movements because she was distracted by her surroundings. The man in front of her had discarded his shirt, and his sweat was pooling on his mat. To Sherry's left, a woman was obviously very well-versed in the required poses, but she grunted with every change of position. Like a preheating oven, the temperature and humidity elevated as the class progressed. The air was stifling and thick with rancid body odor. Sherry's body hadn't been asked to bend in such acute angles since her time in the womb. She would have giggled at the absurdity of her situation if it weren't for the fact she was close to tears. It was as if the walls were closing in on her.

After fifty minutes, Sherry lay spent on her mat.

"We better get up before we can't," said Amber.

"You know something?" Sherry sat up slowly. "Yoga is a metaphor for where I am right now."

"Really?" Amber wiped her brow with her hand towel.

"It challenges you to be flexible, strong, and re-laxed, like the sponge cake I use for a jelly-roll cake, when all I you can think of is giving up. It's given me an idea." Sherry gathered her wet mat, soaked towels, and empty water bottles before she headed toward the car.

"What exactly are you searching for?" Amber peered past Sherry as she navigated different botany websites.

"Just trying to identify a plant I saw recently. It had these wonderful green and ivory leaves." The next strike of the "Enter" key produced a vivid pho-tograph of a potted plant. "This could be it."

A knock at the door prevented Sherry from read-ing the plant's full description. She lowered the screen and pushed her laptop to the back of the kitchen table.

"Are you expecting someone?"

"Not that I can think of."

As the women made their way to the front door, Chutney, already there, was wagging his tail as if he were using it to fan a scalding bowl of soup.

"Must be someone Chutney likes." Sherry picked up her pace. Through the sidelights she spotted the two familiar figures holding out their badges. "What would the day be like if we didn't get a visit from these two?" She opened the door without hesitation.

"Hello, Ms. Frazzelle, Ms. Sherman. This will just take a minute."

The detectives remained outside the open door. Sherry made no effort to draw them in.

"I came to collect Mr. Stiles' photos. I need them back sooner than I thought. I assume you've had a chance to look them over." Detective Bease removed his hat and sunglasses.

Sherry didn't answer. She was concerned her yoga outfit might be wafting an unpleasant odor of dry sweat. She picked up the hem of her shirt and aired herself out, hoping to redirect the scent. Sherry realized her actions may have made the smell more prominent.

Detective Bease's eyebrows shot up, and he blinked as if his eyes were splashed with vinegar. "I also have copies of Patti Mellit's article about the cooking demonstration you were both in this morning. I printed it off the newspaper's website."

"She gets her job done in a hurry." Sherry crossed

her arms to mask the emerging goose bumps. "What did she say about me, I wonder?"

"It was mostly geared toward introducing the Au Natural Market and OrgaNicks products to people who may be unfamiliar with either or both. It was pretty straightforward. Very boring, in my opinion. She didn't even mention the little problem you had with your food. Nice of her. She could have sensationalized the whole thing."

"Glad she didn't. That wouldn't have gone over well with Mr. Andime. They have enough tension between them from what I've witnessed." Sherry put her hand up to stop the conversation in its tracks. "Stay right here and I'll get the photos." She left Amber at the door and trotted to the living room, where she picked up the shoebox of photos.

"Got the photos right here." Sherry made no attempt to deliver the box to the detectives.

"I also wanted to pass along a copy of Ms. Mellit's review of Chef Brock Lee's Splayd and Spork Restaurant." Detective Bease nudged Detective Diamond, who handed the ladies two articles. "The review had a generally moderate tone about it. Ms. Mellit was forthright with her criticism, which was very minimal. Her praise was well thought out, her suggestions for improvement were exacting, and what she had to say about Chef Lee as owner and head chef should please him."

"I will read it as soon as possible." Sherry chose her words as if they were an abundance of red pepper flakes being added to a delicate cream sauce. "Amber and I had mixed reviews of the place. I'm a little surprised you say she was so nice. I think most of her readership enjoys it when she picks places apart. She gives her readers the feeling she's standing up for our rights to get the highest quality for our dollar when we pay to eat out. Her tough words don't win her any friends in the restaurant community, I'm sure, but it sounds like Chef Lee has won her over."

"One more thing. I met with Jamie Sox, the missing participant from yesterday's demo." Detective Bease leaned one arm on the doorframe. "He lives just over the New York State border, not too far from here."

The words, "lives not too far from here," reverberated in Sherry's ears. *Close enough to steal my towel, then return it to my house? Close enough to drop off a tainted apron? Close enough to mess with my ingredients at Au Natural? Crazy enough to have had a run-in with a particular chef judge and taint my recipe with poison?*

"I can't go in to detail, but he was at home, organizing his pencil collection, by color, size, eraser material, etcetera," Detective Bease reported. "It was mind-blowing how many pencils he has. As a pen collector I appreciate a serious collector when I see one. You know he's an actuary, right?"

"I understand that." Sherry handed the box of photos to Detective Diamond. She kept one in her hand. "I didn't think much about him until I found out he broke a contest rule when his recipe ingredients were handled by an unapproved third party. All caught on camera. Patti Mellit witnessed it. Sure enough, in this photo right here it shows Nick Andime's hand extending out toward Jamie Sox. At first glance, it's an innocent handshake between the two, but if you inspect the scene very closely,

Jamie is definitely being handed something. See how the light is reflected off the plastic baggie? Then, right after, Jamie was called out by Chef Birns and Patti. He had real reason to be angry at Chef Birns."

"Interesting," said Detective Diamond.

"So Jamie was crossed by Chef Birns," Sherry stated. "The chef also crossed Kenny Dewitt when he told him he was ineligible for a contest prize. But where's the proof either of those two killed Chef Birns? Nowhere, because there isn't any."

"You realize what you're saying, Ms. Frazzelle?" Detective Diamond lifted his sunglasses to reveal his ocean blue eyes. "If you take the others you mention out of the equation, it puts you solely in the forefront of the suspect list. So, I wouldn't be so hasty making statements on conjecture."

A phone vibrated. Detective Bease stepped off the front porch to take the call.

"Sherry, what are you doing?" whispered Amber. "Why are you reinforcing their idea you might be guilty?"

"It's a risk, but I'm willing to take it. I feel like they're spinning their wheels and that's even worse for me in the long run."

Detective Bease returned, pulled his partner aside, and whispered loud enough for the ladies to hear. "Andime called. It seems he would like to have Brynne Stark investigated by our department because she is, in his words 'harassing him with nonstop threats.' He also thought I should know he's been dating both Brynne Stark and Olivia Baker over the last few months, in case the issue should come up in the investigation. He wanted to be the

one to tell us in case Ms. Stark blurted it out. Let's go."
Detective Bease faced Sherry. "Ms. Frazzelle, heed my
warning and stay away from any cook-off-related
people or activity. It's for your safety. Do you understand me clearly?" He enunciated each syllable in a
firm monotone. "There's a farmers' market fifteen
minutes west of here in a town called Eastport. Do
you know when it closes?"

"Of course, six p.m.," answered Sherry. "Getting
something for dinner?"

Detective Bease put his hat and sunglasses back
on. "Good afternoon, ladies," he mumbled.

Detective Diamond followed close behind his
partner, cradling the box of photos. Sherry closed
the door behind the detectives and collapsed on to
the couch in the living room. Amber sat across the
room in the recliner, phone in hand.

"I'm going to call OrgaNick's and check on my
apron." Amber punched the keys on her phone.

"Hello, I was a contestant at the OrgaNicks Cook-
Off, and I wonder if you knew how I can get my contest apron sent to my home address. I heard they
were being held for us. I see, thank you." Amber put
down her phone. "The word is all of them were
thrown out right after the contest because it was
thought no one wanted them."

"Strange," said Sherry. "Wonder how Brynne
managed to salvage one for me? I'd be happy to
give it to you when, or if, it arrives."

"Thanks. I appreciate that."

Sherry studied her friend's face for a moment.
"You know, I was thinking. We could use some salad
items for your farewell dinner and what better place
than a farmers' market for freshness and quality?"

"I was afraid you were going to say that," said Amber. "The detectives aren't going to be happy if they see us there."

"Hey, we're just going to get ingredients for an early dinner before you're off to the train station."

Chapter 16

Sherry and Amber discussed which salad to make for dinner. The consensus was to find some tender, sweet lettuces to serve as the foundation for a goat cheese, cranberry, pistachio salad with honey-cider vinaigrette. Sherry also mentioned her love of adding grated horseradish and mustard to her salad dressings. She liked the way they lent a pop of heat to the dressing but only enough to balance any sweet elements in the salad, like dried cranberries.

Sherry was also on the hunt for artisan bread. Last time she went to the outdoor farmers' market, she brought home a round country loaf studded with olives. She grilled it, then kissed it with her best olive oil. It was crusty, chewy perfection. Later, she baked the crusty end pieces for croutons for one of her salads.

When they arrived at the parking lot, Sherry spotted Detective Bease's car. She knew better than to alert Amber to her sighting. The ladies began shopping in earnest at the very first vendor they came to. Homemade, wheat-free, organic, non-GMO dog treats were the featured items.

"This is a bit pricey for me." In an attempt to exercise financial restraint, Sherry's budgeting trick was to only bring a predetermined amount of cash with her. "I'd get a bag of 'Simply Pawfect Cookies' for Chutney in a snap if they weren't twelve dollars for twelve treats." Sherry moved on toward the next vendor.

"I'll meet you there in a minute," Amber called out.

"You don't even have a dog. But okay, meet me next door."

Sherry strolled a few steps to the produce vendor. She studied the selection of greens as she waited for Amber to join her.

"I just passed Brynne," Amber whispered, when she found Sherry stroking a tomato.

A few feet away, in the open area between the sales stalls, Brynne Stark was holding a tray featuring various specimens of local goat cheese. Her alpine green dirndl was hard to ignore among the pants and cardigans most of the cliental wore. As potential customers passed, Brynne pivoted to lure them in. It gave Sherry and Amber the chance to sneak around to the next vendor without being detected.

"I bet she's the one the detectives are coming to see," said Sherry.

"We can't let them see us here." Amber bumped into a set of toddler twins as she shimmied to the side. "You promised you'd lay low."

"This isn't a cook-off or a cook-off-related activity, and I had no idea Brynne would be here. They can't restrict me from getting food for dinner, can they?" Sherry shrugged and ducked behind the sign decorated with vegetables from the Fun E Farm.

"We've struck gold." Sherry was close to euphoria when she studied the variety of lettuces the farm offered. There were multiple shades of green featured, along with reds and even browns. Some lettuce seemed destined to hold up better if dressed with lighter vinaigrettes, while others could bear heavier dressings, such as Blue Cheese Ranch, and not wilt under the weight.

"Aren't these gorgeous?" Sherry held up a frilly leafed lettuce and a smaller red lettuce.

"Yep, gorgeous," a deep voice echoed. "What a coincidence finding you two familiar ladies here."

"You startled me!" Sherry jumped back when she saw the two detectives within arm's length. "We just thought your idea of coming down here was so good, we hopped in the car, and here we are."

"I'm going to take it at face value you two are not here for any other reason than to shop," Detective Bease said.

Sherry's cheeks flashed hotter than sriracha sauce.

"Are you buying those or just taking them out for a test drive?" The Fun E farmer circled his booth and approached Sherry.

"Sorry, here you go." Sherry handed the overalls-clad man eleven dollars to cover the cost of the produce she was handling.

Detective Bease rumbled from his throat and walked over to Brynne where she was busy presenting her goods to the approaching duo. Sherry and

Amber sidestepped their way to the edge of the Fun E Farm's booth closet to Brynne.

"What a surprise! Detective Bease," Brynne gasped.

"We just need a moment of your time, Ms. Stark," Detective Bease said.

"I assume if you're still asking questions, the investigation of the murder of Chef Birns hasn't concluded?"

"That's correct."

"Would either of you like a sample of herb-rubbed goat cheese or possibly a dollop of goat cheese, pesto, and fig spread on a cracker? How about some goat cheese with locally crafted chorizo sausage? The cheese is lovingly made from the freshest goat's milk from free-range grass-fed goats located only twenty minutes from here at Roamin' Empire Farms. It's as local as local goats, I mean gets."

Before the detectives could respond, Sherry and Amber stepped forward for cheese samples.

"Yes, please, we'd love to try some," Sherry said.

"Ms. Stark," Bease began, ignoring the interruption. "We realize you're working, but if you wouldn't mind answering a few questions, we can make this quick." Bease shifted his position and shot Sherry a heated glare, the intensity of which could have melted Rocky Road ice cream instantly.

As the detective spoke, Brynne thrust her platter of samples at anyone who was in close proximity. Her abundant colorful hair ribbons trailed across the cheese as she whirled about in an effort to entice potential customers. The recipients always smiled and gave a satisfied "yum, thanks" or "where can I buy this" inquiry after a nibble. Brynne handed out a tri-fold informative pamphlet on the

earthy cheese, the happy goats, and the idyllic farm
where the animals were raised. Sherry admired
how masterful Brynne was at coordinating the re-
sponses to Detective Bease's questions while performing her job.

"When was the last time you saw or conversed
with Nick Andime from the OrgaNicks Company?"

"Um, we used to talk a lot, don'tcha know."
Brynne's Midwest twang wrapped around her
words like the golden dough that envelope Pigs in
a Blanket. "Mr. Andime, I mean, Nick, helped me
get the job as hostess at the recent cook-off. I'm
very grateful for his generosity and belief in me.
But I'm not sure why he continually calls me, leaves
voice mails, sends texts, and sends e-mails. He
doesn't really say much. Sometimes it's just a garbled grunt or moan."

Brynne greeted a small clan who expressed interest in her product. "Please take a brochure, which
will provide you with all the facts about our wonderful cheese. Goat cheese can be enjoyed by even the
most lactose intolerant individuals because goat's
milk's makeup is very similar to human's."

Without losing a beat, Brynne turned her focus
back to Detective Bease. "I don't want to start any
trouble with the man. He's just feeling a bit of stress
with his new job." Brynne's smile brightened. "Nick
mentioned he might put me in a commercial for
OrgaNicks. It would be a wonderful advancement
in my career, but until the ink is dry on the contract, I need to make a living. That's why I do what
I do. Plus, I don't have a lot of time to devote to listening to him talk about his on-again, off-again,

relationship with Olivia Baker. It's gotten to the point where I'm not replying unless it's work related, and I know he's angry with me. So to answer your question, I have only spoken directly to Mr. Nick Andime once, maybe twice, since the cook-off."

"I see, sparse communication." Detective Bease scribbled on his notepad with the New England Patriot's logo pen he'd pulled from his pocket. "How is your relationship with Chef Olivia Baker?"

Sherry and Amber couldn't restrain themselves from having another sample. Detective Diamond joined them as well.

"I'm so glad you enjoy our goat cheese." Brynne did a half dip, half curtsy.

"I really need to buy some," said Amber.

"If it's your first purchase of goat cheese, we recommend the simple log form." Brynne tipped her head toward the brochures on her tray. "In the pamphlet we've supplied recipe suggestions, all the ingredients of which can either be found here at the farmers' market or at your local grocery store." Brynne paused. "Hey, I'm talking to two of the best cooks in the country. You should be giving me advice on how to use the product."

"Thank you, Brynne. I wasn't sure you'd remember us." Sherry smiled and pointed to the cheese. "My dad is coming over for dinner in two days, so I think I'll surprise him with some of your delicious herb goat cheese. He loves to spread it on crackers with a bit of mango chutney."

"What a delicious idea!" Brynne was all smiles when she turned her attention back to Detective

Bease, who had begun tapping his pen on his notepad.

"I don't have any problem with Olivia Baker," said Brynne. "She seems to be in a tough spot at the moment, losing her job and all. I wish her well. I saw her fairly often for a while because we always seemed to work the same venues. I was often the event hostess when she catered it. She didn't hide the fact she thought catering was well beneath her talent level. I'm guessing her snobbish attitude may have led to fewer and fewer jobs. I'm sure things will turn around for her. In a weird way, we root for each other's success.

"But if you want to talk to her directly, she happens to be here somewhere, shopping for Chef Brock Lee's restaurant. She passed by me about ten minutes ago."

Detective Diamond stepped forward. "Ms. Stark, Chef Birns was hired by Nick Andime to judge the Hillsboro Cook-off. That seems somewhat odd because Mr. Andime was also a financial backer of Chef Lee's restaurant in Stamford. It's the same restaurant where Chef Birns was employed as executive chef, a position from which he was ultimately terminated. The restaurant has been struggling to make a profit, some say due to the tumultuous atmosphere in the kitchen. You'd think Andime would want to cut ties with the man. Has Mr. Andime ever mentioned Chef Birns in a disparaging way? Do you believe Andime holds any animosity toward the chef who may have lost him the money he needed to fund his new organic business venture?"

Brynne rearranged a few items on her tray before

answering. "Not for a minute." A bead of sweat trickled down her temple. "I'm not saying he isn't moody, but Nick is anything but vengeful." Brynne made three stuttering attempts to get the word vengeful from her tongue.

"By the way, I have yet to receive my apron from the cook-off," Sherry stated.

Sherry watched Brynne's eyebrows squeeze together.

"Sorry? Apron?"

"You called a few days ago asking for my address so the sponsor could send me the apron I left behind at the cook-off."

Brynne shook her head, causing her hair ribbons to brush across the cheese and send crumbles airborne.

"The one with the OrgaNicks logo on it?"

"Yes." Brynne answered with hesitation. "So many things to do. Seems like ages ago. I'll follow up and see what the holdup is."

"No rush. Just checking." Sherry winked at Amber.

Detective Bease grumbled. "Where's your computer, Diamond?" Detective Bease whipped his pen back and forth to get the ink flowing, but it wasn't working.

"I saw you holding your notepad, so I left it in the car," replied Detective Diamond. "Is there a problem?"

"The problem is you're not prepared for all scenarios. Next time, don't come empty-handed." Detective Bease kicked a pebble.

"Need this?" asked Brynne, as she handed Detective Bease a child-size souvenir pencil with a goat's head eraser.

"Thank you." Detective Bease plucked the tiny pencil from her hand and held it with the tips of his fingers. He finished up his notes before relinquishing the pencil to a little girl who was ogling it. "I appreciate your insight, Ms. Stark."

"My pleasure." Brynne served a gaggle of young mothers and their children. "Is Nick in trouble?"

Sherry froze in anticipation of the detective's reply.

"I am not at liberty to answer, Ms. Stark. Have a good day."

Detective Bease and Detective Diamond left, while offering a dismissive hand wave. "Good afternoon, ladies."

"Follow me." Sherry motioned Amber forward in the opposite direction.

"Right behind you." Amber tagged along behind Sherry as she made a beeline for the artisan bakery. "How in the world can you explain Brynne's answer about the apron? If they all got thrown out, how can she be sending you one?"

"We'll have to wait and see if one really does arrive. I'm not too optimistic after seeing the vacant expression on her face when I mentioned it," said Sherry. "C'mon, let's keep moving."

"I can't resist baked goods." Amber doubled back to the Yeast Coast Bakery. "Not good for the waistline, but I'm thinking of taking up jogging so this could be just the motivation I've been missing. I'm going to grab an apple coffee cake with maple glaze. Who can resist that combo?"

While Sherry waited, she realized Amber was

standing behind Detective Bease in the checkout line.

Sherry tapped the detective on the shoulder. "I promise we're not following you."

"Just a small sidetrack." Bease held up his intended purchase. "Nothing here should make headlines." Detective Bease handed Detective Diamond his bread bag, and they disappeared into the crowd.

"Okay, last stop, the Biz E.B."

"Welcome! I'm Evan Bumble, this county's sweetest beekeeper and purveyor of honey products." A stout man with hair sprouting from all exposed skin swooped in and addressed Sherry. He was dressed in a yellow and gold striped T-shirt. "My favorite singer is Sting and my favorite color is amber. Now you know all about me." The man began humming a one-note tune.

Sherry nudged Amber. "You're his favorite color."

"Very funny."

"Hey, check them out." Just beyond Mr. Bumble, Sherry spotted the detectives approaching a woman in a chef's coat.

Detective Bease sidled up to Olivia Baker.

"We need to get over there." Sherry waved to the purveyor of honey. "We'll buzz back soon, Mr. Bumble."

"Bease is going to kill us," Amber said.

The women positioned themselves behind the detectives' backs.

"I just have a few more questions for you," Detective Bease began. "It'll just take a moment of your time."

"I've been waiting for the follow-up interview," Olivia said. "Now is as good a time as any."

"Okay. First, it's come to my attention you had a close relationship with both Tony Birns and Brock Lee. Is this a correct statement?"

Olivia nodded.

"Please use a verbal response so we clearly understand," stated Detective Diamond. "Engaged to Mr. Lee and a business associate of Mr. Birns. Are these correct facts?"

"Yes, you could say that. Those things have been true at one time."

"How would you describe your relationship to Mr. Nick Andime at this moment?" asked Detective Bease.

"We have an understanding," replied Olivia.

"You're currently unemployed but were once an investor in the Splayd and Spork Restaurant in Stamford. Is this accurate?"

"I have a few part-time gigs. I still am an investor in the restaurant, as is, I mean was, Tony. The three of us disagreed on certain business practices, so rather than pull out my investment, which was basically my life savings, I chose to terminate my employment there. Ironically, because funds are now extremely tight for me, I'm reduced to doing the shopping for Brock's evening specials. I have, for all intents and purposes, been left with nothing, unless he's able to turn a profit very, very soon. I think it'll happen. Tony Birns was a large part of the problem at the restaurant, even after he left as head chef. I imagine with his passing, things may settle down there and run more smoothly."

Detective Bease made some notes with a pen painted like a rhubarb stalk.

"Don't get me wrong. We were all still friends up until the time of Tony's death, but money can drive a big wedge between relationships at times. Brock had to make a choice between his friends and growing his business. That's why I'm never going to let a man, or anyone for that matter, make me dependent on him or her for anything again. You guys are trouble. Not *you* specifically, but guys in general. I'm going to work any way I can to get back on my feet and no one, not even someone with deep pockets, will tell me what to do and when to do it. Anyone who lets that happen to them will wither on the vine like a tomato after the first frost."

"Are you referring to anyone in particular?" Detective Diamond tamped down his windblown hair.

Olivia frowned. "Next question."

"Have you been in contact with Nick Andime since the cook-off?" asked Detective Bease.

"I've talked to him for a second on the phone, but this week our dinner was canceled. His doing. You may want to ask his friend, Brynne, what he's up to. I bet she's in contact with him. She's here right now, as a matter of fact, if you want to ask her in person. Don't get me wrong. I really don't mind too much how much time she spends with the guy. Nick gets a bit overly possessive sometimes."

"I have another meeting set with Andime tomorrow morning. I'm not sure why he wants to see me again, but you can be sure I have a few more questions for him. Okay, Ms. Baker, we have the information we need from you." Detective Bease made eye contact with Sherry when the group she was attempting to blend in with dispersed and her hiding place became transparent.

"Is Nick in trouble?" Olivia asked.

Sherry elbowed Amber, picked up her bags, and strutted away.

Chapter
17

After an early dinner, Amber rolled her suitcase to the front door. Sherry scooped up Chutney and Amber's OrgaNicks gift basket, and took her seat in the car.

As they drove, Amber reached in the backseat and rifled through her packed clothes. "I almost forgot the present I picked up for you two at the farmers' market." She presented the gourmet dog treats. "Thanks for being the perfect hostess. I learned so much during my visit and have created some tremendous memories, not all good but memories, nonetheless. I'm going to send you something special from Maine to remember me by, but in the meantime, I wanted Chutney to miss me, too!" She hoisted the package of canine cookies so Sherry could see them as she drove. "Chutney's going to need these for extra energy if he's going to take my place as your partner in crime. Oops, I mean, solving crime."

"You shouldn't have!" said Sherry. "He'll absolutely love them! Thank you!"

Sherry's car pulled up to the Amtrak station, with only minutes to spare. Amber leapt from the car with her bag and basket, waved, and scurried off toward the train platform. Sherry lingered in the "no parking" zone to watch the train pull away from the station. Behind her a short siren wailed. A police car pulled up next to her, and the officer inside rolled down his window.

"Keep moving forward, ma'am, you're holding up everyone behind you."

Now there's an understatement if I've ever heard one. I've got to get moving.

When Sherry returned home, she was forced to steer her car in a tight turn to get into her driveway. A full-size SUV blocked the normally easy access. *Not a great parking place for such a massive car. The driver must need glasses or is just downright inconsiderate.* She inched her car along, hoping not to clip the other car's side mirror with hers.

Safely in her driveway, she unbuckled Chutney from his car restraint and carried him up the steps to the front porch. "Why didn't I turn the porch light on?" She fumbled inside her purse for the car key set she had tossed inside when she needed both hands to carry Chutney. "Stay very still, boy, and I won't drop you." She lowered her chin and wedged the handle of her purse under her jaw. One hand fingered coins, dollar bills, granola bars, and a tube of emergency moisturizer at the bottom of her purse but wasn't able to locate the keys. If she could activate her phone's flashlight app, she would stand a chance of finding the darn key. It was going to take a third hand to accomplish that, though. A bead of sweat rolled down Sherry's forehead. A dull ache was radiating through the side of her head from holding it cocked at an awkward angle.

Just as her search became more of a test of endurance, Chutney began to struggle. Sherry feared hurting him as she squeezed hard to control him. "Chutney, stop wriggling."

Chutney yelped a piercing cry. She heard a rustling in the giant holly bush next to the porch. She turned toward the noise, just as a dark figure sprinted up the steps. A hard shove knocked the air out of her lungs.

"Mind your own business!"

Opening her eyes was as herculean a task as prying apart an oyster shell with a chopstick. When she finally muscled her eyelids open, she was stunned to see only branches. She tried to lift her head to identify where she was, but her body wouldn't cooperate. The arm she lay on felt oddly disconnected from her body, and she couldn't move her arm.

"This must be what it's like to have the weight of the world on your shoulders, literally."

Sherry's legs straddled a holly limb, and the jagged leaves were embedded in her bare legs. She regretted her decision to wear a skirt to the train station. She also regretted not heeding Ray's warnings to stay out of the investigation. A tear rolled down her cheek. She couldn't even lift her hand to wipe it away.

Sherry wiggled the fingers of her free hand.

"Well, something works." Blinking hard to clear her thoughts, she pieced together how she could have had ended up laid out like a butterflied leg of lamb.

"Oh my God," she exclaimed with a violent, painful shudder. "Chutney. Where are you?" Her brain was pulsing with fear for the safety of her pup. "Chutney, Chutney, here boy," she whimpered. Speaking sent shockwaves of pain through her bruised head and shoulder. The sound of his jingling collar was nowhere to be heard. "If I could move this shoulder, I could get out of here." Sherry squeezed her eyes shut then whimpered, "Phone!"

Not only was her battered right shoulder pinned under her, but also her cell phone. In her prone position, using her unhurt left arm to reach her skirt's right hip pocket was impossible. The pain limited her ability to contort in such a way to get at the pocket, but she kept at it. With each attempt, she bit the inside of her cheek to help counter the searing pain.

"Got it," she exclaimed. She hit the phone's activation key with her thumb and then cursed. "My right thumbprint is the pass code. How's that going to work? I can't even begin to move my right hand." The phone rejected her left thumbprint, so she was forced to type in a numerical pass code. She straddled the phone on her left hip and managed to type the four-digit passcode on the last try before the phone locked her out completely. "Technology, ugh!"

Sherry hit the speed dial key for Charlie's cell number. She felt a sliver of relief as the phone rang. "When he answers, how am I going to explain my predicament?" She decided on a simple, "I'm in trouble," but after she counted the fifth ring, she began to lose hope of contacting him.

"You have dialed the Charles Frazzelle law office. I can't pick up right now, so please leave your name and number after the beep, and have a great day."

"Charlie, it's me . . ."

"The recipient's mailbox is full. Good-bye." The dial tone marinated her battered brain with bitterness.

"Why didn't I remind him to clear it out?" Sherry whined. "Because I'm not his mother. That's why."

"Okay, nine-one-one." Sherry punched in the numbers. The screen was black before she got the second "1" pushed. Dead battery. She closed her dripping eyes and began counting backward from one thousand to get her mind off the pain.

". . . Eight hundred sixty, eight hundred fifty-nine. What if no one finds me and I become the compost in my own front yard?" Sherry whispered. "Eight hundred fifty-eight, eight hundred fifty-seven."

"Sherry, are you down there? What are you doing?" Erno jumped off the front porch and squatted down next to his daughter. "Can you move?"

"If I could, Dad, I wouldn't still be here." Sherry was swamped by her misery.

Erno pulled out his phone. He dialed 911 and gave the address and some vague information concerning what the medics were going to find when they arrived.

"You've got some explaining to do." Her father

set about removing the prickly branches from atop her body.

"I called Charlie, but his phone went to voice-mail." Sherry's voice was as weak as the taste of refrigerated tomatoes. "What are you doing here?"

"I thought you might be lonely after Amber left, so I was just checking in. Lucky thing I did."

With sirens blaring, the ambulance pulled up to the house. The driver and his crew lifted Sherry out of the bushes and placed her on a stretcher before transporting her to the emergency room.

Just as the EMTs were closing the vehicle door, Sherry called out to Erno with her last drop of energy, "Chutney's gone. Please find him."

On the drive home from the emergency room, Sherry, feeling much improved thanks to powerful painkillers, attempted to apprise her father of the events of the past few days. She was careful to script it so as not to alarm him unnecessarily, but as she told him the details, she herself grew increasingly concerned for her own safety. She noted he listened in silence without asking any questions.

When she finished her story, Erno released an extended single-note hum. "Sherry, I appreciate your efforts to clear your name and move the investigation along at your speed, but you're done now, right?"

"Dad," Sherry said, "my recipe contests, not to mention my good name, mean a lot to me. I'm sure they'll find who is behind all this very soon."

Reclined in the backseat to keep the weight off her injured shoulder, Sherry closed her eyes because the throbbing in her head increased with the words she spoke.

"Like I always say, 'If you don't know where you're going, you'll probably pack the wrong clothes.'"

"Thanks, Dad. I'll keep that in mind."

"Sherry!" Charlie held her hands in his. "Sherry, can you hear me?"

Sherry opened her eyes. She tried to lift the throbbing arm, but it was as difficult as peeling a butternut squash. She coaxed her fingers to investigate what hurt so much on the side of her head. She discovered a bump the size of a walnut.

"Aw! That hurts," Sherry moaned. "Charlie, is that you? I was dozing. Where are we? Where's Dad?"

"You're home. I brought you in from the car. Erno couldn't lift you by himself so he called me to come help. He was exhausted so I sent him home." Charlie pulled up an ottoman next to the sofa Sherry was lying on. "Can you tell me what happened?"

Sherry blinked until her vision cleared. "I remember searching for the keys in my purse and having so much trouble finding them. I guess I forgot to turn on the porch light before I took Amber to her train. It was pitch black. Suddenly, someone yelled something at me, and boom, next thing I know the medics are helping me out of the bushes."

"This neighborhood is so safe. I'm shocked." Charlie shook his head.

"I'm not really clear on any more details." Sherry

rubbed her forehead. "Somehow I was flung off the porch. Right now things are a little fuzzy. I had to give the police as much information as I could at the hospital, but there wasn't much to go on. No one broke into the house. There were no fingerprints on me, and I didn't see any face. I remember a dark SUV parked in front of the house. Didn't even occur to me to get the plate numbers. Whoever shoved me off the porch screamed something, but it was so fast. Definitely a man's voice and a man's strength in the push. I can't recall much else."

Charlie touched her shoulder with a light hand.

"My shoulder will be okay. Only a slight separation, and this lump on my head will shrink soon enough, so no worries." Sherry attempted a smile, but her mouth sagged instead.

"Listen, if it's okay, I'll stay here for a few days until you're up and mobile. I owe you that much." Charlie's words swept across Sherry's head like a smoky grease fire, and her breathing slowed. "You just take it easy for now. I'm here to serve. Just call me Nurse Frazzelle."

"Thanks, but I'll be fine." Sherry attempted to sit up. Halfway up, she let out a hair-curling groan and slunk back down. "Well, maybe one or two days. What about Chutney? We need to call every animal rescue center around here. It's my fault he's gone. He'll never survive out in the wilds of suburbia. He can't hear or see well!"

"Your dad and I have called all the vets, shelters, and animal clinics we could think of," said Charlie. "Nothing yet, but it's only been half a day."

Sherry frowned and closed her eyes. A tear dripped from the corner of her eye. "It's all my fault."

The next morning, Charlie barged through the patio door as Sherry lay on the sofa.

"Charlie's back, Marla. I better go. Thanks again for calling, I'll be fine in a few days. No need to come. Love ya." Sherry placed the phone down next to her pillow.

"Jackpot in the backyard. Chutney's collar, leash and a chunk of cloth that looks like material a man's blazer would be made from, but no dog." Charlie displayed the items in his outstretched hands for Sherry to see. "They were just inside your garden."

Sherry stared at Charlie, not daring to understand the implications of his find.

"I'm sorry." Charlie softened his tone and continued. "Fragments of that old pull cord you asked me to replace were wedged in the door lock. The gate couldn't shut properly, and most of your plants were clear-cut. They didn't stand a chance when whatever animal it was got in and had free rein of the place. I should have fixed that stupid cord when you asked me. On the other hand, if Chutney was locked in your garden or chased in by someone, that broken cord gave him the chance to escape."

The murder, the accusations, the assault, the lost family member, and now the garden devastation. Sherry shut her eyes tight and made a silent vow.

"Where's my key?" Sherry questioned as she fished in her purse that was the size of a tall kitchen garbage bag. She used her other arm to control Chutney as he tried to wriggle free from her grasp.

As hard as she tried, she couldn't feel the cold ridges of the metal key because her purse kept expanding in size.

The next thing she knew, Chutney leapt from her arms and disappeared into what was now a bottomless purse.

"Chutney! No!" Sherry cried.

After she called him, Chutney peeked his head out of her purse with a mouthful of food. He began vomiting seafood tomato sauce. A second later, he was coughing, and his eyes were rolling back into his head.

"Chutney, breathe!" Sherry pleaded, but it was too late.

The dog collapsed back into the huge purse and disappeared.

"Mind your own business! Mind your own business," a commanding voice chanted. That sounded like Detective Bease.

Sherry recognized she was at the entrance of the Hillsboro High School auditorium. The school was nearly unrecognizable though, as the structure was in a serious state of neglect and enveloped by a colossal overgrown plant. The next thing Sherry knew, a severe gust of wind blew in and knocked her over. She began a lengthy slow-motion free fall. She knew she was falling to her death but had the presence of mind to strike a pose because Mac Stiles was photographing her.

"What happened?" Charlie came bounding across the room. Sherry's coffee mug lay shattered on the floor next to the sofa. "Are you all right?"

"I had a nightmare," Sherry mumbled. She blinked a few times. "My arm jerked up because I was falling."

"I'll take care of it. Where's the dustpan? By the way, no calls about Chutney yet, but someone will call soon, I know it."

"Wait, Charlie, can I ask you something?"

"Of course."

"What would you do if everyone around you saw

something one way but you saw it dramatically different? Would you throw in the towel and join the crowd or would you speak up in your tiny minority voice?"

"First of all, I'm a lawyer. We're paid to see things differently. Second of all, you're not asking because you want my opinion. You know the answer." Charlie laughed. "Sherry, you're the easiest person in the world for me to read. I think you know something, something very important, and you need to speak up." Charlie went to the kitchen to find the dustpan.

"He's so aggravating." The phone on the side table sang out. "Charlie, the phone's ringing, can you help me pick it up?" After listening for a reply and receiving none, she rolled over to find her phone. She used her less-painful arm to feel for the device. She lifted it up with a groan. When she saw the caller, identified as "blocked," she prepared herself for a scolding.

"Bease here. Got a call from the police saying you were assaulted at your home. Do you have anything to add to the statement you gave them?"

Sherry closed her eyes. "Why did they call you?"

"I'll ask the questions." The detective's insistence stung Sherry's ears.

"Fine. That's right, I was. I told the police all the particulars I could remember except one thing. I remember now what the guy shouted as he was tossing me like a bag of beans into the bushes. It was 'mind your own business.'" Sherry cringed when Detective Bease sighed.

"Sherry, did you call me?" Charlie trotted into the room.

"You okay?" Detective Bease asked. "Whose voice is that?"

"My husband, ex-husband—I mean my almost ex-husband—is here taking care of me." Sherry lowered the phone and put her hand across its speaker. "I did, Charlie, I was having trouble reaching my phone, but I did it." Charlie lifted the edges of his mouth, turned, and left the room.

"Lucky you," Bease said. "Be well." The phone call ended.

Sherry thought she heard a parting hint of sarcasm in the detective's voice.

Sherry held the phone in front of her face and stared at the screen. She tapped it and found the number Bease had provided her with.

"Bease here," the detective answered.

"Detective Bease?" Sherry inquired.

"On the line," he stated. "You called me, why are you so surprised I would answer."

"Sorry, my brain's a little dull right now. This is Sherry Frazzelle, again." She shifted her position to relieve a throbbing that had developed.

"I know. I can see the caller ID. I'm listening."

Sherry could hear her heartbeat in her ears. "I was thinking you should check out something while you're meeting with Mr. Andime, if you're in his office over at the OrgaNicks facility."

"I don't think I mentioned to you I was meeting him." Detective Bease spoke deliberately, letting the individual words stand on their own merit. "Anyway, what do you think I should check out?"

"I may have overheard you mention it yesterday to Chef Baker at the Eastport farmers' market." Sherry fidgeted. She didn't like getting caught eavesdropping. She prided herself on being more discreet than that. "Inside Mr. Andime's office was a large potted plant, by his desk. It might be worthwhile to get a leaf sample."

"Ms. Frazzelle," Bease began.

"Humor me." Sherry raised her eyebrows until she felt a tug on her cheeks.

"I don't work for you, Ms. Frazzelle, and I'm extremely busy. May I remind you of my warning to stay out of the investigative end of things?"

"Hey, Sherry, need anything before I go work on my computer?" Charlie's commanding voice startled Sherry, and she dropped the phone. With a moan she scooped it up. "Oops, I didn't know you were on the phone. I'll wait." Charlie stood by Sherry's head and tapped his foot on the floor.

Sherry waved her hand at Charlie. "No, I'm fine. Thanks." Sherry raised the phone to her ear as she watched Charlie head toward the front door. She was surprised to hear the detective still talking. ". . . and take your latest mishap as a sign to lay low."

"I literally couldn't lay any lower if I tried." Sherry cleared her throat and gathered her breath. "And one more thing, have you ever considered Chef Tony Birns wasn't the intended victim? Detective? Are you still there?"

Chapter 18

Sherry's eyelids burst open as her phone's ring-tone played on. The window across the room framed a setting sun that transformed the clouds from white to the color of blood oranges.

"Hello, Sherry, it's your sweet-as-pie dad," Erno began, while Sherry blinked herself lucid. "I wanted to give you a heads-up I'm walking in the front door in two seconds. I didn't want to startle you. Here I come! I called Charlie and he told me he's working in the patio and can let me in."

In the time it took Sherry and her medicated brain to make sense of the conversation, Charlie rushed to the front door. Erno and Charlie made their way over to Sherry on the sofa, the elder of the two carrying a furry white bundle.

"Chutney!" Sherry sat up as straight as a celery stalk. "What happened to his leg? Where did you find him?"

"His leg is broken," Erno said. "He was found about a half mile from here. Tough little guy went a long way on three wheels. Something must have really spooked him. But I'd like to think he was going for help to save his gal. Like Lassie would."

A warm tear trickled down Sherry's cheek.

"Anyway, he'll have to wear this leg contraption for about a month. But the vet says dogs' bones heal pretty quickly. He also has this gash, maybe where the collar yanked off, but it's hard to say. A Good Samaritan brought him to the vet. I found him at the fourth vet office I called today. They were so happy to have him claimed."

Sherry was never so ecstatic to see anything in all her life.

"Are you feeling better?" Erno asked. "You've got some color back in those cheeks. Always a good sign."

"More like an adrenaline rush flush. I wasn't sure I'd ever see my dog again, and here he is."

"Now I just have to figure out how to get Chutney-boy to do his business with this cast on." Erno held the dog at an angle. "Want to hold him for a minute? Don't get up. I'll deliver him to you."

"I can hold him." Charlie extended his arms.

"Don't you dare," warned Sherry. "I need him."

Charlie backed off with his hands raised.

As Erno carried Chutney over to Sherry, they passed his collar, leash, and the torn piece of material Charlie had left on Sherry's side table. Chutney snarled as his nose twitched frantically.

"Did you see his reaction?" Sherry pointed to the dog's collar. "Show him those again. One by one."

Charlie picked up the collar. Chutney's tail rotated faster than a handheld mixer at full speed.

"He likes that." Sherry smiled.

Charlie picked up the leash and brought it over

to Erno. Chutney attempted a three-legged jump from Erno's arms while jerking his body left and right.

"Don't drop him. He's precious cargo." Sherry lifted her head higher. "I think that's a very familiar belonging. He definitely associates his leash with a good time."

Charlie set down the leash and picked up the piece of cloth and waved it in front of the dog's nose. Chutney curled up his lip and bared his teeth.

"The person who belongs to that piece of cloth is on Chutney's bad side." Sherry reached out her hand. "As a matter of fact, let me take a closer look."

Charlie handed Sherry the cloth. Sherry flipped it over twice. She rubbed it along the skin of her arm. The hairs on her forearm stood up. She gasped.

"Sherry? What is it?" Erno gripped Chutney tighter.

"Can someone get me a resealable plastic storage bag and a Sharpie, please?"

"I will, then I'll give it a go outside with our furry tripod." Charlie went in search of Sherry's requested items.

Erno rubbed the top of Sherry's head just as Charlie returned with a clear bag. "Sweetie, I'm heading home unless you need me to do anything for you."

"Here's the Baggie and the Sharpie." Charlie handed it to Sherry, who put the piece of cloth inside before pinching the seal shut. She wrote "For Bease" on the edge of the bag with the pen.

"We'll be back when his business is complete."

Charlie, with Chutney in his arms, left through the back door.

"Do you want me to wait with you until Charlie gets back inside?" Erno asked.

"I'm fine, Dad. Sorry I can't see you to the door, but thanks for bringing back Chutney. I'll talk to you soon." Sherry sunk her body down lower on the sofa and closed her eyes. "If you see Charlie outside, tell him to take his time."

"See you soon, honey, and no more hunting for clues, please. Leave it to the professionals."

Sherry's eyes darted open. "If I hear those words one more time . . ."

Erno waved, gave a wink, and let himself out the front door. Sherry's phone rang as the door closed behind her father. "Blocked caller" flashed on the screen.

"Hello." Sherry clicked the speaker setting on. She propped the phone on a pillow next to her ear.

"Bease here. I'm in the OrgaNicks parking lot. Met with Andime in his office. He got called out of the room for a few minutes, and Diamond and I scanned every inch of the place. Nothing green or leafy anywhere. You're sure of where you saw it?"

"Positive." Sherry blew out an extended breath. "It was next to his desk. Don't you remember seeing it when you met with him? That's why you should have brought Detective Diamond in with you last time. He was top of his class at spotting details. You couldn't have missed it. It was a large plant in a blue ceramic pot."

Bease huffed.

Sherry rubbed her forehead. "I have something else to tell you."

"Hold a minute," cautioned Detective Bease. "Something's going on here. A fight just broke out!"

Sherry waited for what seemed like several minutes, while listening to garbled voices in the background. She could make out Detective Bease saying, "Yes, Diamond, that's Andime and Mellit. Write this down in quotes. Andime's words. 'Journalist integrity,' something about 'destroying the chef's career with the stroke of a pen,' and 'my brother is an idiot.' Mellit's words. 'Egomaniac and con man.'"

Sherry imagined a scene similar to the one she witnessed when she visited the OrgaNicks office. She visualized the smirk on Nick's face in one of the photographs she retained.

"Patti Mellit is here, too," said Detective Bease.

"What? Patty Melts? I think they're the perfect comfort food." Sherry flipped her palm upward.

"No, Patti Mellit, the food writer who covered the cook-off."

Sherry raised her eyes to the ceiling then back down to her phone. "She's Nick Andime's sister-in-law."

"I understand that. Doesn't seem like they'll be spending Thanksgiving together this year. No, don't write *that* down, Diamond."

"Detective Bease, did you give any consideration to what I mentioned in our last phone call? I don't think Chef Birns was the intended—"

"Here we are!" Charlie came through the front door carrying Chutney. "I got him to do his business, despite his cast. And we brought you a present I found at the door!"

Sherry put her hand over the phone. "I hope it's something to eat. I'm starving," said Sherry. She lifted her hand and said, "Sorry, Detective Bease, my nurse and my dog have returned."

"Who?" the detective snapped.

"Charlie and Chutney. Anyway, did you hear me say, I don't think Chef Tony Birns was the intended victim?"

"Ms. Frazzelle, you're making a very strong statement. The victim seemed to have a number of people in his life who could be categorized as enemies and now you're saying he wasn't even the intended target? He died from, and all current evidence points to this, intentional asphyxiation. Your food may have been what transported the offending substance that basically choked the chef to death, may I remind you."

Sherry shifted her position to relieve an unpleasant tightening in her stomach.

"Off the record, why would you now say the substance was meant for anyone else? Consider your words, because you, of all people, have a huge stake in the answer."

Sherry rubbed her temple with her index finger. "Right now it's a feeling, but a strong one."

"Okay, well, I've made a mental note of your statement."

"I have to go, Detective Bease, Charlie's waiting."

"Wait, I think I see something back by the dumpsters. Is the plant you referred to earlier about three feet tall with green and white leaves, in a light blue shiny pot? Ms. Frazzelle, are you there?" The detective's voice grew distant.

"Detective? That sounds like it. Can you hear me?" Sherry arm twitched and brushed the phone off the pillow. It slid under the sofa. "Ugh."

"I'll get that." Charlie handed Sherry a legal-size envelope. "This was at the door when we returned." He retrieved the phone from under the sofa. He showed Sherry the blank screen. "Battery's out of juice. I'll get the charger."

On the top left corner of the envelope was the return address: OrgaNicks Foods, Division of Hillsboro Industries, Hillsboro, CT. Sherry drew in a deep breath to combat the pain and ripped open the seal. Inside was a neatly folded, spotless cook-off apron. She held it as high as she could and watched it unfold. She let her breath out in a long, slow stream.

"Very nice," said Charlie. "Yet another apron to add to your expansive collection!"

Dinner was a pleasant surprise of takeout items re-imagined by Charlie, with help from Sherry side-lined on the couch. Purchased tomato soup was elevated with a touch of garlic and herb spreadable cheese, stirred in until it was creamy. Parmesan crisps on top of the warm soup added salty cheesy goodness. Sherry talked him through making the paninis, and the result was gooey rich Brie, smoky country bacon, with a snap of watercress in each satisfying bite.

When she was full, Sherry handed Charlie her empty plate. "Charlie, do you think I'm boring? I'm thirty-five, single, and a part-time employee at a hooked-rug store. I like to garden, walk my dog, and enter food competitions. The lamest dating profile ever."

"Hold on. What's this all about? Did the bump on the head not knock some good sense into you? You know I never would have married you if you were boring."

"But a little boring, right?" Sherry plumped her pillow and laid her head back.

"You scared the life out of me when I got the call Erno found you crumpled in the bushes. There's proof you're anything but boring. Let's never go through that again, promise? Just stay out of the detective game, please, and find something else to make you exciting. Enough of this negative talk, I have dishes to do."

"That's my goal, very soon." Sherry was dissatisfied with Charlie skirting her question. Her ringing phone broke her sulk. She answered on the third ring and put the phone on speaker so she could lay it down next to her.

"Hi, Sherry, it's Amber," said the friendly voice on the other end of the phone. "Just wanted to say I made it home safely and thank you so much for being such a kind and generous hostess."

"Hi, Amber. You're very welcome. I should mention I had a bit of a mishap after dropping you off at the train station. I'm recuperating from a bump on the noggin. Luckily, Charlie has been taking great care of me."

"Car accident?"

"No. Someone seemed to be waiting for me

when I returned home from the train station, and it wasn't with a welcoming plate of brownies."

"What?" exclaimed Amber. "I can't believe it!"

"Whoever it was wanted to really get a point across by screaming, 'Mind your own business' just before pushing me off the porch and into the front bushes." Sherry saw the creases form on Charlie's forehead after hearing this previously undisclosed detail. "I'd like to keep that detail from my dad, please."

"Didn't hear a thing." Charlie carried Chutney to the back door. "We'll be outside for a few."

"Sherry," Amber warned, "Please be extremely careful! This has gotten very serious, and you made a promise you were done snooping around."

"Consider me warned." Sherry rolled her eyes.

"But while we're on the subject, is there anything new in the investigation?"

"Amber, let me run something by you."

"I'm ready, I think."

"Remember Mac Stiles' photo with Nick Andime and Patti Mellit in the background involved in an unpleasant discussion?"

"Sure do."

"Before I returned the box, I pulled a few more pictures from that sequence. One, in particular, had a time stamped about ten minutes later where Nick is showing Patti the contestants' display table of their completed recipes. Nick's face in the picture wasn't as sour as the previous shot, but he did seem, well, constipated. Patti, on the other hand, was all smiles. She had a small fork in her hand, poised to taste the most delicious food ever. I saw that scene unfold in person, too. What I didn't see, at the time, was I don't think Andime was happy that the photographer was capturing the moment on film. I specifically remember him tell Patti that it should remain a 'secret' when she taste-tested off the display table. He was insistent. In the photo Nick Andime was sneering at the camera lens and, let's just say, 'if looks could kill.' The time-stamp sequence shows she sampled the food a good fifteen minutes before the judges began their tasting. Remember how the waiting was interminable? It was excruciating. Anyway, my gut feeling is whatever killed Chef Birns was meant for Patti Mellit instead."

"You have to tell Detective Bease."

Sherry inhaled to relieve the tightness under her ribs. "I did tell him I thought Birns wasn't the intended target, but I'm not sure he's a believer. I stopped short of saying Patti's name, though. There must be something more concrete to base my theory on, but what?"

"I wanted to ask if you've checked in on Kenny Dewitt's blog?" Amber said. "Today he wrote about a cook-off he recently participated in. He doesn't specifically name it as OrgaNicks, but it's obvious it is. He describes how he was disqualified for having a blog.

"Then he questions why a fellow contestant's dish took on two different appearances, depending on whether it was on the judging table or the display table. He points out the fact the recipe in question probably also broke the rules. Of course, he was talking about Jamie Sox's plates of food. He slams OrgaNicks for not being consistent with their rules enforcement and calls the contest, and I quote 'as fake as the crabmeat in California Rolls.'"

Sherry stared at the ceiling.

"Sherry, are you still there?"

"Amber, I have to go. I need to revisit one more photo." Sherry's voice trembled.

Sherry hung up just as Charlie came in holding her dog.

Chapter
19

The next morning Charlie entered the kitchen with a look of severity that could frighten the bumps off a dragon fruit. "Sherry, you scared the life out of me. You have to stop doing that. I couldn't find you anywhere. What are you doing in here?"

"And good morning to you. Hope you were comfortable sleeping on the mountains of clothes in the blue room." Sherry removed two eggs over easy and turkey sausage from the skillet, with her sore arm resting at her side. "Your cooking was great while it lasted, but this just feels right. I'm back in the saddle."

Charlie joined Sherry at the stove, where she wrapped the eggs and sausage on an English muffin in foil. "I don't know if I can give it up. I was getting pretty comfortable with a spatula in my hand. I might be the competitor to watch out for at your next cook-off. Just kidding. I'm not cut out for all the measuring, seasoning, heating, and timing. I don't know how you do it. I can convince a jury a man is innocent, but I would never be able to convince a panel of judges my cooking deserves a prize. And your point is well taken. I'll take my clothes with me when I go."

"Thanks, Charlie, and thanks again for your help. Don't worry, I'm not going to be that delicate woman who needs an e-husband rushing over all the time because she can't live without a man."

"Do you mean ex-husband or e-husband?"

"E-husband. You know, a man I text or e-mail to come change a lightbulb because I haven't ever learned to do it myself. I guess you could call him an e-male, spelled E-M-A-L-E." Sherry giggled. "I don't want that either. Hopefully this episode is a one and done and you're free to return to your single life."

"Good, because that would get old really fast. I'd have to 'unfriend' you, as my ex-wife. But before I go, can you also promise me you'll stop snooping around for the murderer?"

"Let's not get crazy. If I don't finish what I started, you'll be bringing me your homemade brownies in jail on visiting day." Sherry recognized by the vacant look on Charlie's face his brain had gone into workplace mode and tuned Sherry's attempt at humor out.

"Thanks for the portable breakfast sandwich. I've got a huge caseload today and I need energy." Charlie opened the front door. "I have to say, you're not exactly sending me away with a calm feeling."

"Just get going. You've got your own clients to keep out of jail."

"Definitely. Take it easy today. Don't overdo." Charlie stepped out the door and proceeded down the porch steps.

"Yes, boss." Sherry's fingers were crossed behind her back. "Have a good day." She began to close the door but reconsidered. "Wait, you should take all your clothes with you."

Charlie raised one hand over his head and, without looking back, waved away Sherry's suggestion.

Sherry pursed her lips and shut the door. She flipped the dead bolt. As she turned her back to the door, the kitchen filled with the sound of her cell phone ringtone.

"Hi, Amber! What's cooking?" Sherry put her phone on speaker and laid it on the kitchen counter. She tore off a paper towel and began wiping the granite surface.

"Not too much. Would it be an imposition if I stayed with you during the awards dinner?"

"You're coming to town for an awards dinner? Academy awards, Grammy awards, which awards?"

"Have you checked your e-mail this morning? The OrgaNicks Cook-Off is finally ready to announce the winners. They're paying for us all to make a quick return back to the area. I can stay at the hotel they're offering up if it's a bother to have me stay again so soon. No problem."

"I'm way behind on sorting out my e-mail. You miss one day and suddenly there are thousands unread. Hold on one second." Sherry gathered up her laptop, moved it to the kitchen table, and searched her In-box for anything containing "OrgaNicks."

Sherry studied the message on her screen. "Amazing. It's at Nick Andime's own house. Do you think people are just going to turn around and come back to town?"

"I know I will," said Amber. "Did you see they're throwing in a bonus travel expense check for any miscellaneous meals?"

"Very generous. Of course. Stay here. Hopefully Marla will be here, too. Keep me posted on your arrival time."

"Off the top of my head, I'm guessing mid-morning Monday, but I'll definitely keep you posted."

Chutney began barking, which shook his little body off course as he limped his way to the front door. To add to his impairment, his cast leg kept slipping out from underneath him on the smooth wooden floor. He gave up his journey and lay down, barking all the while.

"There's someone here, Amber. Talk to you soon."

Sherry returned to the front door and peeked out the sidelight windows. Recognizing the slender man outside, Sherry let her father in. "Hi, Dad. I'm getting a funny feeling you and Charlie are tag-teaming me. Are you two keeping an eye on me?" She led her father to the living room.

"Just doing the Dad thing." Erno plunged his hands in his pockets. "I missed seeing you at work the last couple of days."

Sherry sat down, but Erno remained standing. "Tomorrow is my grand return to the store. Although I could come in today if you really need me."

"Tomorrow is just fine. Anything new with the investigation of the murder at the cook-off? I mean, unless you don't want to talk about it."

Sherry's eyelid fluttered the way they always did when her father was stern with her. "Dad, I've told you all I know." Sherry's tone was as sweet as fudge. "There are two very capable detectives on the case, and I have no doubt it will be resolved soon." Her eyebrows sank as she searched her father's face for signs of belief. "There is some big news other than the murder, though. The cook-off awards ceremony has been scheduled for next Monday at Mr. Andime's home. He's the head of OrgaNicks. I'm guessing the more intimate setting speaks to honoring the chef who passed away. They didn't want to make it a huge public relations spectacle."

"That is big news." Erno rubbed his hand against his facial stubble. "I'd be more excited if I didn't have to report the Foody Dude is at it again today, making speculations and accusations. I don't like it, Sherry."

Sherry shifted in her seat. "Stop reading it. Out of sight, out of mind."

Her dad began to pace back and forth. "Easier said than done when it's my daughter's life that's involved. Do you remember anyone acting suspiciously toward the end of the cook-off? That has to be the most important time to focus on."

Sherry tried hard to unravel her tangled thoughts, but the mild remnants of a headache made it difficult. She squinted her eyes and concentrated. "The final minutes of the cook-off were pretty action packed. Let me think. My strongest memories were of Patti Mellit for some reason. She wasn't intimidating the way she conducted her interviews for her article. On the contrary, she was so engaging as she spoke I was distracted from my cooking. I wanted to hear other contestants' answers to her interesting questions. And then there was Kenny Dewitt, who was intent on riling people up. He had a running commentary going the entire time and was very distracting. Jamie Sox had a meltdown, and Nick Andime skulked around losing patience with people. I was pretty stressed toward the very end of the cooking process, so my recollection is a bit blurry. All in all, nothing really stands out that I would label as suspicious. It's frustrating me."

Erno faced his daughter. His expression was open and encouraging. "Sounds like there was a lot going on that morning, but you're still not hitting on a motive for premeditated murder. Which cook came into the cook-off already wanting the chef dead? As I always say, you can't brine a chicken without vinegar."

"Well, actually, brine is often just water and salt." Sherry didn't like to question her father's wisdom, but sometimes it was a bit too subtle for her. "I don't know. Nothing's hitting me at the moment." She rubbed the tiny remnant of the bump remaining on her head. "I just can't shake the thought Chef Birns wasn't the intended target."

Sherry patted the seat cushion next to her. "Have a seat, Dad. We need to call Marla and make sure she's coming to the awards ceremony."

Chapter
20

"Dad, stop worrying. You're more agitated than a hungry vegan at a pig roast. We'll be fine." Sherry picked up her cell phone and checked the battery level before putting it in her purse. "It's just a dinner and awards ceremony. What can go wrong?"

"Listen, before last week, I never even considered there would be a murder at one of your cook-offs, and now it's happened. So I think I have every right to be concerned."

"Fine. I see your point."

"Good, because I want you, Marla, Amber, and the grand prize check to come home in one piece."

"I second that," Marla shouted as she descended the stairs. Midway down, she hiked up the legs of her denim jumpsuit to make the trip less cumbersome.

Sherry watched her sister bypass the last step with an athletic leap. "We should be back by ten at the latest, I'm guessing, hopefully with a couple of big checks, not just one. A little something for all of us."

Amber came down the stairs after Marla, dressed in a sparkly silver blazer and pleated black skirt. "Should I wear something more colorful?"

"No, you're fine." Sherry's pesto green pants and lemon yellow shirt flashed brilliance in the hall mirror as she walked by. "Dad thinks I'm dressed like a citrus salad. I don't think it was a compliment. Your outfit is much more fitting for a dinner out, but then again, I've never had much fashion sense. I clearly get all my wardrobe inspiration from the produce aisle. Marla, on the other hand, is setting the fashion world on fire with her evening overalls. I've never seen anything quite like it."

Marla twirled around in a full circle. "Representing Oklahoma, we'd like Marla Barras to step forward and receive the ten-thousand-dollar winning check." She took a bow. Amber applauded.

"No one's winning if we don't leave soon." Sherry collected her purse and the car keys. She turned to her father. "And thanks again for keeping Chutney company. I hope it's not too much trouble carrying him in and out to do his business."

Erno smiled as if with resistant lips. "We'll be fine. Good luck, girls. Bring home the bacon!"

"Wait a minute. I forgot something. I'll meet you at the car." Sherry dropped her hand from the front doorknob and ran to the kitchen. She returned carrying her cook-off apron.

"Why are you bringing the apron?" asked Amber, as they climbed in the car.

"I just have a feeling it might bring us some luck."

Sherry tucked the folded apron under her purse. "Okay, copilot, would you mind setting the GPS?"

Amber typed the address in and hit "Start navigation."

"Route recalculation," GPS Woman insisted after only two miles. "Make a U-turn when possible."

"That can't be right," Sherry tightened her grip on the steering wheel. "But I'll do it. This thing has fooled me before."

Sherry had just completed her third U-turn when she heard a siren. "Ugh, now what?"

Sherry looked in the rearview mirror and sucked in a deep breath. A police car flashed its lights from behind. From the backseat, Marla put her hand on Sherry's headrest. "Pull over, and just relax. They don't like conversation, just stick to 'yes' and 'no.' Not that I've ever been pulled over or anything."

Sherry guided the car to the curb.

"Uh oh." Sherry tracked the female officer in the side mirror as she approached the open driver-side window.

Marla laid her hand on her sister's wrist.

"License and registration, ma'am."

Sherry opened her glove compartment, grabbed the paper-clipped organized papers, and handed them to the uniformed woman.

"Your papers are in order here, but your headlight is out. I could write you a ticket, or you could promise me you're on your way home and will take the car in first thing tomorrow to have it fixed."

"The second choice works best for me, ma'am," said Sherry. "I mean, Officer."

"Well then, stay safe." The officer handed back Sherry's documents. "Enjoy your evening, ladies."

"Good job, Sher," Marla said.

"Are we really going home?" Amber asked.

"Well, yes. After dinner. That is if we can get this GPS working."

"Use my phone's mapping app. I've never had any trouble with it." Marla handed her phone to Amber in the front passenger seat.

Under the guidance of Marla's phone, the trio drove past gorgeous one-acre properties with meticulous landscaping and white-pebbled driveways. The houses were well-maintained and well-loved examples of the rewards of upper-middle-class pride and hard work. Each structure along the route was illuminated with inviting outdoor lighting. The homeowners' attention to detail was repeated house after house.

"Nice neighborhood. Nick Andime must be doing well."

"Right turn onto Cobra Bend in one-quarter mile," the GPS instructed.

"Is this right?" Sherry rolled down her window as they neared the instructed turn. She craned her head and double-checked the makeshift gravel road. "That's definitely not even a real road."

"Ugh! We lost the signal. The program shut down. Must be a dead spot." Amber fiddled with the phone but wasn't able to restart it. "The house is on Cobra Bend, so I think we can find it from here."

Sherry cleared her throat and closed the window to keep the dust out. "Let's just drive a little way down the street and see if there are any numbered mailboxes. We're looking for '113.'"

Sherry's car continued on the bumpy narrow surface.

"I could really use a full set of headlights now." Sherry clicked on her high beams. She was forced to reduce them when the branches of the giant oaks crowding the road reflected the intense light back into the car and nearly blinded her. "With a headlight out, I can't see anything on the left side. We'll just go slow and hope for the best."

An untrimmed tree limb scraped the roof of the car with a goose-bump-inducing screech. Even traveling at ten miles per hour, the car kicked up a cloud of dust, which encircled the car. Sherry squirted wiper fluid on the windshield, in order to proceed safely, only to have the grime build up a moment later.

"This is crazy," said Amber. "It seems like we've left civilization. Let's turn around."

Marla caught Sherry's gaze in the rearview mirror. "We can make it. I'm sure we're almost there."

Just as Sherry was mentally assessing the possibility of the car's ability to make a K-turn without plunging off the skinny road into the drainage canal, which ran on either side, when a mailbox came into view; "113" was painted in blood red on the box. The post it rested on was rotted and cracked and the whole mechanism sat askew.

Sherry slowed the car before making the left into the driveway.

"I think this is it. Sure seems the Andimes aren't keeping up with the Joneses," Sherry quipped.

Amber began tapping her foot on the car floor.

"I still can't see the house." Sherry strained to make out a building at the end of the dark driveway.

"Would putting in a driveway light or two really kill him? Strike that comment. Kill is a poor choice of words."

Sherry took the turn. She pulled the car up into what she interpreted as a parking spot. When she and Marla got out of the car, they found themselves under a giant apple tree that had seen better days. The full moon set in the clear sky lit four monstrous tree limbs, giving them the appearance of grasping arms.

"Those shadows are hard to ignore. They almost look alive." Sherry hugged herself to warm her chilled arms. "Too cold out here. Let's get inside."

"Sherry, I have a really bad feeling in my stomach right now. Where are all the other guests' cars?" Amber stayed seated until Sherry made her way around the car to Amber's door. Amber's hands were shaking.

Sherry coaxed her friend out of the car by offering a hand.

"We must be fashionably early. Come on, guys." Marla jumped back when one of the tree limbs scraped up against another, resulting in a monstrous snap when a branch broke off.

"Hold on a minute. I forgot the apron." Sherry left Amber and Marla frozen in place until she returned with the apron.

"I don't know why you insist on bringing that," Marla said.

Sherry just shrugged. From a distance, Sherry heard a repetitive squeak, followed by a bang. A lone path light guided them up to the front door of the dark gray ranch-style house. The source of the noise seemed to be a loose shutter, painted a darker shade of gray than the house. Each time the shutter scraped then slapped the side of the window, Amber grabbed Sherry's arm.

"Is there even a doorbell?" The women ascended two rickety steps in need of a good sweeping. Sherry ran her hand down the molding around the door in search of a button but only got a handful of paint flakes. As she shook out her hand free of debris, the door hinges cried out a hellish wail.

"Welcome," boomed a voice just inside the open front door.

Sherry seized Marla's forearm to steady herself. She sucked in a huge breath and willed herself to reply.

"We're here for the dinner," Sherry squeaked. She extended her hand to the man inside the door.

He left her holding it in midair for what seemed like an eternity. Finally, a reciprocating hand jutted forward. It was awkward to shake someone's left hand with her right hand, but it was all he offered, so she accepted.

"You're Mike, from OrgaNicks," said Sherry. "We met a few days ago."

"Yes. Follow me."

As he turned to walk away, Sherry noticed Mike's right hand was heavily bandaged. A shiver rippled down her body. She hugged her arms tight across her waist and fell in line behind the blocky man. She elbowed Amber. Amber stumbled forward. Marla stayed a step behind Amber.

The women followed Mike through the hallway. The man was mute as they walked but pointed out the frayed edge of an area rug as if to suggest they should watch their step. He stopped in front of a closed door. There, he turned the knob and wrestled with the warped door until it opened, at which point he fell inside the room, severing his grip on the door.

"I am *not* going in there." Amber put her hands on her hips. "I've never had claustrophobia until this very minute, but it's full-blown now."

Before Sherry could respond, Mike proclaimed, "This way."

Sherry linked her arm with Amber's and guided her into the dimly lit room. Marla scurried in behind them. Without uttering a word, Mike turned and left the room, yanking the door shut behind him. Sherry scanned the room to get her bearings. The dark laminate floor was partially covered with a moss green rug. The windows in the room were streaked with smudges. The sills were bug graveyards with no room for more bodies. Dotted across the surrounding gray walls were a number of charcoal portraits of various old-timey people interspersed with mounted animal heads. Sherry saw the growing panic in Amber's eyes and made it her mission to counter it.

"I think those are meant for us." The shrill voice that escaped from Sherry's mouth was unrecognizable to her ears. She pointed to a corner table set up with various drink offerings.

"I guess so." Amber cleared her throat. "But, I'm not thirsty."

"The decorator needs to be fired." Marla pointed to the numerous animal heads on the wall. "Andime must not be a vegetarian."

Sherry took a step closer to inspect a rabbit head. "Well, what do you know? You were wrong, Marla. These are stuffed animals, literally. They're made of felt. He has a sense of humor after all."

Sherry walked over to a sofa angled to best enjoy what appeared to be a boarded-up fireplace. "Should we sit? I'm sure the others will be here soon."

Sherry took a seat and refolded the apron in her hand to smooth out any wrinkles. She switched on the small lamp on the side table but realized it had no bulb in its socket.

"Maybe this will help." Marla flipped a wall switch. Nothing. "Good way to save on the electric bill, I guess. This whole house should be called 'Nick's Man Cave' it's so dark. I believe I heard he's never been married."

"Ouch!" Sherry leapt up. Caught on the back of her shirt was a crusty metal spring that had popped through the sofa's slipcover. She unhooked herself and frowned when she saw the hole it left. Sherry pointed to a door beside the fireplace. "Do you think that's a bathroom? I've got rust all over my hands. I need to wash them."

"If it is, you're not leaving me alone." Amber jumped to Sherry's side. "Consider me Velcroed to you."

Not letting her more than an arm's length away, Amber followed Sherry to the doorway. Sherry turned the knob and when the door opened, they were stunned at what they saw. Inside, was a closet piled high with miscellaneous items, which appeared to have been tossed in with no regard to organization. The skin under Sherry's eye twitched. Two large plants housed in cracked terra-cotta pots were slumped over, dehydrated beyond salvation. Brown, withered leaves littered the closet floor. Leaning against one of the pots was a shovel caked with dirt. Sherry took a step closer. Amber pulled her back.

"No way, Sherry," Amber warned. "Don't go in any farther." Amber grabbed Sherry's arm.

"Just want to see something," Sherry powered out of Amber's grip. She stepped just inside the closet, knocking over a "Happy Halloween" sign. A second later a human skeleton collapsed down on her.

"Amber, help," shrieked Sherry. "We have to clean this up. Now! Marla, get over here. We need your help, quick." Sherry waved Marla over.

The trio got down on their hands and knees and collected as many bones as they could manage. Sherry hurled the lightweight bones back into the closet. "At least they're plastic. I would be in a full flop sweat if these were real."

As the last bone flew through the air, Amber gasped when the stomping of footsteps reverberated from the hallway.

"Someone's coming," Sherry managed to spit out. "Get off the floor." Sherry jutted out her hand to help Amber up. She slammed the closet door with a surge of adrenaline-fueled strength. A moment later Mike entered through the door as it burst open.

Kenny Dewitt was dressed in a yellow and turquoise Hawaiian shirt that announced his arrival before he did. "Hey, ladies. Long time no see. Why are you so shocked to see me? You've got to know I wouldn't miss the end of this saga for anything."

Behind Kenny followed Diana Stroyer, Jamie Sox, and Patti Mellit.

Sherry's chest was heaving. "Hi. Of course, it's great to see you all." She brushed the last residue of dust off her hands and pants.

Mike gestured toward the limited drink selection. He then turned and left the room, this time without closing the door.

"Man of few words," said Kenny. "And judging by this dump, he seems to work for a man of poor taste. It's a fixer-upper even the Addams Family wouldn't put a down payment on."

"Hi, all. Do I detect some negative reviews of my brother-in-law's interior design skills?" Patti cocked her head to the side as her gaze panned the room.

"It's missing a woman's touch," said Sherry. "He's not married, right?"

"Are you making an offer?" quipped Kenny.

"Honestly, I've only ever been to the front door of this house to pick up Nick for his step-father's funeral," Patti said. "I had no idea what the interior was like until now. Unusual is the word that comes to mind."

Diana and Jamie joined the group, drinks in hand.

"Have you been here long?" Diana glanced at Sherry's empty hands. "You're not drinking tonight?"

Sherry and Amber made eye contact.

"This might sound crazy, but I don't think anyone should put any food or drink in their mouth tonight," Sherry blurted out. She had not yet discussed with Amber or Marla about making their discovery public.

"Let me get this straight." Kenny tapped his

temple. "We're all invited to the OrgaNicks CEO's personal house for dinner and awards, and you're thinking we should all fast instead? Yes, I do think that's crazy."

"Well, speaking of crazy, you came all this way even after being disqualified," said Marla. "How come?"

"I consider it a business trip." Kenny fingered his shirt collar. "Can't leave my readers hanging. I'm glad you're a fan of my blog now, by the way."

"Is there a problem with the meal?" asked Jamie.

The group took a step closer together and formed a tight circle.

"Nick's not a bad cook, I've heard," said Patti. "Growing up, the two brothers, or half-brothers to be accurate, had a revolving door of parent combinations, so they had to learn to fend for themselves in the kitchen and other places. Rafe is a great cook. I have a hard time believing Nick isn't also. I don't see a problem."

"It's not about his cooking skills. See the closet over there?" Sherry pointed to the closed door. "If you open the door and see what's in there, tell me you don't think the same thing that happened at the cook-off could happen again tonight. I wouldn't even recommend having a drink."

"What?" Diana held up the glass of wine she'd just sipped from to eye level.

"Let me check it out," Kenny strutted over to open the closet door. A turn of the knob did nothing. He yanked and still the door didn't budge. "Jamie, we need some muscles over here."

Jamie ambled to Kenny's side and tried the doorknob. No movement. "Locked," Jamie said.

"That's impossible. We were just inside," said Sherry, "unless Mike somehow got over there on his way out."

"I think you're just being dramatic." Kenny made his way back across the room to the beverage table.

Diana sidled up to Sherry. "What exactly was in there?"

Before Sherry could answer, Mike marched in to the room. "This way to dinner."

The guests made their way down a dim hallway to a room furnished with a long rectangular table and chairs. Behind the head of the table was a makeshift podium and above it was a portrait of Nick Andime lit with spotlights that bathed the entire room in a harsh glare. A woman was seated alone at the table with her back to the door. When the group walked in, she turned and stood to face them.

Chef Olivia Baker was dressed in a tight black dress, gold sandals, and a matching gold headband. Her wavy brown hair, which Sherry had only seen drawn up in a passionless bun, cascaded down her back like a chocolate fountain.

"Hello," the chef said. "Come join me. Chef Lee couldn't make it tonight, so I'm your judge representative. Don't stress, though. All contest decisions have been made, so it's time for fun."

Sherry flashed a forced smile the chef's way. She beckoned Marla and Amber over with a curl of her finger.

"I forgot the apron in the animal head room. I'll be right back." Sherry trotted to the door, where Mike met her. She softened her pursed lips and wrestled with her quivering cheek muscles to draw up the corners of her mouth. "I forgot something in the other room."

"Was it this?" Mike pulled Sherry's apron from behind his back.

Sherry sputtered an unintelligible reply, cleared her throat, then tried it again. "Yes, thanks." Sherry took the apron from Mike. "What happened to your arm?" She reached forward and as she did her fingers brushed the sleeve of his nubby blazer. The touch of the abrasive material jogged her memory.

Mike turned on his heels and left the room.

"Rude." Sherry rejoined the others at the table. There was only one seat left for Sherry, placing her next to Kenny and across from Amber and Marla.

As Sherry sat, Kenny said, "You're not really sticking to your fasting plan, are you?"

"I'm not eating a bite."

"Me either," said Amber.

"You want to tell me what was so horrific in that closet that it's going to keep you from dinner?" asked Kenny.

Sherry widened her eyes. "For starters, a skeleton and dead plants."

"That's nothing. You should see my closets," Kenny laughed. "That would really spook you."

All heads turned as the lights were dimmed, and Mike began a round of applause. A thunderous "good evening" was bellowed from the doorway. Nick Andime walked through the doorway dressed in a black suit. He wore a lime green tie that provided a splash of color. Around his waist was a cooking apron covered in what appeared to be meat juices.

"Ladies and gentlemen, may I present Mr. Nick Andime, chief executive officer of the OrgaNicks Food Company of Hillsboro, Connecticut. He will be your master of ceremonies for the evening," Mike announced.

"Thank you, thank you." Nick began his trek toward the seat at the head of the table. He glanced at his portrait as he neared it.

"Okay, things are getting a little weird now." Kenny turned to Sherry. "Maybe you're on to something."

Chapter
21

Sherry's gaze followed Nick as he approached the head of the table. Out of force of habit, she pulled her phone from her purse and checked it to make sure the battery was fully charged. She relaxed a bit when she had completed the ritual.

"I'm so glad you all made it. I hope I gave everyone enough time to make the trip back for the awards dinner." Nick walked up behind Chef Baker's chair. "Good evening, Livvie. I'm so happy to have you represent the judging panel this evening."

Olivia leaned away from the hand that brushed her back.

Nick continued on toward Sherry's seat.

When he neared, Sherry sputtered, "Would you like to borrow this?"

Nick studied the clean apron Sherry presented and then glanced down at his stained one.

"Very kind of you, Ms. Frazzelle." He maintained a constant smile. "But I like to show off the work I do in the kitchen. It's a badge of honor, you could say. If you don't mind, though." He wiped his soiled hands on Sherry's spotless apron, leaving a dark reddish brown smear across the OrgaNicks logo.

Nick turned and faced Kenny. "And welcome to you, Kenny Dewitt, or should I call you The Foody Dude? I've been following your blog all week."

Kenny squirmed in his seat as Nick's expression morphed from jovial to sour.

"Amber Sherman, one of my recipe demonstrators. Nice to have you back." Nick delivered a smile across the table.

Amber delivered a return smile that quickly faded.

"And next to you, Ms. Barras. Welcome. Diana Stroyer, we're thrilled you could join us." Nick continued circling the table. "And, Mr. Sox, thank you for coming."

Jamie Sox bowed his head. "Hello. I wouldn't miss it. I always see things through to the very end."

Nick floated by Patti's seat. They mumbled an indiscernible salutation to each other before he continued on.

"Has anyone seen Mac Stiles, our photographer?" Nick called across the room. "He should be here by now."

Sherry searched the room for Mac. Her gaze darted back to Nick. Without waiting for a reply, Nick spun on his rubber-soled, imitation-leather dress shoes, creating a noise that could be misinterpreted for passing gas. Disturbed by the twirl, Nick's gold chain rose up and struck him in the mouth. He scowled then took his seat. Nick signaled to Mike, who stood just inside the doorway. Mike left the room. A moment later, he returned with a tray of salads.

"Shrimp and avocado wedge salad for starters.

My own creation. All organic, of course." Nick stood and opened his arms wide. He sat down as Mike distributed the plates.

Any discreet conversations died away as soon as the appetizer was served. The silence in the room was as heavy as day-old Béchamel sauce. Sherry took note of who began eating and who did not. Diana tackled her salad with vigor, while Jamie picked his apart and ate only the avocado. Kenny's was gone as fast as he was served. Chef Baker nibbled at hers, all the while inspecting each element on her fork before it entered her mouth. It was only Sherry, Marla, and Amber who scraped their lettuce leaves from one side of the plate to the other, without ever raising their forks to their lips.

Kenny broke the silence. "You must think you're going to win, you're so dressed up." Kenny gestured toward Jamie's three-piece tropical weight suit.

"It's the suit I wear sixty-six percent of the work week, usually Tuesdays, Thursdays, and Fridays, so I weighed my options and made my choice to wear it here."

"I thought actuaries didn't like choices or options. I mean, aren't you supposed to base your decisions on fact, stats, and numbers?"

"True. Past performance can certainly be a predictor of the future in many cases. I felt I should dress in my most successful outfit because with five cooks eligible for two prizes, I have a forty percent chance of winning fifty percent of the prizes, thanks to your disqualification. If I was to place an insurance value on my chances of winning, I would have to begin by setting the premium quite high because even though, statistically speaking, I have been a top prize winner zero percent of the time, this being my one and only cook-off, it will only take one win to make my winning record one hundred percent. So the premium must be high to cover the likelihood of a payout."

Sherry tapped Amber under the table with her shoe. "Did you hear that? Once an actuary, always an actuary." Sherry winked at Marla, who winked back.

"Did anyone else not understand the logic there?" asked Kenny. "Jamie, you were wacky at the cook-off, and you're even wackier in real life."

"And the same goes for you." Jamie said. "By the way, I would appreciate it if you kept me out of your blog."

Sherry extended her leg in Marla's direction and kicked. Marla jumped in her seat when the aggressive foot landed on its mark.

"Diana, do you like your salad?" Sherry leaned in toward the center of the table.

Diana was checking her cell phone between bites. She continued scrolling until Sherry cleared her throat. Diana raised her head.

"Do you like your salad?" Sherry pointed her fork at Diana's salad plate.

"Sure, it's not bad." Diana poked a shrimp and displayed it. "Same exact salad is offered at Chef Lee's restaurant. I wonder if he gave Mr. Andime the recipe. And, someone should advise Mr. Andime there's no such approved label for any seafood as quote-unquote organic."

"Interesting. There's a possibility Chef Baker made the salad, isn't there?" Sherry peered down the table at the chef. "Although, she's not exactly dressed for cooking."

"I'm not sure I would be up for cooking a dinner a few days after my husband unexpectedly died either," whispered Diana, with hands cupped around her mouth.

Amber's dropped fork had a violent collision with her plate. All eyes shifted to her.

"Oops," Amber said, "Slippery devil."

"Wait." Sherry's body tilted so far forward in her seat, she put her elbow in her salad. "Whose husband died?"

"Olivia was married to Tony Birns, or should I say, she's his widow now," Diana said. "Word is, their marriage was more of a business arrangement for the tax benefits than a union of love. They couldn't actually afford to get a divorce."

"I'm so confused," sighed Sherry. "Diana, why didn't you mention that the day we had lunch together?"

"I think I told you they were cozy at the first cook-off I saw them at and distant at the next. Come to think of it, I didn't hear you ask if they were married." Diana touched her hearing aid.

"So Mr. Andime was duo-dating Brynne Stark and a married Chef Baker? Actually, I shouldn't be surprised. I spent my professional life being paid by one-half of an unfaithful couple to explore the issue of infidelity. I've seen it all." Amber arranged two shrimps side by side on her plate, before separating them to opposite ends of her salad.

"I'm not here to judge, no pun intended. I'm just telling you what I know. With Nick Andime a principal backer of their restaurant venture, I guess he deserved special privileges, if you know what I mean." Diana wiped the corners of her mouth with her napkin and then slid her empty plate toward the center of the table.

With a swoosh and a bang, the double doors to the dining room flung open. The table conversation halted as all eyes were trained on a woman hobbling in. Sherry was stunned at the sight of a disheveled Brynne Stark holding one of her high heels in her hand. It appeared to be missing its heel. The bottom of her black cocktail dress was ragged and her knee was bleeding. Without saying a word, she limped around the table. As she passed each guest, they were provided a view of the back of her dress, which revealed her zipper was spread open a good four inches from the top of the dress. A hair extension on the side of her head was unclipped and dangled from her scalp like the feathers of a partially plucked chicken. Once at her chair, she appeared to be waiting for Nick to pull it out for her, but when he didn't, she yanked it away from the table herself.

"Would someone please pass the wine," Brynne called out.

Nick and Brynne huddled in a private tête-à-tête. When they were done, Brynne was all smiles and Nick appeared to be sulking. Brynne drained her glass of wine. She waved off the salad Mike offered and gestured for more liquid refreshment.

When he seemed satisfied everyone was done eating, Nick motioned to Mike to clear the salad plates and bring in the main course. The dinner menu consisted of roasted Cornish game hens, wild rice, and caramelized Brussels sprouts. The wine was self-serve, but there were only two bottles on the table to be split among all the guests, and Brynne was hoarding one of them.

Kenny nudged Sherry. "Kind of stingy with the alcohol, don't you think? Brynne polished off the first bottle in no time. What's her deal anyway?"

"If my lip-reading skills are as good as they used to be, I gather Brynne didn't get the word about this dinner until an hour ago. Also, she fell in the parking lot running from her car to get here on time. She thinks Nick needs to install more outdoor lighting. She couldn't zip her dress by herself and, finally, she was mad she didn't get to make the introductions she was hired for."

"Wow, you should work for the CIA or something. You're missing your true calling. You'd make a good detective," Kenny said.

"Thanks. I try." Sherry kept an eye on Mike as he returned to his post at the door after making multiple trips to and from the kitchen.

On his final trip, Mike carried a brown paper bag while balancing Nick's dinner plate on his unbandaged arm. He left the bag by Nick's side when he served him.

"I'm really hungry, Sherry. I'm going to try my food." Amber trapped a vegetable with her fork, sniffed it, then put the fork down. "Can't do it."

"Hang in there," Sherry said, "there's plenty of time to eat later."

A hollow chime of an empty wineglass caught Sherry's attention. Patti pushed back her chair and stood, a newspaper in hand. Sherry followed Patti's line of sight to Nick, who was slumped in his chair.

"Good evening talented home cooks and those

associated with the OrgaNicks Cook-Off." Patti held up the newspaper. "It's been my pleasure to cover the event for the *Nutmeg State of Mind Gazette*, and I've brought a final mockup of the article. It's just missing the winners' names, to be added very soon. The article will be out on newsstands tomorrow. Pay particular attention to the sidebar article on the OrgaNicks Company and its value in the organic-food industry. I, like the rest of you, remain saddened by the circumstances of the cook-off, and I dedicated the article to Chef Birns. I would also like to say—"

"Patti, that's enough," Nick interjected. "If there's more to say, and I don't think there is, it can wait. Wouldn't you all prefer to get right to the winners' announcement?" Nick rose from his seat, walked over to Patti, put his hand on her shoulder and guided her down in her chair.

Sherry pulled her phone from her purse and crafted a text message.

"No electronics at dinner," Amber called across the table. "Remember the Frazzelle family rule."

"Right." Sherry forced a smile. "I'm almost done." She hit the send button and set her phone down.

"Okay, ladies and gentlemen, the time has come." All heads turned Nick's way. He stepped on the small podium under his portrait. The painting's lights cast irregular darks and lights across his face, giving it the appearance of a slice of cinnamon swirl bread.

"I'm just going to get right to it. You've all waited long enough." There were numerous dings and clangs as forks and knives were put down in unison.

"Without further ado, the winner of the OrgaNicks Cook-Off is . . ."

Diana pushed her seat back with her knees and rose, catching the hem of her dress under the chair, fragmenting it with a loud rip. Sherry placed her hand over her mouth to stifle a gasp.

"Jim Sox and his Chicago Style Bison Sausage and Greens Pizza on Whole Grain Crust."

Diana crashed back down in the direction of her seat.

"Come on up and receive your prize."

Jamie curled his hands around his mouth. "The name's *Jamie* Sox."

"Well, dude, all your crazy worrying paid off, big time. Congratulations." Kenny reached across the table.

"And the second prize goes to Sherry Frazzelle," continued Nick.

The back of Sherry's neck prickled with discomfort. Bile bubbled up her throat like hot seltzer water. She couldn't feel the tips of her fingers.

"Step right up."

Sherry's first attempt at standing failed when her knees buckled. She labored to propel her body upright.

"They're not the winners we chose," Chef Baker called out. "When did the decision change?"

"Good job, Sherry," said Amber. "I think."

"This couldn't be more ironic. I don't believe it," said Kenny. "You're the one who should be disqualified for poisoning one of the judges."

The piercing screech of Jamie's chair as it slid across the floor punctuated the room's silence. As they neared each other, Sherry considered bracing herself on Jamie's arm, but he was so slight and the feet she saw beneath her were so unsteady, she squashed the idea. It was then she realized the grayish brown stain on her pants had grown to the size of a dinner plate and was so wet her pant leg was stuck to her thigh. Throughout the dinner, Sherry had scooped small amounts of food into her napkin so it would appear she was eating. Halfway through the main course, her napkin had surpassed its capacity and leaked onto her pants. Sherry rushed back to her seat, grabbed her apron, and tied it around her waist to conceal the mess.

"Well, that's product loyalty for you." Nick pointed to the OrgaNicks logo on Sherry's apron as she neared.

At the podium, Jamie and Sherry stood on the step below Nick.

"Here are your trophies. Ms. Stark will present you with your checks," Nick said.

Brynne wiggled out of her chair and, with only one functioning shoe, stumbled to Nick's chair. She pulled out two bank checks from the bag on the floor.

After presenting the awards, accompanied by a subdued round of applause, Nick had one more presentation. "I have a special piece of cake for the winners." He motioned to Mike.

Sherry shivered as Mike approached Nick's chair with a plated wedge of cake in each hand.

Sherry waved both palms. "Very kind, but no thanks. Maybe I'll doggie bag this for later."

"Cakes are my specialty," Nick said. "I'll be offended if you don't try it."

"I don't eat sugar." Jamie angled his head away from Nick.

"Yes," said Nick, as he put down one plate of cake. "Your dietary restriction was brought to my attention, forgive me. Well, more for Ms. Frazzelle."

Nick held the remaining plate of cake closer to Sherry's face.

"Please. I'm very full." Sherry's eyes glistened as her head began to pound.

"She says she's not hungry," a man called out from the opposite end of the room.

"There you are." Nick shouted to Mac Stiles, who was jostling past Mike. "Ever heard of punctuality? Why are you so late, and why the hell aren't you taking pictures?"

Nick turned back to face Sherry. "Just eat the cake."

"I brought some pictures you might be interested in, Mr. Andime." Mac stayed in the back of the room, positioned near the door, just out of the security guard's reach. He opened his portfolio and held up two enlarged photographs.

"This isn't a good time to be having a show of your work, Mr. Stiles." Nick stomped his foot. "Go get your damn camera and do your job."

"Now is the best time, Mr. Andime." Jamie swiveled his head around to face one of the contestants. "It has been brought to my attention I broke two cook-off rules on the day of the event. I shouldn't be the winner."

Sherry followed Jamie's line of sight to Kenny, who sat bolt upright.

"Since the cook-off, I have spent numerous hours mentally reviewing the final moments of the event. I am blessed with an eidetic memory. I can recall numbers I have seen at any time throughout my life. That trait is both my blessing and my curse."

"What you're telling us is all well and good, Mr. Sox, but ancient history as far as I'm concerned." Crumbs flew off the plate of cake as Nick's hand began to shake. "Can we get on with this so everyone can get home at a reasonable hour?"

"Bear with me. Let me complete my thought," said Jamie. "I was so nervous throughout the cook-off that near the end, when my printed recipe sheet became so stained with food spills it was unreadable, I had to recall my garnish amount from memory. But I couldn't. The problem was, I had tested my recipe so many times, both with and without garnish, before I finally chose which version to enter in the contest. Both recipe versions were lodged in my brain. So when panic set in, I couldn't come up with the proper garnish measurement. It wasn't my memory for numbers failing me, but that the garnish wasn't supposed to be there. The recipe I selected had no garnish. May sound trivial, but rules are rules, no adding or subtracting ingredients."

"Garnish on, garnish off." Nick set the cake down. "I think we'll all agree we can forgive your slight error."

"Please, Mr. Andime, let me finish. In my panicked state, I had wrongfully doubted my special gift. So when you, Mr. Andime, handed me storage bags filled with garnish labeled with my assigned plate, 'Number four,' it was such a relief. You were so specific about which bag to put on which plate, I didn't question it."

"Jamie, did you even notice they weren't the same greens in each bag?" Sherry made sure her voice was clear and powerful.

The audience murmured in unison. Jamie shook his head no.

Nick scanned the room. "Why does any of that even matter? You'd have to be obsessive-compulsive to notice these things, Ms. Frazzelle. Unless, of course, you were trying to transfer the blame of a terrible criminal act you committed onto someone else to get your neck out of the noose. Wasn't it your recipe that sickened poor Chef Birns?" He panned the dinner guests with an icy gaze. "That was just a joke. Let's get back to the awards, shall we?"

With a crack and a crash, the doors to the dining room sprang open and two men, as intertwined as tossed spaghetti noodles, fell through. One of the men landed with a hard thud on the ground. Sherry sighed with relief when she recognized Detective Bease brushing himself off. At the detective's feet, Mike was struggling to pick himself up off the floor, while cradling his bandaged arm.

"Welcome, Detective Bease," said Nick. "You've made quite an entrance."

Chapter 22

"Detective Bease, you're as persistent as ants at a picnic. And like those uninvited bugs, you weren't on the guest list tonight. Since you're here, please, have a seat so we may move this thing along." Nick dabbed at his glistening forehead with his soiled apron, leaving behind a red smear.

The detective stayed put. Sherry saw Brynne beckon Nick over with her index finger. Nick leaned in. During the subsequent exchange, he shook his head as Brynne spoke, just as she nodded hers when he spoke. Loosened by all the head bobbing, another of Brynne's hair extensions cascaded to the table. Without hesitation, she brushed the hairy accessory onto Nick's chair. The two separated then turned to face the guests at the table.

"Regretfully, ladies and gentlemen, Mr. Sox has made such a compelling case in opposition of his cook-off win it has been decided he should forfeit his Grand Prize." Brynne plucked the gold trophy out of Jamie's hands. Jamie, head held high, put the check on the table in front of Nick's chair and returned to his seat.

"The Runner-Up will now move up a spot and become our Grand Prize Winner. The checks will need to be rewritten, so they'll be a slight delay in receiving those. Congratulations, Sherry Frazzelle," Brynne added.

Amber clapped, but she was the only one applauding.

"Our runner-up is Amber Sherman and her Seafood Flatbread." Brynne tore a slip of paper she held in her hand into scraps.

Chef Baker threw up her hands. "What? Who's making these decisions?"

Amber didn't move from her seat. Sherry saw Amber reading her phone and took the cue to check hers. She reached in her pocket but it was empty. Her chest iced over when she spied her pink cell phone next to her napkin on the dinner table.

"Ms. Sherman," said Nick, "did you hear Ms. Stark announce your name?"

Amber raised her head but remained seated. Nick cleared his throat. Brynne followed suit and cleared hers.

Detective Bease rushed over to Amber's chair. He banged his hand twice on the table. "Mr. Andime, are you aware labels with a counterfeit organic certification have been confiscated from the printer in the OrgaNicks warehouse? Are you also aware one of the bags you handed Mr. Sox to garnish his food with at the cook-off contained leaves from the houseplant Dieffenbachia? The same plant you had in your office up until three days ago and the same variety of plant that can be found dead in your living room closet? The leaves of which are lethal to a sensitive individual consuming them. Anthony Birns had a sufficient amount of these leaves in his throat to cause his death.

"I'm in possession of photographs which sequentially document you retrieving the bag of deadly leaves from the refrigerator then handing them to Mr. Jamie Sox to use as a garnish. In addition, two more photos show you directing Patti Mellit, your sister-in-law, to consume the food off the cook-off display table. Unfortunately for Chef Anthony Birns, it was he who ingested the leaves."

Nick banged his hand twice on the podium. "Detective Bease, your interruptions are becoming intolerable. But, in an attempt to not be as rude to you as you have been to me, I'll respond. Labels are printed at the warehouse as a cost-cutting measure. It saves the consumer money in the end, and that is not a crime last time I checked. And to address the remaining issues, I am president of an organic-food company, not a botanist." Nick loosened his tie and undid the top button of his shirt. "Let's face it, the problem here is with Mr. Sox, who clearly had an issue with Chef Birns. I was just helping out a contestant who was struggling to complete his dish. I had no idea I was handing the murderer his weapon." Nick snickered then turned toward Sherry. "You're off the hook, Ms. Frazzelle. It wasn't you after all."

There was a collective gasp. Sherry's legs vibrated with adrenaline.

Detective Bease placed a hand inside his coat. "Thanks to the keen eye of one of the contestants, who is an expert gardener, a positive identification

of the offending plant leaves could be made from
Mr. Stiles' photos. Yes, it was Mr. Sox's plate that
went to the display table with the deadly leaves, but
he is not the murderer."

Nick jerked his head in Sherry's direction. His
astringent breath made her eyes water more pro-
fusely than dicing an onion did. Sherry tried to
take a step away from Nick, but the limited space
around the podium restricted her movement.

"I think Jamie Sox needs a good lawyer," said
Nick.

Patti rose from her seat. "I witnessed Chef Birns
take the garnish off Jamie Sox's plate as he passed
the display table on his way from the men's room.
He put it in his pocket. The judges are very familiar
with the finalists' recipes. He knew a garnish wasn't
written in the recipe and that Jamie would be pe-
nalized for having added one at the last minute. I
believe the chef was truly trying to help a struggling
contestant during the crucial final moments of the
cook-off. The chef ate what he thought was a harmless herb and died a painful choking death. Isn't
that so, Chef Baker?" Patti turned in the chef's
direction.

The chef nodded, while wiping tears from her
eyes. "He paid the ultimate price for trying to help
someone."

"What garnish was on the plate when it went to
the judging table? Why didn't they all get sick?"
Kenny called out.

"The plate the judging panel tasted had a basil
chiffonade garnish," said Sherry. "There's a photo
proving it."

"Idiot!" Nick shouted. "Patti, you just said he put

the leaves in his pocket. That means he didn't eat them. Patti is leading the investigators on a wild goose chase. I'm sorry she wasted your time, Detective Bease."

Patti hissed at Nick. "Shhh."

Chef Baker stood up with her hands over her heart. "We discussed what to do when we received word of Mr. Sox's mistake. We thought at the very least if his dish was photographed on the display table it should be consistent with his written recipe. Chef Birns had the perfect opportunity to remove the garnish during his bathroom break. We didn't think it would hurt to help Mr. Sox out for committing such a modest error. The fact we okayed Tony's good deed breaks my heart because it killed him. If the Dieffen . . . whatever the plant was, was on the judged plate, too, I might not be alive today either." She lowered her head into her hands.

"It was lucky for me Chef Birns got to the display plate before I did, or it would have been me who died." Patti shuddered. "If only he had just left the leaves stuffed in his pocket."

"I'm guessing he ate them to clear his palate just before eating the stuffed pork tenderloin dish," said Chef Baker.

"Why all the fuss over some green plants?" Nick shook his fist. "Ms. Sherman, do you want your award or don't you?"

Amber remained silent and seated.

"Mr. Andime," said Detective Bease, "I have evidence you knew precisely what those labeled garnish bags contained and that you intentionally chose the contestant so overcome by nerves he would unknowingly carry out your plan to harm someone, at the same time becoming the prime suspect. In the photographs taken by Mr. Stiles, it's as clear as white vinegar."

Sherry appreciated the food reference and nodded her approval in the detective's direction. The gesture didn't appear to go unnoticed by him.

"You have the Dieffen . . . the plant, in your office," said Patti. "The big one alongside your desk. I saw it during our last meeting."

"Me, too." Sherry pointed to herself. "Then it mysteriously disappeared. But there's no mistaking you have one in your living room closet."

"It's all ridiculous," said Nick. "First of all, there was no 'plan.' Second, the plant is sold at a million nurseries. Lots of people have one. They just don't eat them. That was the chef's big mistake. I had nothing against Chef Birns. I liked the guy."

"Did you know plants can be identified by their DNA the same way humans can?" probed Detective Bease. "The same accomplished cook and gardener supplied me with valuable information about your Dieffenbachia plant." Bease's gaze danced toward Sherry. She blushed.

"With a leaf collected from your plant and a sample from the remains of food storage bag 'Number four,' we were able to establish a match. The chef even had a trace of the plant left in his pants pocket lining and in his throat. And it all matched."

"Nope, you're wrong. Houseplants are propagated from parent plants. I know that much about raising mass-produced plants. They would all have the same DNA, if so. So my plants have many, many exact relatives, I'm sure. Tell him, you're the resident expert!" Nick shouted in Sherry's face. Droplets of spittle rained down on her.

Sherry puffed out her chest and raised her chin. "Sorry to correct you, Mr. Andime. I inquired about where your office plant was purchased with a call to your secretary. She was only too happy to share that yours was a one-of-a-kind plant imported from the best plant nursery in Argentina. You paid a premium for it, she boasted."

"Patti, you did this." Nick slammed his hand down. "You ruined me!"

"My food didn't kill the chef. I knew it." Sherry pumped her fist. "The poor man ate my pork right after he ate the noxious leaves. It probably helped lodge them in his throat, but I can't help that." She bent over at the waist as a combination of relief and dismay washed over her.

"Mr. Andime, I'd like to have a word with you in private before this matter escalates any further." With a hand inside his jacket, Detective Bease took a measured step toward Nick.

"No!" erupted Nick. "Stay right where you are."

Nick jumped off the podium and ripped the unclaimed statue out of Brynne's hands. He shoved Brynne before grabbing Sherry around the neck. Brynne went down in a heap.

Nick held the statue, poised to bash Sherry on the head if someone made a move. "Not one more step, heroes, or this lady's toast."

Detective Bease held his ground.

"Nick, how could you do this to me?" cried Brynne. "I tried so hard to protect you. I don't even know why I bothered. I was never your first choice, anyway. Right, Olivia? You scored big. You got a husband and a boyfriend."

"Truth is, sadly, I'm just a sucker for the wrong kind of guy," Chef Baker called out from her seat. "Thanks for the good times, Nick, but we're done."

Nick tightened his armlock on Sherry. She struggled for a breath.

"As soon as the chef was murdered, your behavior became so bizarre I knew you had something to do with it. Then I saw this one closing in on you." From the floor, Brynne pointed to Sherry. "I did my best to try to buy you some time, you know, hoping you'd make the right decision to get out of this mess. But she couldn't be scared off. What a wasted effort." Brynne struggled to sit up. "Nick, you're a monster!"

Nick let out a cry that seemed born from deep in his gut.

Sherry's eyes widened when she saw Detective Bease edge forward.

The detective's voice softened. "Okay, Mr. Andime. Just relax."

"It wasn't the chef I wanted taken out. It was my idiot brother's wife." Nick released his grip on Sherry and pointed at Patti.

Sherry's jaw dropped and her chest deflated. She began to back away from Nick, while keeping her gaze on the trophy in his hand. "I knew it! That was the reason you two were fighting when I saw you together. There's even a photo of you two arguing at the cook-off." Sherry placed her hand on the table to steady herself. "Patti was way too nice in her article about the cook-off. I was suspicious she felt threatened by you. No offense, Patti, but you're famous for your bite, not your bark, when it comes to your writing." Sherry peered down the table toward Patti.

Patti put up her hand and waved. "None taken," she mouthed.

Nick thumped the trophy on the side of the podium. "Patti's been trying to publish a scathing article for weeks about my business. Why is she trying to ruin me? I'll tell you why. From the day she and my brother became editors at the high school paper, their life has been 'happily ever after.' I wanted that. I deserved that. But I couldn't even get 'Editor' in our stupid high school. I think she recognized I was now finally hitting my stride, and she was jealous. She was the only obstacle between me and the success I deserved. I wanted her gone. How was I supposed to know Tony would swipe the stupid garnish off Jamie Sox's plate on his way to the restroom before Patti got to it? I told her to go taste test the display plates, but she was too late. He'd already eaten it. She's been late to every appointment since I've known her. Why should the day of the cook-off have been any different? Then people really started sniffing around my personal space, and that made me very angry."

"Time to give up, Nick. Face it. Your company's based on a lie," Patti shouted. "You can't throw around the term 'organic' if it's not true. Certified organic labels are never yellow and blue. Security records show OrgaNick's never had a visit from a certifying agent. I had to tell the truth because you wouldn't. But to try to kill me for that?"

"Patti, don't be so dramatic. I only wanted to make you sick enough to keep you from publishing your exposé article. I never meant to kill anyone. The information I read about the plant claimed you'd only be knocked out for a few days. Just enough time to tidy up a few things, like the hard drive on your computer, right, Mike?"

All heads turned to the back of the room where Mike, still rubbing his bandaged arm, faintly muttered, "Yes, sir."

"Okay, there may have been an asterisk in the article that mentioned some people had fatal reactions to the leaves," added Nick, "but come on, usually side effects are exaggerated. The chef must have had a weak constitution.

"And you, Sherry Frazzelle." Nick's voice raised an octave. "You just wouldn't quit tracking me. You're as persistent as gas after a chilidog-eating contest. Why is the world out to ruin me?"

"I'm lost." Diana refitted her loose hearing-aid battery. "What did Patti know about Nick's business, and why would it ruin him?"

"We'll fill you in later," yelled Kenny.

"Does this look familiar, Mr. Andime?" Detective Bease held up a round blue and yellow piece of paper. "To the untrained eye, it's a label, but in reality, it's a smoking gun."

"Mr. Andime," called Detective Diamond, from the back of the room, "you're under arrest for the murder of Anthony Birns."

"This isn't going to happen," Nick screamed and leapt off the podium.

Just as he jumped, Mac raced forward from the back of the room, met Nick halfway, and knocked the trophy out of his hand. Mac struck him in the midsection, with his fist. Nick slumped forward.

"Throw it," yelled Kenny.

Heads turned as Diana stood and threw the entire hem she had managed to tear from the bottom of her dress to Kenny, who used it to tie Nick's hands behind his back as he writhed in pain on the floor. Diana clapped, hiked up her new mini-dress, and sat back down.

"We've got our confession." Detective Bease waved uniformed men into the room. "Come on in, Officers. We've got our man."

Six police officers rushed into the dining room with their weapons drawn.

"You okay, ma'am?" the female officer with the familiar face asked Sherry when she reached her side.

"I think so. I've never been happier being called ma'am in all my life." Sherry's eyes welled with tears. "Thank you." Next thing Sherry knew, she was hugging the policewoman who had given her the great advice to "stay safe" earlier in the evening, instead of a ticket.

Chapter 23

"I'm going to have to sign off, Charlie. I just pulled into the Augustin farmers' market. Good luck in your golf game today. Shoot low. And yes, I'm sure your new friend will enjoy herself. Just tell her how I couldn't hit the ball past the tee box and still had fun playing with you. On second thought, don't mention me at all."

"And good luck to you today. Pickles may just be the ticket to fulfillment you've been searching for," Charlie replied.

"Ha. Bye, Charlie." Sherry ended the call.

With the majority of the parking spots cordoned off for some unknown reason, Sherry was forced to wedge her SUV into a tight parking spot sandwiched on either side with oversized child movers. The door of one slid open.

"Allie Grace," a shrill voice wailed from the driver's side. "Never open the car door before you know it's clear. And stop unbuckling the car seat while we're moving. It's not safe."

"Sorry, Mommy," the child whined. Her tiny leg

was dangling out the sliding door. Her booster seat strap spilled out of the minivan.

Even after the apology, the little girl neglected to close the door, and Sherry was forced to hold her car's angled position. Sherry now had a front-row seat to the lengthy unpacking procedure of all the necessary equipment involved in transporting, entertaining, feeding, and watering of Allie Grace during the family's time at the market. "I must be patient. Everyone is a potential customer."

With her thoughts deep in the throes of uncertainty about how her day would unfold, Sherry missed the "all clear" signal from Allie Grace's mother. For her oversight, Sherry was rewarded with a horn blast from the car behind her. Unfortunately, the "all clear" signal was premature. The strap on the diaper bag the mother attempted to hoist over her shoulder snapped and spilled its contents, once again suspending Sherry's progress.

"Some things about being a mom I'm not sure I could handle." Sherry watched as Allie Grace's supply-packed stroller passed lethargically in front of her. The little girl was attempting to be helpful by pushing it through the bumpy field, which served as the car park, but moving the unwieldy stroller proved impossible for her underdeveloped muscles. Another horn blast from the driver behind Sherry suggested to the mother to take control of the stroller. Finally, Sherry was permitted to pull her car in. She maneuvered her SUV into a parking spot that left as much wiggle room as a pimento stuffed in an olive.

"I better leave ten minutes earlier next week." Sherry turned the car off and gathered up her information packet, a reusable shopping bag, and her purse. "First-day jitters." She checked her face in the rearview mirror. "I hope I'm not the oldest apprentice here."

When she opened her door, the edge of it gently kissed the not-so-minivan next to hers. "I'll never be able to get out of here."

After assessing her chances of exiting her car without mishap, Sherry sucked in her stomach, contorted her torso like a pretzel, and squeezed through the sliver of an opening her door provided. She shimmied down the sides of the cars toward the walkway, where she tied on her new "Perfect Storm Pickles" apron over her cucumber green shirtdress. She was surprised to feel a vibration from her purse. She parked herself to the side of the walkway and found her phone.

"Hi, Dad. What's up?" Sherry checked the clock on the phone. "I don't have much time. I have to find some volunteers to help me unload the car."

"Just wanted to say good luck on your first day and remind you to not be shy about taking notes," Erno said. "And don't be nervous. Make eye contact with your customers and remind them they should buy an extra jar for last-minute gift giving and . . ."

"Dad, wow! You're way more anxious than I am. I'll be fine. I'll call you tonight and tell you how it went. Are you missing me at the Ruggery?"

"I'm doing okay with your trimmed-down schedule."

"It's only one less day a week. You should be fine. I better get moving."

"I feel like I should leave you with one more pearl of wisdom. So here it is. Pickles are just cucumbers with a longer shelf life."

Sherry cocked her head askew and puffed out her lips. "Dad, I'm a big girl now. You raised me right." Sherry pictured the little girl pushing the monstrous stroller and felt a pang of empathy for the toddler's struggle and the woman raising her. Her mom was doing the right thing, supporting her daughter's independent spirit.

"Message received. By the way, can you send me any zucchini recipes you might have?" Erno asked.

Sherry thought she detected a hint of neediness in her father's tone. Her mouth curled into a smile.

"I have a date tonight," he added.

Sherry's reply caught in her throat for a split second. "Of course, Dad. I'll check when I get home. Love you, but got to go now. Bye-bye."

Lost in a cloud of thought thicker than the vichyssoise she had prepared the night before, Sherry came close to not spotting the casually dressed man in a crumpled hat waving in her direction. Not sensing any immediate familiarity, Sherry checked behind her to make sure it was she being summoned. The number of people shopping was low this early in the morning, so she had no trouble confirming the man wanted her attention.

"Miss Frazzelle, um, Sherry, over here." The man trotted toward her.

Dressed in khaki shorts, a collared white sports shirt, and tennis shoes, Ray Bease was more appropriately dressed to ball boy for the Wimbledon finals than to shop for farm-fresh produce. The ancient hat, though, divulged the fact he might be over the job's age requirement.

"Detective Béase, fancy meeting you here." Sherry smoothed her apron and replaced an errant lock of hair. It was nice to be labeled "Miss." "Are you working today? I don't see Detective Diamond with you."

"Thursday's my day off, doctor's orders." Ray removed his hat, primped it and put it back on. "After the OrgaNicks investigation concluded, I had a mild medical scare and, long story short, I need more downtime or my life will be a lot shorter than it should be. Diamond's been transferred to data intelligence, so we're not together anymore."

"I'm sorry to hear about your scare, but I'm glad you're listening to the doctor." Sherry began edging away. "I have to get over to the pickle stand. Today's my first day volunteering there."

"Pickles. I see. Sounds like a great position for someone with all your gardening knowledge." Ray kicked a stone with his rubber-soled boat shoes.

"The current pickle maven has declared this is her last year selling, so I'm testing the waters as a possible replacement. The OrgaNicks Cook-Off check is financing my volunteer status, in the meantime." Sherry wondered what was so interesting on the ground that kept Ray from raising his head. "Stop by if you can, and I'll practice my spiel on you." Sherry waved and began backing up before Detective Béase could say another word.

"Which way to the vegan desserts table?" she heard the detective ask a woman with an official customer-service badge on.

Sherry passed the beaded-crafts table and neared

the goat cheese booth that stood next to her Perfect Storm Pickles location. In a million years, she never thought she'd see who she saw offering goat-cheese samples. The woman's dirndl was a different color and the ribbons in her hair were updated to a new color scheme but none of the pageantry deflected from the fact Brynne Stark was standing between Sherry and her brined-cucumber table.

"Sherry Frazzelle." Brynne presented her tray. "May I interest you in a goat-cheese sample?"

"Brynne Stark." Sherry glorified the woman's name with excessive use of her tongue and lips. She had no idea what Brynne had been up to since the investigation had concluded. She only knew the woman's friend and employer, Nick Andime, had gone to jail.

"I'm sensing seeing me makes you apprehensive," said Brynne, "but let me put your mind at ease. I would never have done anything to hurt you or anyone else. At the time, I was just so sick about the likelihood Nick had involved himself in something illegal. I sent you the doctored apron as a warning you might be getting into some hot water with a man who had a screw loose. From then on, Nick and his buddy Mike worked together to try and make your life a living hell in hopes you'd back off. I regret caring for a man with such evil intentions. As for me, my lawyer worked his magic and convinced the skeptics I had nothing to do with Nick's plan."

Brynne's accent was thicker than Sherry had heard before. The girl wasn't even trying to mask the twang the way she had at the cook-off.

"Something's different about your face." Sherry studied the location on Brynne's face where a removal scar remained. She found the matching location on her own face with a light touch of her finger.

"Oh, this." Brynne tipped her head upward. "I had my mole removed. My whole life I was proud of the fact I had inherited my granny's birthmark. Employers tried to have me remove it, and I refused. But I think Gran wore it better than me. As long as it was my decision, I was going to go through with it. So, it's gone. You know, next month I'm heading back home where I belong. I've accepted a job as the Channel Fourteen weather woman. I needed a new start. And I get to keep my accent, don'tcha know! I have spent so much time and money trying to not be the person I truly am. Turns out going home could be my biggest break of all."

"I'm sorry Nick used you," Sherry offered.

"I let him. He and his sidekick Mike will have a nice long time behind bars to think about what they've done. No hard feelings between you and me then?" Brynne presented the tray of cheese.

Sherry assumed if she took one, it would solidify the deal. Sherry studied the tray and then captured the tall, naive young lady's gaze. Seeing an honest driven woman just trying to make it in the world behind those big brown eyes, Sherry put her hand out, but instead of taking a sample of cheese she waved off the cheese tray.

"No thanks. But no hard feelings." Sherry turned and walked the final few feet to her pickle table.

It wasn't long after Sherry finished organizing her product into a geometric grid consisting of sparkling glass jars housing green spears swimming in tangy brine that Ray Bease reappeared.

Seeing his eyes lapping up her display, she began her pitch. "The Perfect Storm Pickle comes in dill, garlic dill, and zesty dill. We offer whole pickles, spears, and chips depending on your needs."

The detective examined the various jars, whose labels were decorated with dramatic storm clouds. He handled one jar at length, prompting Sherry to ask, "Is there any other information I can give you to help you decide?"

"Yes, actually. Would you ever want to go to dinner? With me, I mean." Ray shuffled his feet while he waited for Sherry's answer.

Sherry drew in her breath. "You know, I'll never forget when you told me the apron I brought to the awards dinner was the 'nail in the coffin' for the case against Mr. Andime. My friend Amber was wondering why I brought it. I just had a feeling it was an important thing to do. Kind of the same way I know when my cucumbers have married with their garlic brine long enough to called pickles. It's intuition, I guess. I just knew the logo on the apron was the smoking gun. Patti Mellitt proved Nick never went through the proper organic certification process. OrgaNicks had no record of inspections or the paperwork that must be completed to get the proper label on a product. Nick master-minded printing his own labels, but they were the wrong color. He chose yellow and blue labels because they were his high school colors but those are not USDA-approved certified organic label colors. The apron sealed the deal, you said."

"I did say that." The detective rocked back and forth from his heels to his toes.

"You didn't believe in my innocence at first, did you? Okay, I get it. You were just doing your job with the facts as they presented themselves. But I'm not sure I'm ready to socialize with someone whom I had to work so hard to prove my integrity to. Do you understand where I'm coming from?"

"Fair enough. Offer stands, as is. Just keep it in mind," Bease said.

"Thanks, I will." Sherry pointed to the pickle jars. "Have you made a choice?"

Detective Bease checked a piece of paper he held in his hand. He took a pen out of his shorts pocket that Sherry could see had a flamingo and an alligator on the shaft and made a notation on the sheet of paper. "Nothing today. Maybe next time."

Sherry pointed to the detective's pen. "Florida?"

Ray nodded. "Did you get a chance to read Patti Mellit's article on OrgaNicks last month?"

Sherry picked up the smallest jar on the table. "The article was great. 'No M'OrgaNicks' was a perfect title. Bottom line, Nick Andime tried to short-cut the organic product process by printing his own labels without going through the proper certification process, but he got caught. Tried to take a lot of people down with him during his cover-up, but you were too good for him to get away with it. You must be very proud. Here." Sherry handed the detective the miniature jar of pickles. "Free sample. You'll be back after tasting these. I guarantee."

"Miss Frazzelle," the detective began.

"It's Sherry."

"Sherry," Ray said. "The ingredients you added to my investigation made for a complete recipe."

Sherry pulled something out of her cash box. She extended her hand and gave the detective a shiny green object. "For your collection."

He smiled and walked away admiring his new pen in the shape of a cucumber, inscribed with "If you're ever in a pickle . . ."

*Recipes from
Sherry's Kitchen*

Roasted Asparagus
with Spring Harvest Butter

Makes 6 servings.

1 pound fresh asparagus, rinsed, tough ends
    trimmed
1 tablespoon olive oil
2 tablespoons grated Parmesan cheese
¼ cup butter, softened, not melted
¼ cup fresh radish, chopped fine
2 tablespoons fresh chives, minced
1 tablespoon fresh lemon juice

Preheat oven to 450 degrees F.

Place asparagus across an 8 x11-inch baking dish
and toss with olive oil and Parmesan cheese. Bake
12–15 minutes.

Meanwhile, prepare butter by stirring together
with radish, chives, and lemon juice in a small
bowl. Cover butter blend with plastic wrap and
refrigerate until ready to use.

Serve roasted asparagus by placing each serving
of 6–8 asparagus on each plate and top with a
dollop of blended butter.

Sticky Peppered Maple Steak
with Pumpkin Pancakes

Makes 4–6 servings.

1 tablespoon salt
2 tablespoons pepper
4 boneless beef chuck eye steaks, cut 1-inch thick
     (about 8 ounces each)
4 shallots, peeled, chopped
½ cup pure maple syrup
2 tablespoons apple cider vinegar
¼ cup dried cranberries

For the pumpkin pancakes:
½ cup canned pumpkin puree
1 cup buttermilk "complete" dry pancake mix
½ cup buttermilk
¼ teaspoon grated nutmeg
1 tablespoon unsalted butter, plus more if needed
     when cooking pancakes
¼ cup toasted pepitas (pumpkin seeds),
     as a garnish

Combine the salt and pepper and rub seasoning
over both sides of steaks. Heat a large nonstick
skillet over medium heat and add the steaks to
the skillet. Cook steaks 8–10 minutes, flipping
once until desired doneness.

Remove steak to a plate, and maintaining skillet
heat, sauté shallots for 1 minute then add maple
syrup, vinegar, and cranberries to the skillet.

Bring skillet contents to a low boil and simmer until thickening begins.

Add the steak back to the skillet and continue simmering until steak is lightly coated with peppered maple sauce, 1–2 minutes. Remove skillet from heat and let rest.

Meanwhile, prepare pumpkin pancakes by combining pumpkin, pancake mix, buttermilk, and nutmeg in a bowl. Heat 1 tablespoon butter in a large nonstick skillet over medium heat. Working in batches, spoon the batter into the skillet to form each of eight pancakes and flip when lightly browned and bubbly on one side, adding more butter when needed with each batch. Cook until set and remove pancakes to a plate.

Assemble each serving by giving each of 4–6 dinner plates 1–2 pancakes. Cut steaks into strips and top each pancake with 4 steak strips and sauce, and sprinkle with toasted pumpkin seeds.

New England Harvest Chicken Cassoulet

Makes 4–6 servings.

2 tablespoons olive oil
6 boneless, skinless chicken thighs
2 cups applewood smoked chicken sausage,
    cut in ½-inch segments
1½ cups diced carrots, celery, onions (about
    ½ cup each)

1 teaspoon fresh rosemary (or ½ teaspoon
   dry rosemary)
1 teaspoon fresh thyme (or ¼ teaspoon
   dried thyme)
1 cup "original" canned baked beans
½ cup chicken broth
2 cups canned fire-roasted diced tomatoes
1 cup sourdough bread crumbs
2 tablespoons melted butter
½ teaspoon garlic salt
2 tablespoons chopped parsley and lemon wedges
   to garnish

In a large ovenproof skillet heat 2 tablespoons
olive oil to medium hot. Add the chicken
thighs and brown for 5 minutes. Reduce heat
to medium, turn thighs, and sear on the other
side for 2 minutes. Remove chicken to a plate.

Maintaining heat, brown the sausage for 3 minutes.
Remove sausage to the plate with the chicken. Add
vegetables, rosemary, and thyme to skillet, and
sauté for 4 minutes. Add the baked beans, chicken
broth, tomatoes, and the chicken, sausage, and
any juices from the plate to the skillet and simmer
over medium-low heat for 30 minutes, uncovered.

Heat oven to 350 degrees F. In a bowl, toss
together the breadcrumbs, butter, and garlic salt
to coat and sprinkle across skillet contents. Place
entire ovenproof skillet in the oven for 15–20
minutes to brown topping. Carefully remove
skillet (please don't touch hot handle!)

Serve each portion of cassoulet garnished with a sprinkle of parsley and a lemon wedge.

Bronzed Bluefish with Artichoke Salsa and Sweet-and-Sour Guacamole

Makes 4 servings.

2 pounds bluefish fillets, skin on one side
1 teaspoon garlic powder
1 teaspoon smoked paprika
1 teaspoon marjoram
1 teaspoon sea salt
2 tablespoons cooking oil

For the artichoke salsa:
½ cup marinated artichoke hearts, chopped
½ cup chopped tomato
½ cup chopped red onion
2 tablespoons jalapeño pepper, chopped
2 tablespoons lime juice
½ teaspoon sea salt
½ teaspoon ground pepper

For the sweet-and-sour guacamole:
1 ripe avocado
1 tablespoon lime juice
¼ cup diced ripe mango
Cilantro and lime wedges, to garnish

Combine the garlic powder, paprika, marjoram, and 1 teaspoon sea salt. Rinse fish fillets, and rub both sides with garlic powder blend. Heat cooking oil in a large frying pan over medium heat until it's hot. Place fish nonskin side down and fry for 3 minutes. Flip fillet and cook skin side down until skin is crispy. Remove to a plate.

Combine salsa ingredients in a bowl.

Prepare the guacamole by mashing the avocado and lime juice until smooth. Gently stir in mango, taking care to leave chunky.

Divide the fish on 4 serving plates, and serve with a helping of salsa and a spoonful of guacamole. Garnish with cilantro and lime wedges.

Please turn the page for an exciting sneak peek of
Devon Delaney's next Cook-Off mystery

FINAL ROASTING PLACE

coming soon wherever print and e-books are sold!

Chapter

1

"You'd think winning recipe contests was a matter of life and death. All the other contestants, except one, stormed out of here in such a huff I didn't get to try their appetizers." Erno Oliveri put one arm around his daughter, while snaking his free hand toward the plate loaded with crab stuffed mushrooms. He popped one in his mouth. "If your recipe beat these beauties, you must be a great cook." He released his daughter and went back, double-fisted, for more.

As Sherry touched her warm cheek, she envisioned her face glowing radish red. "Thanks, Dad, but you're exaggerating a bit. I don't think anyone was in a huff. And if you think I'm such a good cook, why haven't you had more than one taste of my Spicy Toasted Chickpea and Almonds?" Sherry untied and removed her new *Watch Sunny Side Up with Brett and Carmell weekdays at 8 am* apron. She folded the cloth to the size of a dinner napkin. "I have to say, the way you've been scarfing down my competitor's food, I'm glad you weren't one of the judges." She used the compacted apron to swat her father's head with loving restraint.

Sherry set the cloth on the polished acrylic table she and her fellow cook-off competitors had displayed their competing dishes on. The spills and splatters each cook produced during their thirty-minute time allotment were mopped up, and Studio B was ready for whatever broadcast segments were coming up next.

"Congratulations, Sherry, great recipe," the woman who crafted the crab mushrooms said as she headed toward the building's exit, appetizer platter in hand. Her kind words couldn't mask the sagging frown on her face.

As she passed, Erno's hand jutted forward to hijack one more bite. A moment too tardy, the plate traveled beyond his reach and his hand remained empty. His arm collapsed down to his side and his chest deflated.

"Yours were great, too," Erno called after Mushroom Lady. He turned back to face Sherry. "Forgive me. I'm not a chickpea fan, but obviously your appetizer was perfectly executed." Erno's gaze followed the exiting tray of fungi across the TV studio and out the door. "Farewell, delicious ones, I'll miss you."

"Dad, you're so transparent. Can you get your mind off the crab long enough to help me gather my stuff, please?"

A block of a man with a head full of wavy salt-and-pepper hair approached Sherry as she placed her baking sheet inside her rolling carryall. She lifted her head and smiled at the imposing News Twelve station owner, Damien Castle. She began to utter a greeting before she realized he was talking on his cell phone. Sherry swallowed her "Hello" and continued packing her cooking supplies.

"I'll be there. Yes, of course. I haven't missed one yet, have I? Thank you for being so accommodating." Damien put the phone in his breast pocket, lifted a mixing bowl off the counter, and handed it to Sherry. "Your cook-off win today is the biggest thing to happen at News Twelve since the Governor's motorcade stopped by unannounced to use the men's room last month. We had to interrupt our broadcast because his entourage created such a stir." Damien pursed his lips and handed Sherry her serving spoon from the pile of rinsed silverware.

She blew a wayward lock of hair from her face. The hairstyle she had begun sporting recently was taking some getting used to. She hadn't worn a shoulder-length cut, without clips or barrettes, since she was in her twenties. "Thanks, Mr. Castle, I love these smaller cook-offs." Sherry arched her eyebrows skyward as she reconsidered her comment. "I didn't mean this was a small cook-off in any negative sense."

Sherry sucked in a deep breath, in hopes of washing away any lingering taste of the foot she had put in her mouth. "Certainly it was one of the most fun appetizer competitions I've been a part of in a long time. Your TV station went above and beyond to make all four of us contestants feel well taken care of."

Erno cleared his throat with a rumble rivaling a food processor set on full power. Sherry gulped down the emerging words she was about to relay, rather than continue rambling. Instead, she watched her father relocate to the edge of the room, where he found a seat.

Sherry resumed collecting the kitchenware she brought from home. Some contests provided all the supplies needed to complete a recipe while others required participants to bring supplies needed for success. Sherry preferred the former but was resigned to the growing popularity of the latter. It was a more economically sound way for the sponsor to run the contest, but for Sherry, always a juggling act to get supplies to and fro.

"Please, call me Damien. I may own this place, but I don't put on airs. On airs, on-air. That's quite punny if you think about it."

The chuckling man took a step away from Sherry, only to be replaced by a woman in a pinstripe blazer and pencil skirt.

"Damien's right. You proved once again you're Augustin's most decorated home cook. Thanks for entering our contest. You elevated the level for all the others who tried and failed to beat you. For your information, there were close to one hundred and fifty recipes our staff whittled down to the final four, who competed this morning, so you should be proud to come out victorious." Carmell Gordy edged backward until she was alongside Damien.

"Thank you, Carmell." Sherry thrust her platter of appetizers toward Carmell. "Would you like to try some? I don't think you got a chance to try them during the cook-off." Sherry's second attempt to lure the News Twelve personality into a taste test was thwarted with a wave of Carmell's elegant hand.

"I'm careful about what I eat." Carmell patted her concave core with one hand while clutching a vibrant green smoothie in the other. "Television anchors think they can sit behind a desk and hide extra pounds, but savvy viewers know when you've let yourself go."

"Hard to break my urge to want to fill bellies." Sherry set the platter back down. She wedged the tips of her fingers just inside her straining waistband and sighed as she struggled to fit more than one finger in. She untucked her shirt and yanked the hem over her stomach bulge. "I'm thinking of taking up Zumba. Lately I've been doing too much cooking and not enough sweating. I need to get back in shape."

Carmell glanced past Sherry. With no real intention of taking up the dance exercise du jour, Sherry was glad her comment was ignored.

Carmell rotated on her heels for a close encounter with Damien. "Are you behind in your e-mails? I'm waiting for a reply. There's time sensitivity involved." The words hissed from Carmell's mouth like escaped steam from a pressure cooker.

Damien winced and pulled out his phone. He began talking into the device.

"Ugh. He's not fooling me. He puts on that act when he wants to avoid a conversation, especially one involving me." Carmell craned her neck toward Sherry. "Did you hear his phone ring? I didn't. Did you see him dial out? I didn't."

Sherry scraped her shoe along the ground. "It could be on vibrate. We were told to shut our phones down when we came in the building."

"He owns this place. He plays by his own rules. I've heard his phone ring during a broadcast plenty of times. And if he's talking to someone right now,

I'm the Queen of England." Carmell took a noisy pull on her straw. "Time to get back to the anchor desk. We have a segment coming up on Augustin's Andre August Dahlback Festival. As you probably know, he's the legendary, and possibly slightly embellished, founder and namesake of the town of Augustin. If he hadn't brought those first onion bulbs over from his native Sweden and made this land the prosperous center of the onion universe, who knows what this town would be famous for today? Tune in for more information." Carmell's sweeping wave brushed Sherry's arm as she turned and walked away. "Bye-bye."

Sherry watched Carmell hop over the camera cables crisscrossing the floor of the studio before slipping through the studio doors.

Damien returned his phone to his pocket. "I've got to run. Need to stay ahead of the next mini crisis brewing. Sorry I can't offer more clean-up assistance." He helped himself to a cluster of Sherry's chickpeas and almonds and marched away in Carmell's footsteps.

"Carmell, wait." A young man in an oversized flannel shirt trotted over. On his head, a haphazard man bun fidgeted from side to side with each step he took. A shorter man, who reminded Sherry of a beet, bottom heavy and red-faced, tailed him.

"That woman sends me on a wild goose chase to find a certain kind of treat for her dog, and now the picky canine won't touch the pricey biscuit," Man Bun said, stuffing the pouch of dog treats in one of his multiple cargo pants pockets. "What he did eat was the receipt. Now I can't get reimbursed. What am I doing all this for? Certainly not for the big bucks. Interns don't make a dime. Her pooch hates me and, considering all I do for him, he could be a tiny bit grateful." He locked gazes with Sherry. A broad smile bloomed, revealing gleaming white teeth. "Hi, I'm Steele Dumont, esteemed station apprentice. My job description is, if someone wants something done and no one else wants to do it, I'm your man."

"Nice to see you, Steele. I know of you, although you probably have never heard of me. I work for your grandmother one day a week selling her pickles at the Farmers' Market. She mentioned I might see you here. Such a small world, right?" Sherry returned the smile. "I was in the appetizer cook-off this morning. I think I saw you darting around the studio behind the scenes. You're hard to miss." Sherry observed Steele's man bun, which was sprouting free-spirited hair. "And now I'm on my way out. Good luck in your job."

"Much appreciated. Got to go, too." Steele spun around toward the shorter man. "Brett, do you need me to grab any supplies from the closet before I get too involved in settling Dog Treat–gate with Carmell?"

"Nope, all set. I'm on in ten after Carmell finishes her segment, so right now I'm heading to my dressing room for a touch-up. My rosacea is acting up again. Stress related, I'm sure." The man who had served as the moderator of the morning's cook-off, Brett Paladin, brushed his glowing cheek with the back of his hand. "Hard to believe, but I could use a bite to eat, too."

"I didn't get a chance to tell you how much I've enjoyed watching you over the years. I watched your very first broadcast. If I'm not mistaken, you anchored a show called *On the Front Burner with Brett*. That same year you visited my high school and gave a talk in our English class. I was starstruck." Sherry visualized a statuesque powerhouse of a man whose authoritative voice kept the interest of twenty-two willful teenagers for an hour. All those years later, standing next to him, the bridge of her nose was the same height as the top of his head. She had to decline her chin to make eye contact.

Brett massaged his well-fed stomach. "Thank you. Loyal viewership means the world to me. I remember how difficult it was working solo. A partner like Carmell is an invaluable asset." He tossed a glance toward Sherry's plate of food and held up what appeared to be a large cookie. He took a hearty bite. Half of the remaining cookie collapsed to the floor. "I make these energy breakfast cookies myself. I think they're good enough to market. Would you like a taste? I'd value your opinion."

Brett broke off a chunk. Sherry attempted to send a signal of refusal with the wave of her hand, but it was ignored. Her stomach warned, "No more room until I've digested the crab mushrooms, roasted gruyere asparagus, mini sausage sliders, and phyllo spinach quiche the other contestants had me sample."

"Okay." The word leapt out before she could quash it.

The cookie landed in her hand. Brett's lips parted. The cookie entered Sherry's mouth. After a moment of mulling over the flavor and texture, she transported it down her digestive highway. She gulped hard to squelch a rising belch.

"Well? Pretty good, right?" Brett's grin was so expansive, his ears lifted. He took a bite of the remaining cookie.

"If I could give you one suggestion."

Brett's shiny smile went south faster than mayonnaise sitting in the summer sun.

"If you add a spoonful of almond butter, the batter will be moister and bind the baked product better. And maybe add more flavoring. I suggest turbinado sugar. Oh, and some chopped almonds for crunch. Oatmeal would give the cookie a desirable chewy texture and a sprinkle of sea salt delivers a tangy bright note." After analyzing Brett's creased forehead, Sherry added, "I see great possibilities, though."

A man carrying a clipboard jogged over to a scowling Brett. His crew cut was so flat on top Sherry imagined she could rest a stack of pancakes on it without concern for toppling. He pointed out something on a sheet of paper to Brett before proceeding on. Brett grumbled and massaged his temples with his fingertips in a small circular motion.

The building heat of heartburn churned in Sherry's chest. "Boy, a typhoon of constant motion around here. People rushing in, people rushing out. Gives me an uneasy feeling."

The way Brett studied the room from one corner to the other, she knew he wasn't fully invested in listening to her.

"That guy can't make a decision to save his life and he's our producer." Brett exhaled with such force, crumbs came flying out of his mouth. "Truman Fletcher's clipboard is what really runs this place."

Brett's voice reverberated throughout the room. "Where's your dad?"

"How did you know my father was with me, Mr. Paladin?" Sherry's eyebrows rose like popover batter in a hot oven.

Brett's facial hue deepened. "Call me Brett, please. Only Dan Rather deserves the honorific *Mr.*" Brett laughed at length until the color drained from his face. "I recognized Erno Oliveri in the back of the room, off camera, while you were cooking. It wasn't hard to pin him as your father. The resemblance is quite strong. I rushed onto the cook-off studio floor this morning, so I didn't get a chance to say hi. To be honest with you, I thought the kitchen segment was solely Carmell's. Didn't get that assignment until five minutes before shoot time. Not sure how that girl has the wherewithal to make changes for others at the last minute, but if Truman Fletcher okays something, it's as good as done." Brett gestured toward the mountain of a man in chino pants and an oxford shirt, sleeves rolled up, examining his clipboard.

"I had no idea you and Dad knew each other." Sherry shifted her weight from one leg to the other. "Dad's right over there in the back of the room." She pointed out him seated along the dimly lit edge of the studio. Erno was partially obscured by the massive lens of a TV camera. "I'm almost done here. In a minute I'll take you over to him."

After Sherry stored the last of her utensils in her rolling suitcase, she strained to close the zipper but a few failed attempts later, she gave up. Sherry turned to Brett. "Follow me."

"Watch the cables." Brett steered Sherry by the arm as they headed over to Erno.

As she neared her father, Sherry's footstep snagged a thick plastic encased wire, and she lost her balance. Brett's reaction wasn't fast enough to keep her from pitching forward toward a monstrous camera. Her ribs took the brunt of the blow.

Carmell Gordy emerged from Erno's side and steadied Sherry by grasping her shoulders. "Are you hurt?" Carmell's lips were as puckered as a week-old apple slice. "You were almost breaking news. I wouldn't want to have to report the cook-off winner was a casualty." Carmel released her grip, and Sherry teetered for a split second.

"Thanks. I'm clumsy. Old news there." Sherry righted herself. The intensity in Erno's eyes was that which the little girl in Sherry had seen on a few occasions growing up. That uncomfortable energy he transmitted meant a punishment was about to be doled out.

"I'm going." Carmell's clipped tone was fortified by the harsh tapping of her heels as she strutted away. She stopped and turned her head. "Oh, Brett, Damien took you off the Founder's Day feature we're shooting tomorrow. Did he tell you?"

"Yep. Can't count on much around here lasting more than a few minutes." Brett scuffed his shoe on the floor.

"What was that all about?" Sherry leaned over and put her hand on Erno's back. "You and Carmell could have toasted my appetizer almonds with the heat generated between you two."

"Just a friendly chat." Erno avoided Sherry's

glare. "We'd met prior to today and were catching up on lost time." Erno kept his head low and examined the back of his hands before flipping them like burgers on the grill, palm side up.

"I brought Brett Paladin over, Carmell's co-anchor, to say hello." Sherry stepped aside to let Brett slide between them. "He was asking for you."

"Good to see you, Brett." Erno shook Brett's hand.

"Good to see you, too." Brett spoke with such urgency his words blended together as one.

"How do you all know one another?" Sherry pointed from one man to the other. She crossed her arms on her chest.

Brett rocked forward on to his toes. "Most anyone in town knows your father, I'd say. Probably best our acquaintance wasn't broadcast ahead of time, what with you being a contestant and all. Of course, me knowing your father had no bearing on the contest judging." Brett checked his watch. "I've got to get going. Nice to spend time with you both and have a good day."

Brett removed his blazer and slung it over his arm. He ran his hand through his pile of hair, before marching away.

"Ah, there you two are." Damien Castle rushed toward Sherry and Erno. He was able to navigate his short journey without once lifting his face from his phone screen. "We need to get you on your way. Station security doesn't allow visitors, even as esteemed as you two, to stay much beyond your allotted segment time. I've been sent to find you because you haven't signed out at the reception desk. The other three contestants are long gone."

Sherry and Erno returned to the table in the center of Studio B. Sherry snapped up the handle of her carryall. "We're all set."

"Don't forget this." Damien handed Sherry her cook-off trophy. His massive hand obscured the base of the shiny statue. "Do you have your gift certificate to the Au Natural Market?"

"Right here." Sherry pulled a small envelope from her pants pocket and waved it in the air. "All two hundred and fifty dollars' worth. A nice surprise that'll fund my next recipe experiment. Thanks so much." Sherry held the trophy up to eye level. She spun it until the inscription faced her. She read the words aloud. "'Augustin's Local News Twelve TV, You Watch Us Watch You.'" Sherry clutched the bronze replica of an oversized spatula in the crook of her elbow, before realizing she also had to juggle a tray of leftover appetizers, along with her supply bag.

"Can I help you?" Before Sherry could respond, Damien snatched the suitcase handle with a swipe of his hand.

"Thanks." Sherry tightened the crook of her elbow to keep the trophy from slipping through. The base of the shiny statue rested on her hip and shifted with each step she took. At the same time, she clutched the tray of remaining Spicy Toasted Almonds and Chickpeas.

"Right this way." Damien motioned Sherry and Erno toward the studio exit. He pocketed his phone long enough to unlock the door that was shut to unauthorized personnel. "Oh, I almost forgot. If you wouldn't mind leaving the trophy with the receptionist, we'll have the engraver put your name at the base of the spatula handle." Damien let the door slam shut after Sherry and Erno stepped through. "Do you prefer we inscribe your name as Sherry Frazzelle or do you have a middle name you'd like to include?"

With Damien's question delivered, Sherry stopped short. Erno clipped her heels. The front row of toasted appetizer took flight from the platter and winged its way across the hall.

"Sorry, you caught me off guard. I'm in the process of getting my name legally changed back to my maiden name, Oliveri. This'll be the first time I'll officially be an Oliveri again." Sherry corralled some stray chickpeas with her foot into a neat collection before sidestepping them. "So, if you wouldn't mind, I'd prefer Sherry Oliveri." Sherry turned toward a door on her right. "This way?"

"No, that's the control room. The brains of the operation." Damien scooted around Sherry to take the lead again. "Down this hallway. We have to duck through the main studio to get to the lobby."

Sherry noticed her father examining the next door they approached. "This way, Dad."

"Is there a men's room around here?" Erno asked.

"Right over there." Damien indicated the direction with a head tilt as barking erupted from the other side of the door. "Bean, keep quiet." Damien tapped the toe of his shoe on the door. "Carmell's Jack Russell makes himself at home in her dressing room while she does her show. I need to check her contract. I might want to rescind the perk, citing continual noise violations." His words had an edge as sharp as Sherry's favorite paring knife. "Erno, head that way and you'll see a men's room symbol on the door. We'll wait for you in Studio A. Be as quiet as possible when you come in. They're on live now." Damien pointed to the illuminated "Quiet Please" sign at the end of the hall.

Erno shuffled past Sherry and was enveloped by the dark corridor.

"I hope my dad can find his way." Sherry stared in to the dingy abyss in front of her before glancing back. "His vision isn't as sharp as it used to be in low lighting. I guess if the Governor found the men's room, Dad can, too. Minus the entourage."

Damien was too busy checking his cell phone and murmuring to himself to acknowledge Sherry's attempt at humor.

Chapter 2

"What was that?" Sherry's feet refused another step. She braced her quivering arms against her sides to steady them. She bent her knees and assumed the "ready to bear heavy weight" stance. As her hands lurched backward, a few more legumes and nuts were ejected from the platter she carried. "Did you feel a tremor?"

Damien's phone squealed. He scrambled to click a button that ended the shrill alarm. "A tough storm is about to pass over us. I'm getting a tornado warning on my phone. Heavy thunder, intense lightning and hail possible, imminently . . . well, strike that, right now." He brushed his finger across the phone screen. "There's an ominous blob on the local radar. We're in the bull's-eye for the next ten minutes."

Sherry checked the hallway behind her. No sign of Erno. The muscles in her forehead constricted tighter than the skin of a sun-dried tomato. An army of chilling goose bumps advanced up her arms.

"Listen, I've got to run to the control room and make sure operations are running smoothly. Sometimes a surge of electricity creates havoc at a low-power station like ours. I'll get your equipment case to the receptionist, where you can collect it on your way out." Another muffled boom echoed through the hall. "Head straight through those doors and wait in the back of the studio for your dad. Best place is behind the camera operator, Kirin. You won't be in the way back there. And please, no talking."

Sherry jutted out her lower lip. Waves of silent pleas left her brain, begging Damien to stay with her, but his phone was his primary concern.

Damien took off in the opposite direction and was soon out of sight.

"If my ex-husband's connection with me was as strong as Damien's is to his phone, Charlie and I would still be married," Sherry whimpered.

Sherry was left alone, with the challenge of opening the door to the main studio with full hands. Fort Knox didn't have such impenetrable doors. The obstacles facing Sherry were no less imposing than a monolith, and they must be soundproof, so knocking wasn't an option. A quick survey of her surroundings confirmed there was no one else around to help solve her problem.

Sherry's first thought was if she had once solved the dinnertime quandary of satisfying her meat-and-potatoes-craving ex-spouse when her refrigerator contained only one portobello mushroom and a cup of leftover black rice, this dilemma should be a piece of cake. Her second thought was maybe her spontaneous cooking experiments were another reason why her ex-husband, Charlie, was dissatisfied with their marriage.

"Why am I even thinking of Charlie at a time like this? You're on your own, girl."

Sherry set her serving plate and trophy on the floor and leaned on the door latch. No movement, whatsoever. After another rumble of thunder shook the walls, she pounded on the metal door but was rewarded with only a muffled thud and a sore hand. Sherry guided her trophy and plate to the wall with her foot and stared down the unforgiving barrier in front of her.

"Let me help," a boisterous voice chirped.

Sherry rotated around, arms poised to strike, and whacked Steele Dumont on his forehead.

"Sorry. I didn't mean to startle you." Steele waved a laminated card across the sensor. The door unlocked with a resounding click.

"I didn't hear you coming." Sherry picked up her food and hardware and walked through the open door. "My dad should be heading this way in a few minutes. Will he be able to get through without some sort of pass card?"

"There's always someone coming or going. He won't have to wait long before he's let in." Steele closed the door with slow precision. He put his finger up to his lips. "One more minute and the segment's over, so if you'll wait over there, please."

Steele indicated a spot next to the giant camera being operated by a woman in a backward-facing baseball cap. "If I don't get Carmell's change of lipstick to her dressing room by the end of the next commercial break, there'll be hell to pay." Steele's rubber-soled desert boots screeched without mercy on the linoleum floor as he reversed directions.

Sherry took her position in the shadows at the back of the live set. As a result of holding her right bicep cocked in support of her trophy for an extended length of time, a twitch was developing. *Might as well try to relax and enjoy the show until Dad shows up. I wish he'd hurry up.* Sherry turned her attention to Carmell seated at the anchor desk centered on a slick wooden riser. The woman in pinstripes, garnished with a gemstone statement necklace, delivered the words on the monitor with the smoothness of vanilla pudding.

"As you can imagine, making a better life for his family was what motivated Andre August Dahlback, a sack of onion bulbs slung over his shoulder, to settle in this part of Connecticut, and aren't we all better off for his having done so? Augustin's Founder's Day celebration is the brainchild of the town historical society. The festivities promise to deliver as many layers of fun as one of Mr. D.'s onions." Carmell's head bobbed up and down, appearing to agree with her own assessment. Her eyes, the color of kale and the shape of a crosscut carrot slice, enticed the camera lens to move in for a close-up. "After the commercial break, *Sunny Side Up with Carmell and Brett* will be taking a turn from our, thus far, food-themed show to explore the top five habits people have that unknowingly offend others on a continual basis."

Carmell drummed her fingers on the desk. "Wow,

I hope our producer isn't sending me a message with that story."

The camera's red light faded to black. Sherry studied Carmell as the anchorwoman froze her toothy smile until the set lights lowered. As the lights lowered, so did the angle of Carmell's lips. She pulled her cell phone from under the desk, held the device up to eye level, and shook her head. At the same time, Steele hopped up on set, only to be redirected with a wave of her hand.

"Brett, four minutes. Be on set in four minutes," an overhead speaker called out.

Sherry was fixated on Carmell, who was pounding her fist on the wooden desk. Carmell's lips were moving as if she was talking to herself.

"I'm going to roll this bad boy back a few feet to frame a two-person shot. Watch your feet," warned the woman steering the camera. "Kirin" was embroidered on the side of her cap. The camera operator stepped down from her perch and hauled the equipment backward. The woman hopped back up on her elevated seat and began extending and retracting the impressive lens.

"Kirin, is that your name? Can I offer you a snack? I was in the cook-off this morning and I have some leftovers." Sherry tipped the plate to show off the contents.

"Yes, I'm the notorious Kirin of Studio A. I didn't shoot you over in Studio B. My counterpart, Lucky, owns that territory. I see by your trophy you won first prize. Congrats." Kirin pointed her elbow toward the shiny spatula statue without taking her hands off her camera's controls. "I suspect there was no giant game show check to go along with the win. Between you and me, this place is a bit strapped for cash." She released a puff of air. "Thanks for the snack offer. If you don't mind, I'll wait until after the next segment. We're about to resume shooting and if my hands are greasy, controlling this monster could get dicey."

The words "strapped for cash" landed in Sherry's ears with the subtlety of Bananas Flambé.

Sherry pursed her lips. "They're not greasy, but it's your decision. I'm on my way out. I could leave a sampling with the receptionist out in the lobby. Kirin, I noticed the apron they gave me for the cook-off was printed with *Sunny Side Up with Brett and Carmell* but Carmell told me the show's name was *Sunny Side Up with Carmell and Brett.* What's the correct order of names?"

"Both ways have been correct, but Carmell is on top currently. Brett's been the morning anchor here for twelve years. Carmell is in her second year. The youngster swept in like a twenty-three-year-old tsunami and we're all holding on to her coattails for dear life at this point. She made a suggestion, and the show title changed in an instant. Pretty amazing. I swear she has some invisible force making her quite powerful." Kirin shrugged. "If you think the show's name change sat well with poor Brett, think again. Damien Castle is her puppet. Don't even get me started on Truman Fletcher's role in all this."

A thunderous boom turned heads. Kirin mumbled an indecipherable collection of words as she peered into the camera's massive viewfinder. The overhead lights surged with an impossible glow before flickering and dying out altogether. A despondent curse was exclaimed. A resounding crash and a dull thud echoed through the room. Sherry dared not move, visualizing the spaghetti-like maze of thick cables on the floor, the towering microphone boom at head level and a landscape of television monitors conspiring to stage a mechanical coup in the pitch black.

"Attention, people." The room din ceased. "Remain calm. The storm has knocked out power. We're not sure why the generator has failed, but we're trying to locate Mr. Castle to get some answers."

An almost inaudible voice added, "The penny-pinching owner has sure done it this time. You get what you pay for."

Kirin began humming to herself. Sherry wished she knew Kirin well enough to ask her to refrain from her eerie tune, which, in the enveloping darkness, was as unwelcome as grit on spinach leaves.

"Has this happened before?" Sherry paused for a reply, but the woman never removed her face from the camera's viewfinder. *With no electricity to power the machine what is she looking at?*

"I can't hold these anymore, so watch where you step. I have to put my platter down. My arms are on fire."

The lights burst on as Sherry stood.

"Dear God." Kirin leapt away from the camera, grazing Sherry's foot with her combat boot. "Someone help Carmell."

There was a piercing scream and pounding footsteps. Sherry blinked hard to acclimate her eyes to the light. As her eyesight adjusted, she witnessed the monitor come to life. On the screen, she was able to make out the anchor desk amidst a flurry of background activity. Sherry pushed her face closer to the screen, in hopes of clarifying what a pile of clothing was doing in the middle of the camera shot. Upon further inspection, she was able to make out a head and upper torso among the clothes. Behind the desk, someone had his or her outstretched arms blocking full visual access to the scene. Orders were being barked.

"This area must be cleared out. We need space."

Sherry grabbed Kirin's arm. "Is that Carmell Gordy slumped over?" Sherry blinked hard in hopes the scene would present itself in a clearer light. "What's the liquid dripping over the edge of the desk? Reminds me of the red wine syrup I make to go with poached pears."

The tips of Sherry's fingertips went numb as a cold shiver overtook her body. The arm Sherry had a death grip on was shaking.

"She might have spilled her smoothie. Wasn't her smoothie green, though?" Sherry jumped back when she caught sight of someone approaching her from the side. She released Kirin's arm. "Dad, there you are. Thank goodness."

"Sherry." Erno threw up his arms. "You could have picked a more visible spot to wait for me.

"This is where they told me to wait. I had no choice. What took you so long? I was really worried you wouldn't be able to find your way back when the lights went out."

"Listen, I couldn't make out what's happening,

but something terrible may have happened to Carmell Gordy," Erno said.

Sherry's eyes darted back to the television monitor. People were crowding the periphery of the anchor desk, ignoring the directive being given to clear away. Sherry no longer saw any sign of what she thought were Carmell's head and shoulders. She lifted her vision from the monitor to focus on the live commotion.

"I can't figure out what's going on. One minute I'm waiting for you and watching the end of a report on the upcoming Founder's Day celebration, the next I can't see my hand in front of my face because all the power's out. When the lights came back up, the scene was more panicked than the grocery store the day before a February blizzard. We're obviously in the way here, let's get going."

Erno massaged his chin with one hand. "Reminds me of an old saying . . ."

"This isn't a good time for your pearls of wisdom, Dad. We need to get out of here." Sherry huffed and squatted down to retrieve her trophy and plate of food. She regretted not finding plastic wrap to secure the spicy treats on the plate but she hadn't, so a steady hand was required to hold them in place.

A clock on the wall caught Sherry's eye. "Eleven forty. We've got to get to the store. You did leave a sign on the door saying you'd be opening late today, didn't you?"